A WOMAN *of* STRONG PURPOSE

S. M. HARDING

2016

Bella Books, Inc.
P.O. Box 10543
Tallahassee, FL 32302

Printed in the United States of America on acid-free paper.

First Bella Books Edition 2016

Editor: Chris Paynter
Cover Designer: Judith Fellows

ISBN: 978-1-59493-513-8

Other Bella Books by S. M. Harding

I Will Meet You There

Dedication

For Frances and Chamu, two beautiful minds and souls who left way too soon. You inspired my first attempts at fiction and I will always carry your spirits with me.

Acknowledgments

I want to thank all the Bella women who work so hard to bring novels from my hands into yours: Linda Hill, publisher; Jessica Hill, who shepherds the manuscript through production and all those who add their efforts along the way including the blurb writers, book designer, formatters, and proofreaders; Judith Fellows for a lovely cover design; the folks in shipping for always doing their best to get books into the hands of readers.

I want to thank Chris Paynter who as my editor saved me from awful blunders, asked questions and made comments that made me think and stretch my skills. My gratitude for a wonderful job and such an easy process.

My thanks always to "Hawkeye" Halbert and Lena for all the technical support.

Last, but certainly not least, thank you reader for taking a chance on a new author, leaving reviews and coming back for more of the McCrumb County crew.

A Geology Lesson

Here, the sea strains to climb up on the land
and the wind blows dust in a single direction.
The trees bend themselves all one way
and volcanoes explode often.
Why is this? Many years back
a woman of strong purpose
passed through this section
and everything else tried to follow.

-Judy Grahn, *She Who*

CHAPTER ONE

Win

I glanced at my watch to see how much time I had before the Friday faculty gathering called the Sherry Hour. Although I'd never seen any sherry at the bar, every other kind of booze was plentiful. This was the last one of the academic year and Dr. Kemat Fitzgerald had urged me to come.

"It's good politics, Win," she'd said. I'd taken that as a warning.

The longer I knew her, the more of a mystery Kemat was to me. The director of Central Eurasian Language Institute, she was generous with stories about growing up in Cairo and her arrival in the US in the late 1980s. She never spoke about the time between.

Maybe it was just my background in Military Intelligence, but I always listened for what wasn't said. CELI had begun its life as the Army Specialized Training Program for Central Eurasian Languages sometime during WWII. The military still sent their people for training here. She must've been vetted thoroughly. Maybe I was listening too hard. These days, I found it hard to judge.

I packed the unfinished student papers into my briefcase, took a detour and dropped it in my truck. Then I took a deep breath and headed into Sherry Hour. I grabbed a beer from an iced tub and examined the room. Despite the efforts Kemat had made to warm up the place with beautiful rugs and wall hangings, it was a room from the 1960s. Long, narrow windows. No blinds. Minimal white. I wondered where the Boston ferns in hanging macramé had gone.

I knew few of the other faculty because I was part-time, or in academic dialect, adjunct faculty. I only taught Wednesday through Friday and took off when duty was done. Though I'd met a few of the people standing around in groups, they'd remained distant acquaintances. I didn't have time to chitchat because I was trying to learn how to teach the subtleties of a subtle language.

My gaze wandered to a stunning woman dressed in modified Afghani garb of an earthy gray color, her hijab a complicated pattern in gray, brown and red. I watched her talking to two men, both bearded but in casual Western dress. Whatever she was saying, the frown that ruffled her brow told me she was upset. She turned away from them, caught my gaze and steamed toward me.

"Chauvinist pigs!" she said in heavily accented English. "Do you still call them that?"

"Haven't heard it in a while," I said, trying to place her accent. "I'm Win Kirkland."

She smiled. "I know. I have seen you on this campus."

Not much of a window of opportunity to see me. Stalker or spy? I tried to remind myself I was no longer active military. A lifetime of suspicion was hard to overcome. "And you are?" She'd remained looking at my eyes through long lashes. Now she raised her head, opened her eyes wide. "Oh, I am so sorry, how rude of me. I am Noor Bhatti. I am visitor scholar."

Was she flirting? Shit. I should know. But nationality now made sense. The last name was Pakistani. Her clothes, not Afghan but Punjabi. "Are you Pakistani?"

"Kashmiri, from Gilgit in the north."

I nodded. South of where I'd been my last couple of tours, but loaded with Taliban who moved across borders easily. *My* border. I knew it was irrational, but I felt my hackles quiver.

"You teach Tajik?"

I nodded.

"How did you learn?"

"I spent some time in the Hindu Kush, learned from the people." I was beginning to get uncomfortable.

"It is beautiful country, more dramatic than my own. But there are…things alike. Yes?"

"I've never been to Kashmir." A lie. Plus, I'd studied the satellite images, looking for Pakistani Taliban. I glanced around the room. Kemat watched us with an intense gaze. I wondered why.

"I would love to tell you about my country," she said, subtly leaning toward me. "Would you like to go for a drink?"

Oh, yeah. Definitely flirting. I held up my bottle. "I have one. You drink?"

"Only when I am in this country. It seems the, ah, social thing to do."

"How long will you be here?"

"I will remain all of summer." She took a step forward and smiled up at me.

"Well, maybe we can go for coffee sometime." Was that vague enough?

"Do you live in Bloomington?"

"No. Out in the country." I almost laughed. Two years ago I wouldn't have hesitated to take her up on the offer, but now I was a married woman. "It's a long drive. I should get going."

I put the bottle down, smiled at her, found my jacket and began the trek to the door. So much for being political.

Before I got there, Kemat intercepted me. "Leaving so soon?"

What could I say? Noor was hitting on me? Cause Noor problems when I could handle her advances by myself? "It's a long drive home and my dog's waiting for me." In the studio apartment I rented in Bloomington because it cut down on the travel.

She looked disappointed.

"I'm really tired, Kemat. I promise I'll be better next year."

"The first year is always the most difficult." She patted my arm. "I'll be in Greenglen next week. I would like to talk with you then. Could we arrange a time to meet?"

"Sure." I wondered what I'd done wrong. Would I have a next year teaching?

"I'm giving a series of classes to the high school teachers in the mornings, every Wednesday. Could we meet for lunch?"

"I'll pick you up at the high school at noon. If that's all right?" I asked.

"That would be lovely."

"Are you going to fire me?" So much for subtlety. Good going, Win.

"Oh no, Win. This is a private matter. I need to ask you for a favor. Now go, I'm sure you want to get home to your wife. Sarah is a lovely woman."

I grinned. "I think so too."

Her eyebrows edged up. "I should hope so."

* * *

As I drove home, I turned the worn gold band on my left hand. Even though it had been four months, I found it difficult to believe I was married. As word spread among my old marine buddies, so did they. In the most graphic terms.

Sarah, when she'd asked me to marry her, promised we'd make it official. An early January vacation in Vermont at a small inn that catered to gays. Micah, Sarah's Dad, and Nathan, our friend since childhood, had come up to give us their blessing on the union. They'd only stayed overnight, but in the time they'd been there, garnered quite a few "Aw, that's sweet" looks. I didn't think they quite understood. Micah was in his early seventies, Nathan our age.

The Green Mountains had been white, the fire in the fieldstone fireplace welcoming. We'd cross-country skied every day, eaten our way through every restaurant in the area. Loved every part of one another's bodies. Most of all, we spent time together. Unabashedly together. She kissed me at a candlelit table in a restaurant. I'd returned the favor as we tapped snow off our boots at the ski rental place.

That's what hurt. Now that we were back in McCrumb County, we were back living in the shadows. Sarah had started her second term as sheriff. Most weeks during the winter, our time together was on Tuesdays, her day off and one of my nonteaching days. When the weather improved with spring, she'd driven into Bloomington more often. We'd shared movies and music and dinner out. Dancing together at Ruby Slippers.

Doable for the time being, but I knew Sarah chafed at the secrecy. I missed the openness of the inn and environs. Ruby Slippers in Bloomington was a part-time substitute where we were surrounded by other gays. We both wanted something full-time.

I'd put the decision in her hands. When the time came, we'd step forward. Hand in hand.

I picked up Des and a suitcase and hightailed it to the country. I pulled into my driveway, saw Sarah's SUV parked to one side of the clearing that harbored my home. Des leaped through the open window of the truck and barked at the front door before I'd stopped. When I walked through the front door, I put my briefcase down. Sniffed. The aroma of something tomato with spices. Des swarmed Sarah, got a kiss on her snout and went to lap her water.

Sarah stood at the stove, a silly grin on her face as she turned. "Well?"

"Honey, I'm home. What's for dinner?"

This had become a running joke between us because it depended on who walked through the door from work. We had no role we couldn't trade, June and Ward Cleaver be damned. A gentle tribute to our union.

"How was work?" she asked on cue.

I took off my jacket, hung it on a peg. Let my gaze travel down her body. She took my breath away as much now as our first kiss. Not a classically beautiful face, but strong with a jawline I could stroke forever. More silver in her hair than when we'd first met. Her height matched my own, her body as athletic as mine. But her breasts. Ah. I slipped my hands under her Angel Mounds sweatshirt and pulled her to me. We kissed until we ran out of breath.

"Angel Mounds, indeed," I said, moving my hands to her full breasts.

"An archaeological site, Win," she said, leaning into my hands. "Not my breasts."

"Leave me to my own interpretation." I kissed her again.

Finally, she pulled back. "Can you tell what I'm cooking?"

"Me."

"Put that thought on the back burner for now," she said with a raised eyebrow. "Remember when we were kids and you'd come over for lunch? Mom made tomato soup?"

"She'd make us grilled cheese sandwiches to go with it," I said, sniffing again. "Perfect for the weather."

"Go change your clothes and dinner will be on the table." She kissed me, a June peck on the lips.

Over dinner, I told her about Kemat at the Sherry Hour. "I can't imagine what personal favor I can do for her."

"Something from your Intelligence background?"

I picked up the gooey sandwich. Not her mother's. I still couldn't identify the cheese she'd grilled between two slabs of locally made focaccia. "She shouldn't have any knowledge of my background. Bill scrubbed all that stuff from what he sent her."

"Hm. Maybe you've given yourself away in conversation. On second thought, I doubt if that's possible."

I took a bite, reveled in the blend of tastes. Watched Sarah as she spooned her soup the proper way. The low light struck one side of her face. I wondered at the blue of her eyes. How the blue changed from the early morning sky then, when she was upset, to the darker purple gromwell I'd seen in Afghanistan. Right now, they matched the sky at midday. "I was hit on by a gorgeous Pakistani woman."

"You what?"

"She flirted outrageously, wanted me to go for a drink."

"She's Muslim? Then she shouldn't be drinking alcohol." Sarah dipped her spoon into the soup.

"Maybe that's not what she wanted to drink."

"*Win*."

I heard the warning in her voice. "Come on, Sarah. It felt good to have a stranger look at me like I'm attractive. Besides, I made it clear I wasn't interested."

While I was finishing up the dishes, Sarah came up behind, slipped her hand down the front of my sweatpants. "You want to pretend we're strangers?"

My knees went wobbly. I swallowed. "I think we're far too engaged right now for that scenario."

* * *

I no longer had an uncontrollable urge to mess up the Zen sandbox in my therapist's waiting room. Perhaps unreasonably, I was proud of that. The door opened and Dr. Emily Peterson beckoned me in. I sat in the same comfortable chair I'd been sitting in for the past two years as I tried to get a handle on my PTSD. The serious symptoms hadn't visited me in months. Being hypervigilant would probably never leave me, especially married to the sheriff of McCrumb County.

Emily was doing her New Age checking-my-aura stuff through half-closed eyes. "Good couple of weeks?"

"Yep. A gorgeous woman hit on me, and I wasn't interested. Semester's over, my grading's done. I'm a woman of leisure until the intensive begins."

"You like teaching."

Interesting. She skipped the gorgeous woman. "Yeah. It terrified me at first. But once I got into the rhythm, understood the students better, I enjoyed it. I like sharing a culture I love."

"You think of Azar often while you're teaching?"

"I feel like she's by my side, helping."

"Any conflict with that, now that you're married to another woman?"

I shook my head. "I have a really strong sense that Azar isn't just blessing my teaching, but my union with Sarah."

"Sarah? Does she feel the presence of a ghost?"

"No. Sarah realizes if I hadn't had Azar in my life, I wouldn't value what we have." I closed my eyes a moment. Gather your thoughts, Win. "Without loving Azar, I would've seduced Sarah without thought, without meaning. It would've been another fling for me."

Emily nodded. "How's the secrecy going?"

"It's a pain. Sarah's getting restless, but I'm okay hiding until she gives the all clear."

Em nodded and jotted a few notes. She closed the file and laid it on the table beside her. "You've made wonderful progress. You're healing well. Just remember, the PTSD may lay dormant for years. I don't think anyone recovers completely. If you notice symptoms returning, call."

"Are you giving me the brush-off?"

"Never, Win. But I think it's time to test your wings. No more regular appointments. How does that sound?"

"Like I'm being pushed out of the nest, to use your metaphor."

"How does it feel?"

I closed my eyes. Probed my own psyche for an ouch. "Okay. Not great, but generally all right. Makes me sad that I won't see you anymore. But mainly, I feel blessed. I know Sarah and I will hit rougher winds. But for now, I couldn't be happier." I hesitated. "What do I do if things fall apart?"

"With Sarah?"

"No. I don't think they will. We try to talk so things won't build up. It's not our marriage I'm worried about. It's life. I seem to have the ability to attract, uh, situations."

"Both you and Sarah do. Is your antenna telling you something's up?"

"Maybe. Don't know yet."

"If you find that to be the case and you're feeling stressed, call. This doesn't mean an end to our therapeutic relationship. You need to talk, don't hesitate to call. If you and Sarah run into a rough patch, come in for couples' counseling. But I don't think we need regular appointments." She smiled. "Use the money you save to take Sarah out for a nice dinner."

CHAPTER TWO

Sarah

I stared at the bottom of a narrow ravine that had been cleaved by water over eons. Pristine beauty that now was blackened and scarred with the charred remains of a skeletal RV and the chemicals that it had contained.

"Doesn't this creek empty into No Name a mile or so south of here?"

"'Bout a mile and a half," Fire Chief Hubler said, with a spit of tobacco over the bridge. "We got three booms, two hundred feet apart, across the crik. Doubt if anything can get through all three, Sarah."

"I certainly hope to hell not. We're not sure what chemicals they had."

"Meth lab?"

"Yeah. We started calling it the Grey Ghost about six months ago because as soon as we got a sighting, they'd move. I would've liked to catch up with them before this."

Mike Bryer, the head of the Fatal Accident Crash Team, walked up. "Real mess. Don't know how we're gonna get it out."

"You have any idea what caused the crash?" I asked.

"Only a guess now—still have to take statements, like from you, Chief, and whoever answered the call with you."

"We only have one truck with the same volunteers we've had for the past ten years. You know where they are."

I examined Gary Hubler's face. Everything sagged with exhaustion. Even his bushy eyebrows.

"Can you wait until tomorrow morning, Mike?" I asked. "I can sketch in what Gary's told me for you."

"Sure Sarah. No problem." He opened his notebook, looked at the basic diagrams he'd drawn. "At a guess, these guys were traveling too fast for this road in good weather. Last night wasn't good weather. When the storm went through, we had gusts up to fifty-five. Looks to me like this place is a good wind tunnel."

"Too fast, wind grabs them and pushes them over the bridge?" I asked.

"Only a guess at this point. When Doc does the autopsies, I hope he tests for drugs."

"He will. An impaired driver would be the last element for a perfect storm." I turned to Chief Hubler. "Go home, get some rest."

"Gotta shower first." He shoved his helmet on his matted hair and walked away.

"Go on, Sarah, you scram too," Mike said. "The mop-up's gonna take all day. No use you standing around, waiting."

"Okay, but first, any idea how much chemical waste got through before the booms went up?"

"From what I've heard, the water was on fire. So, maybe not so much."

"I'll keep my fingers crossed. You'll have my report from the chief on your desk when you get back."

"You don't have to do that. I'll talk with the Morrowburg VFD tomorrow. This wreck ain't going nowhere."

I turned to the creek for a last look. "Damn, I really wanted to nail these guys."

Mike glanced at me. "They got a longer sentence this way."

I drove back to Greenglen undistracted by the beautiful spring day. I kept thinking how smug Win looked when she told me about the woman who'd flirted with her. No, not smug, more like pleased or gratified with just a tad of preening.

I could hear Dad's voice in my head. "Don't go borrowin' trouble, Sarah Anne." And Mom's. "Keep the green-eyed monster in the basement, Sarah." A little voice in my heart saying, "Don't screw this up with unfounded jealousy. If something had happened, do you really think Win would have told you about it?" Would she?

Maybe I hadn't been generous enough with my compliments, though I didn't think I needed to say anything. I thought my actions showed how much I appreciated her. Her body and her soul. "Tell her, Sarah. Open your damn mouth and tell her how beautiful she is. How generous. And fun. And..." Everything.

I pulled into my parking place in back of the narrow, three-story brick building that housed the sheriff department. My home away from home and away from Win. I tugged out the gold chain that held the wedding band she'd placed on my finger when we'd married. She knew I couldn't wear it at work, so she'd given me the chain I could wear around my neck to remind me of her love. I kissed it, tucked it back inside my uniform shirt and opened my car door. "Don't doubt her. Don't fall into that damn green-eyed monster's trap. Trust her. Period."

Time to keep my mind fully on the job.

* * *

When I got to the early Indiana homestead I shared with my dad, I laid the pizza on the kitchen table and divested myself of all traces of my office except the shirt: jacket, cap and duty belt all went on their proper pegs.

"Bring it on in, Sarah," Dad said from the living room. "We'll pretend we're havin' a picnic an' watch IU whup that dang Kentucky team."

I grabbed a handful of napkins, two plates, piled them on the box and walked into the living room expecting a replay of the IU-Kentucky basketball game on TV. "Baseball?"

"IU got a great team this year," Dad said. "Since we can't be there, thought pizza in here'd be the next best thing."

"When was the last time you went to an IU baseball game?"

"When you was little an' I took you. Big mistake 'cause you was so bored I spent more time lookin' after you than watchin' the game."

I laid out everything on the coffee table and scooted it toward Dad's recliner. "Baseball is inherently boring."

"You're cranky, Sarah." He slid a piece onto his plate. "Heard 'bout the RV crash. Shame they done themselves in like that. Be harder to discover their distribution network now."

"Yeah, but that's not what's really bothering me."

"The leaks that let 'em stay a step ahead of you?"

"I just can't believe anybody from the department would tip them off." I settled on the floor, plate in hand. "I can run the financials, but hell, I hate to do that."

"Been thinkin'." He took a bite and made me wait. "Mac had time in that building after you was elected, afore you was swore in."

"Time to do what?"

"Reckon he mighta bugged the place for sheer spite. You know it's somethin' Mac would do. You might have your friend Bill do a sweep seein' as he owes you."

Yes, he did. Colonel Bill Keller, Marine Corps Intelligence Agency, was rumored to be getting his first general's star, thanks in great part to what my department contributed to his last investigation, not to mention what Win had done. "Good idea, Dad. But, if we do find bugs, how did that intel get from Mac to Larry Fellows and his meth gang?"

"Dang good question, ain't it?"

"I'd love to nail Mac on drug charges. It'd finish his cabal forever in this county." I ate another bite and relished the complex flavors. I settled into dinner, glanced at the TV screen now and then and thought about Rob "Mac" McKenzie. He'd almost bankrupted the trust of the people of the county in his two terms as sheriff. Graft, favoritism and kickbacks were his hallmarks. He'd been behind the candidate who'd opposed me in the last election, busy pulling strings, including trying to out me.

I still didn't know if the people had voted for me in a landslide despite believing I was gay, or because they hadn't believed the accusation. Maybe I'd never know and maybe it wasn't important. Or at least, less important than I keep my integrity. Coming out was a battle still raging in me, mind, heart and soul. I was bone-weary with the issue always looming.

"So what other fleabite ain't you itchin'?" Dad asked.

I glanced at the screen and guessed it was the seventh-inning stretch. Or maybe the game was over. I'd been woolgathering, trying not to think about Win. I sighed and told Dad about Win's meeting with "the gorgeous woman."

"She sound proud?" Dad asked.

"Yeah, a little I think. Why?"

"Think it was her way of sayin' 'I weren't even tempted 'cause I love you too much.' Afore you two got together, I imagin' she woulda viewed a gorgeous lady as a challenge an' not thought twice 'bout acceptin' it."

I thought about it. Win had told me about her footloose days, before she'd met Azar. She'd described it not as an emotional garden, but a barren place of sex only. She couldn't afford attachments, not in the marines. As much as she loved sexual gratification, the lack of a real relationship had left an arid and empty place in her.

"You may be right, Dad. How could I have missed that?"

"You ain't lived long enough, Sarah Anne."

* * *

"So when do I get to call you General Keller?" I asked the next morning. I'd called from a pull-off as I headed back into Greenglen from a meeting with state cops. The spring smells, that light mingling of earth and water and warmth, had seduced me. I'd been tempted to stay on the road this morning as long as possible. I inhaled deeply and felt the rebirth in my bones.

"About two months, from what I hear," Bill said with a laugh. "Where do you get your intel?"

"You'll never know." We both knew Win still kept active contacts. I outlined the possibility of bugs, the electronic variety, in the sheriff's department. "Can you help?"

"Of course. But I'm tied up for a couple of days—preparation for my promotion in D.C.—so would it be okay to send down a couple of my officers?"

"Any help would be greatly appreciated, Bill."

I disconnected and took another deep breath of spring. My phone rang before I'd had a chance to pull out. Win.

"Good morning, my love. Any chance you'll be free Friday night?" she asked. "Wonderful singer at Ruby's."

"Every chance in the world." Unless a pressing case came up, but Win knew that. "You sound chipper this morning."

"Finished my grading and sent them in. I'll have to go in to turn in the paperwork, but for now, I'm a free woman."

"Not too free, I hope."

"Never. I love you, Sarah."

"I love you too, Win."

When I got to the station, the first item on my agenda was meeting with my newly formed SWAT deputies, headed by Willy Nesbit. Although he'd run against me for sheriff, backed by Mac, he'd turned out to be a good guy and someone I trusted. Between us, with Win's input, we'd hired three more members for SWAT who were all ex-military. They were back from the academy for standard police training and ready to pick up patrol duties. I worried how much they might chafe under our procedural restrictions for normal patrol duty.

I walked into the conference room, my notes in a file folder clasped in my sweaty hand. These people were seasoned veterans and I had so little to contribute to their success here. Except the 'here' part. "Good morning and let me officially welcome you to the sheriff's department." I smiled at them as I sat at the head of the table. "Before we start with my notes, I'd like to know what you thought of the academy."

Willy grinned, glanced at the others. "The only one who had an easy time is Thea."

"Easy, my foot," she said, grinning back at Willy. "Being an MP isn't the same."

"A lot of procedure to learn in a short time," Brandon said. "But I think we got the job done."

Andy, the fourth member, nodded.

"Caleb's got copies of the criminal statutes for the county and you'll need to get them down pat." I leaned forward and met the gaze of each of them. "When I interviewed each of you, I think I made it clear you won't be sitting around waiting for ops, you'll be on patrol. You have a high wire to walk. While you patrol, you need to remember that you're not at war with the citizens. At the same time, you've got to realize there's no 'routine' traffic stop or domestic call. You've got to keep your balance. Do you think you can serve and protect—and stay safe?"

Four nods, no hesitation.

"Maybe I realize more than these guys that the most tedious patrol can be deadly," Thea said. She rubbed the table with a long finger. "Yet we can't think about a shoot/no shoot situation every time we respond."

"I couldn't have said it better. I can't emphasize enough the danger if you drift into the complacent zone, nor viewing citizens as innately dangerous and the enemy." I opened the folder. "Here are your assignments. You're partnered with deputies for the first six months. Listen to them. You're the rookies here."

I went through the rest of my list, then asked for questions or comments.

"A four-man unit is small," Willy said. "Can we do some training with other deputies, bulk up our presence some—just in case?"

"Yes. I'd hoped you'd be willing to do that kind of training, but I won't begin it until you've all settled in."

I handed each their shiny new badges and shook hands.

When I walked back to the bull pen, I watched two guys move slowly around the area, gadgets in hand. Bill's troops had arrived.

CHAPTER THREE

Win

The lesbian community in Bloomington had slowly enfolded Sarah into its arms. She'd relaxed into the embrace. Friday night, we'd shared a table on the patio with two other couples for dinner. Sarah laughed and joked with them, no longer fearful of being outed. At least not there. When we'd moved into the back room, the performance space, she'd leaned into my arm. Snuggled while we listened to a pitch-perfect singer deliver her smoky lyrics about women loving women.

Tonight we were staying home. Sarah's turn to say, "Honey, I'm home." My turn to cook. As we ate my version of *narenj palao*, an Afghani dish, I could tell she was preoccupied. With work. Shit. I wished she'd find a job that wouldn't devour her energy. Yeah. Dream on, Win.

"So what's up?" I asked.

"This is so delicious. You're going to have to teach me the names of these dishes so I can ask for them."

"Talk to me, Sarah."

She glanced at me. "Bill's guys found electronic bugs all over the department. I can't seem to stop worrying about them, but they'll keep. Can I enjoy this wonderful dinner now, and after dinner we'll talk?"

I was suspicious that talking was the last thing that would happen later. I was wrong. After dinner, we walked to the garden, Des scampering into the underbrush. As we sat on the bench swing in the garden, watching night come on, Sarah began talking.

"That sonofabutt! He makes me furious, Win. He salted the whole place with hidden mics and listened to every op we planned."

"The sonofabutt—that's Mac?"

"Of course. We have evidence. Dave Howard gave him up." She paused in her outburst. "I'm sorry, Win, I can't remember what I've told you and what's happened since."

"Then let me debrief you. Who's Dave Howard?"

"One of Mac's deputies. I didn't want to 'clean house' when I was elected for the first term and get rid of all of Mac's hires. I thought it'd make me look like a sore winner." She pushed us into motion with a nudge of her foot. "Dave seemed okay, did a good job. Not outstanding, but thorough."

"How'd you turn him?"

"When they found the bugs, Leslie printed them in situ and got enough partials to get a hit. Our own Dave Howard. When we questioned him, he gave up Mac and the whole damn scheme. I should've followed my gut and fired them all, damn the consequences."

"Nothing you can do about that now." I rubbed her arm. "The other end of the scheme? You know where the receiver is? You'll need that for evidence, won't you?"

"You're catching onto this sheriff stuff," she said with a small smile. "Nathan's tracking it, but it's slow because he's doing a grid search. I told him to begin the grid at Mac's, but he said that wouldn't be kosher." She jerked when Des snorted her way between us. "Finally, Nathan and his electronic magic found the damn signal. We served the warrant this morning, and Mac's in jail with a list of charges. DA's having fun searching the statutes for more. We think Mac sold the task force information to the meth dealers, but we haven't got the evidence."

"Good, then it's over."

"No," she said, leaning against me. "When the case hits the news, things are going to explode. Mac still has a lot of supporters who thinks he walks on water."

"You're afraid they'll kill the messenger?"

"It's a double whammy, Win. I hate him because he was not only a lousy officer, but a felon. I can't believe he'd bug the department—well, yes I can. But to sell the info to meth dealers is beyond my comprehension."

"He wanted you to look bad. Probably started out hoping he could find some dirt or incompetence. When that didn't work, he went one step further." I pulled her closer. "Not everyone has a sense of honor, Sarah."

"There was a bug in my office."

I thought back. I'd been on good behavior when I was in her office. Hadn't I? "Are you worried you let something slip about us?"

"I think he probably recorded my end of conversations between us. Maybe that's what he fed that horrible pastor who raised the ruckus."

"He knew you were talking to a woman, but not who?"

"Yeah. Or he knew I was involved with someone and thought if it was a woman, it'd cause a scandal that would sink me."

Des nuzzled Sarah. Giving comfort as only a dog can.

"Mac is the gift that just keeps on giving." She took Des's head in her hands and planted a big kiss on her muzzle. "Let's go in, Win. Maybe you can distract me, help me forget this train of thought."

I kissed her. "That's a distinct possibility."

* * *

We'd gone hiking Tuesday, a long trail that wore out both of us. Which was the purpose. It's hard to worry about something when all of your concentration is required to set one boot after another. When we'd gotten home, we'd gone to bed. To sleep. We'd made up for it this morning.

Then Sarah went to work. Back to the buzzing of doom in her head. So little I could do to help her lift the load.

I wanted to catch Kemat's presentation at the high school, part of a broad-reaching "tolerance for difference" campaign they'd embarked on after a young girl committed suicide. She'd been targeted because she was gay by a gang of boys who'd raped her. I didn't think "tolerance" was a strong enough term.

Kemat stood in front of the assembled faculty and students. She'd dressed in Western garb from head to foot. Red power suit, hair swept into a tight French twist, higher heels than were safe. The only clue was a small golden pin on her lapel. The ankh. Kemat's presentation should've been called "myth busting." She tackled all the boogeyman rumors about Middle East countries and the Muslim faith. Well done, Kemat.

I met her afterward, asked where she wanted to eat.

"Are there any vegetarian places here?" she asked.

"But if you want good coffee, we'll have to go to another place after we finish eating."

I took her to the restaurant where I'd met Emily once or twice. At least their wraps were decent. When we'd settled at a table, she fussed a bit. Moved her purse and tote bag from one chair to another. When she'd finally settled, I asked what favor could I do for her.

"I need your help to find Bassir."

"An Arab? Why me? You must have an extensive network of your own."

"I do, but I have made little progress." She frowned, examined my face. "I am well aware of the pattern of your deployments. You were not military police, at least, not for long. Yes?"

I stared at her.

"All right, I can accept you cannot talk about what you did. But I believe you were part of MCIA. Or perhaps, CIA. You did not learn Tajik so well policing military personnel."

I was grateful the waiter chose that moment to deliver our orders.

We began eating, a little chitchat between bites. When we finished, she took the bill. "Now, if you have time, let us go for coffee."

Kemat restarted her earlier conversation as soon as we'd placed our order and found a quiet table. "I want you to find Bassir Sadeeq Zulficar." She handed me a file. "All that I have found is in this file."

"Kemat, even if I'd been involved with MCIA, I'm no longer an active military member. There's no intelligence service I have access to. At the very best, I could only hand over the file to a friend who's still active."

She shook her head. "I trust *you*. I have spoken with Tajik friends about you. You have garnered acclaim and affection. That is what

I trust, not Bill. Do what you can, and if you fail, then let it be on my head."

I scanned the first few pages of the file. Journalist, got out of Syria. Disappeared. I looked at Kemat, tried every argument I could think of. She was adamant. No one but me. Finally I said, "I'll try, but I'm not sure I can do more than ask around about him."

"Do what you can, Win. That is all I ask."

* * *

I didn't refuse because I couldn't. It was part of the hospitality code in the Middle East. I lugged the file home, set it on my desk. Went for a long walk with Des who was ticked at me because I hadn't taken her with me for a ride. She loved riding in the truck. I wondered if she thought every time we went out, it was a job for her sensitive nose or killer teeth. Retirement didn't have meaning for her. How could it?

When we got back, I went through the file as I started making dinner. Wished Sarah was here to share it. As I chopped, I wondered how the hell I could find anyone now. No access to MCIA database or any of the dozen or so databases it opened. Bill had access, but I hesitated asking him. Kemat knew him. How well? But she'd asked me to dig. Conundrum. Depending on what the whole file contained, I could poke around on my own. Kemat asked for my help. I couldn't say no. Period.

I'd finish reading the file tonight.

My phone rang. I leaned over as I wiped my hands. Sarah. "Are you checking up on me?"

"No, should I?"

"Funny. You find more bugs?"

"No. I just called to ask if I can come over."

"I'm just finishing up dinner prep. Hungry?"

"Always. Be there in five minutes."

She disconnected. Hadn't sounded upset. But we usually kept her visits to a minimum. She was worried that neighbors would think the sheriff was patrolling here way too much. By the time I'd chopped extra veggies to sauté, I heard her car coming up the drive. When she walked through the door, Des gave her a greeting that said, "I haven't seen you in such a long time!"

Sarah grinned at me. "Dad's 'bowling' night, which means he's hanging out with Dog. So I won't stay the night, but I missed you."

We kissed. Certainly not a June and Ward peck.

"We have to eat first," I told her. "The *quorma*'s almost ready."

"You're no fun, although eating is a pleasurable pursuit too. Tell me what goes on the table." She cupped my breast and gave my nipple a tweak through my sweatshirt.

"So why are you so restless tonight?" I asked as we ate.

"We're transcribing all the stuff Mac recorded. I'm nervous what'll come to light."

"About us?"

She nodded. "I'm not doing the transcription. John Morgan and his detectives are."

"We can't backspace time, Sarah. Just hope you were oblique enough. That they're more interested in nailing Mac. You're working on his phone records aren't you?"

"Nathan and Caleb are. I'm trying to stay away from the hands-on investigation—why, I don't know. I named Caleb my chief deputy, gave John Morgan his promotion and Nathan's a best friend. All my people. When the shit hits the wind, it's going to land on me." She ate a few bites, smiled. "What's up with you? Just tell me every detail so I can listen and not think."

I understood what Sarah was feeling. It's the moment before you begin the op with no idea of what you'll really face. Or maybe an actor waiting for the curtain to rise, not knowing if an audience is out front. Keep the action going. Don't think about taking a bullet. Or a curtain call. "Emily cut me loose."

"Wow. That's great…isn't it?"

"Yeah. She thinks I'm healing well enough to fly solo. But I can return to the nest if I need to."

"It hasn't been easy, has it?"

"Still isn't. At times. Having you in my life has made it possible for me to move forward, stop living in the past. I love you, Sarah."

She smiled, a lovely opening of eyes and lips.

"I have a side job." I outlined the quest Kemat had given me. "I can't say no. Hell if I know what I can do. Except try."

"If you need help, Win, ask. As long as it's legal."

For a lot of my life, asking for help had been a nonstarter. I didn't depend on anyone else for anything. Survival. That had begun to change when I started working with small units in the field. We had to depend on one another. Had to ask for what we needed. For all the nightmares those missions caused me, they had pushed me onto the road toward trust. So had the kids, the beautiful and trusting kids I'd met in dusty villages.

That road had led me to Azar. She'd pushed me farther along. To Sarah.

We cleared the table together and settled on the couch.

"I need to feel you in me, Win," she said, wrapping her arms around me. Straddling me. "It's in those moments I feel most *me*, centered, in balance."

CHAPTER FOUR

Sarah

"So we have a link between Mac and Larry Fellows from phone records, but no physical evidence?" I asked.

"We've got the calls exchanged between the meth head and Mac," Caleb said. "We've got proof Fellows purchased the phone, both from the clerk and surveillance photos. We just don't have the physical evidence Fellows was the one using it, or that he was using it for drug deals."

"I may be able to help," Leslie said.

I turned to her, and so did everyone at the conference table. "Go on."

"Vincente found the remains of a cell phone in the RV wreck. It was in a cell holder on the visor on the driver's side. We can't do diddly with it, but the FBI lab may be able to."

"Call Tony Garcia at the FBI office in Evansville and ask his help in expediting the turnaround time," I told her. "And, Caleb, go back to the phone records from Mark Jarek's bust. I seem to remember a Fellows/Jarek connection. If it's there, talk to Susan Jarek for verification. She owes us for not including her in the charges, or filing child endangerment charges."

"We'll get right on it, Sarah," Caleb replied. "We need a tight noose for Mac or that fancy lawyer'll get him off."

"Anything else?" I asked.

"Something Vincente found," John said. He put a couple of photos on the table. "Damage on the RV that looks like contact with another vehicle." He nodded to Leslie.

She continued his line of thought. "We're running paint samples from the damage, but don't hold your breath. I think it's going to be a long list of vehicle models. Now, there's a possibility the damage occurred sometime before the RV crashed, but scientifically speaking, the likelihood is that it happened very close to the time the RV went off the road. We've got damage on the other side from the barrier that shows the same characteristics."

"You think the RV was run off the road?"

"Yes, ma'am. So does Vincente."

"I concur," Mike Bryer said. "In fact, I was going to bring it up. We thought it was a wind gust at first. But the more we studied it, the less possible that became. I won't bore you with a lot of data, but angles of trajectory were all wrong. It's in my report." He slid a file across the table.

Well, this was a curve ball. "I doubt if Mac did his own dirty work, so check with body shops to see who's brought in a vehicle for front-end repair." I looked at John. "How're the transcriptions coming?"

"Slow work. When we get a mention of the RV sightings, we start a time line and match Mac's phone data. I think we have a start date. But, Sarah, we're not even halfway through."

"You need more ears?"

"No, it'd just get confusing," John said. "Unless you want us to go faster."

"You've got it organized, keep on going." I closed the file. "Nice work, folks. Now let's get back to work."

I motioned Nathan over as the others filed out of the conference room. "Win needs some help from you."

"Yeah, she called this morning. Gave me a name to search."

"Please, don't do anything illegal. I don't want to have to arrest either one of you."

A smile split his solemn face into one huge grin. "Gotta catch us first."

* * *

By Friday morning, we had enough to bring Susan Jarek in. Her two kids were in the break room with Dory and I watched her fidget through the interrogation room's one-way mirror.

"How do you want to play it?" Caleb asked.

"Straight." I had the urge to giggle and hoped Caleb didn't notice. "When we arrested her scumbag husband, I was the one who found her a place to stay with her kids. I won't let her forget she owes me, but I won't bully her. She's had enough of that."

I tucked the thick file under my arm and entered the small, soulless space where we pumped suspects for information or confessions. "How are you Susan? The kids look healthy and happy."

"They're good, Sheriff. I can't thank you enough for getting me out of that hellhole."

"You're more than welcome. I just wish you'd called us earlier, well, called us for help. We're here to help. But there's a way you can help us. If you will?"

"Sure, but don't know anything about his business," she said, folding her hands on the table. "He wouldn't talk about none of that stuff."

"We're trying to get a line on some of his phone calls. Especially the ones to Larry Fellows."

"That guy was scary. He come by a couple of times." Susan shuddered.

Nice acting job? She might not have been involved in the business, but I'd bet my paycheck she'd kept tabs on her husband. "If I gave you some dates, could you remember if he talked to Larry Fellows on the phone that day?"

"I suppose you want me to remember what they were talking about," she said, with a jut of her chin. "Fuck it. When he wasn't in the shed, he was talking on his damn phone. With two kids running around, it wasn't hard to ignore him."

"Try, Susan." I shoved a calendar across the table. I'd marked the dates with the times the calls had come in. "Your continued cooperation is important to us. Think. See what you can remember. Please."

She examined the calendar, flipping from one page to the next and then back. “I really don’t know. One day was like the one before it and the one after it. Clean, cook, do laundry, take care of the kids. And I never had anything to write down on a calendar. If things got to be too much, I’d call Momma and go over to home.”

Interesting choice of words. Momma’s was home. I sighed because I believed her. While we’d had the house under surveillance, the only time she left was to go grocery shopping or visit her mother.

“I suppose you found his recordings,” she said. “I don’t know what I can add. I really don’t.”

“What recordings?”

“He had this little digital recorder he attached to the phone and only used it when it was a business call.” She frowned. “You didn’t find it?”

I shook my head. “Where is it?”

“I honestly don’t know, Sheriff. Cross my heart. He’d hide it in a different place every night, and since I was at Momma’s all day the day you busted him, I got no idea.”

I tore a clean sheet from my notebook, passed it and a pen to her. “Write down every single hiding place you saw him use.”

I left the room and met Caleb in the corridor. “Get Leslie, Vincente and John down to that house right now. It’s been under seal since the raid, but if someone knew he’d been recording, it’d be easy enough to slip in the back.”

“We searched the place the day after the raid, Sarah,” Caleb said.

“But we weren’t looking for a small, digital recorder. We had no reason to then, but we do now. I’ll text the list to John when she’s finished.”

* * *

“It was so disgusting, yet simultaneously gratifying, to hear Mac’s voice delivering the news of our next raid to a convicted drug dealer,” I said, placing the pizza box on the counter. “His own damn voice, Win, selling us out to drug dealers.”

She gave me a quick grin. “Do you always get this excited about a bust?”

"No. I keep worrying that this is my form of revenge, but it isn't. If anything, it's retribution. You wouldn't believe the mess I found when I took office. Sweetheart contracts with his cronies that ate up most of our budget, no update training for deputies, sloppy casework and in a couple of cases, either letting somebody off or faking evidence to convict an innocent person."

"Why hasn't he been brought up on charges?" Win asked.

"He's a slippery sonofabutt. We couldn't prove any of it. That's why this is so sweet. A direct connection between Mac and Jarek."

"I don't get it. How come Mac didn't warn Jarek about the raid that took Jarek down?"

"Speculation for now, but we think Mac figured we were too close to nabbing Jarek, so he hung him out on the nearest limb and put his bet on Fellows. Remember, Fellows never showed the night of the raid."

"He might've financed the RV for Fellows. Something you might want to look into," Win said. "What about the other transcripts that had you so worried? Have you read them?"

"I've stayed away from all of that, besides, I asked our DA what to do with the transcripts we won't need in the case and he said to store them in the basement."

"The place that floods?"

"Yep." I watched Win get plates and napkins, the way her muscles moved in her forearms as she reached. I took the pizza to the table and got the pleasure of watching Win walk.

"What?" she asked.

"You're a beautiful woman, and I like watching you."

She kissed me. "If I heard that from anybody else, it'd be creepy."

After I inhaled the first piece, I thought about what she'd asked. "Why'd you ask about the transcripts?"

"Because they bother you. You're afraid of what they contain. Yet you're willing to bury them. Let them ghost you." She took a second piece, laid it on her plate and licked her fingers. "I'd think you'd want to know what your detectives heard."

Bull's-eye. "Chicken woman, that's me."

"You'd stop worrying if you knew, Sarah."

"Or maybe be incredibly embarrassed in front of them."

She took another bite. I waited for a comment, but it was long to come. She finally looked up. "If they know, they know. Face the fact and read the damn transcripts. In tae kwon do, you have to know where you stand before you can defend yourself."

"Oh, hell. I think I should take out a full-page in the *Sentinel* and announce our marriage. Then all of this would be over."

She grinned. "I'll chip in half. I'm impatient with you about this because there's a simple answer to 'Do they know?' It's waiting for you in the station's basement. You don't futz around when you're at work. You go for the essence of the matter. You charge into it. Stop being a wimp."

"Not fair, Win. This is personal."

"Bullshit. Fortify yourself. March bravely forth." She accentuated the last phrase with her pizza slice.

I laughed.

She was right. Face the boogeyman straight on. The same way I did every day, in every arrest, in every traffic stop.

After we cleaned up, we settled on the couch.

"You have any hot movies we can watch?" I asked.

"Are you spending the night?"

I shook my head. As much as I wanted to, I had work tomorrow. "I'm taking the early shift for Caleb."

"Then let's make our own movie—without a camera."

CHAPTER FIVE

Win

I lay in bed the next morning, well past my normal up-with-the-dawn. When Sarah had left last night, Des jumped up on the bed and nestled close to me. I awoke with my arm thrown over her, her head nestled into my shoulder. Psychic dog. I needed to cuddle. Around eight, Des indicated her duty was over and she needed to go out. I threw on my robe, walked to the deck door and watched the warming sun.

Wondered if Sarah and I would ever get to wake up together every morning.

Des charged past me and waited at the door. Impatiently. Just like last night when I told Sarah to face the boogeyman in the basement. Impatiently. I'd trust her to have my back in a firefight without a thought. But it frustrated me that she could pretend something didn't exist so she didn't have to think about it. "Chicken woman" was right. When we first got together, she'd told me she didn't want to think about repercussions. Just be in the moment. In other words, have sex and close out the world. I thought she still wanted the same thing.

Emily had taught me how to ask questions of myself. Probe. But that had only happened because I'd been a basket case. I didn't want to see Sarah get to that point before she'd look squarely at her coming-out issues.

Des whined. I let her out, started the coffee. I showered and wondered what I wanted to do today. An absolutely delightful feeling. One that took adjustment. Sometimes I wanted a plan for the day handed to me so all I had to do was follow it. Freedom was hard to get accustomed to.

While I drank my coffee, I opened the files I'd found for Bassir Sadeeq Zulficar. From those and the file Kemat had given me, I'd learned that Bassir was a journalist based in Jordan and working for Reuters and the Associated Press. He'd filed stories from inside Syria, but the last one was nearly a month ago. Silence since then.

I studied the files for what they didn't say. He'd earned his journalism degree at Northwestern University. Nothing in his bio before that. No place of birth, nothing about his parents. I'd asked Nathan to concentrate on his early life. What echoes he could pick up from Syria of Bassir. I thought it strange Reuters hadn't made any announcement. Maybe they didn't know if he was dead or being held by one side or the other. Too many unknowns. Like where he was now.

I'd put out a few feelers to old MCIA friends, asked them to quietly probe for intel. I hadn't heard back from any of them. Yet. Nor had I heard from Nathan. I thought about contacting some of my old informants, but I didn't want to stir up a hornet's nest until I had more definite intel. Shit.

I rinsed my mug and coffeepot, put them in the drainer. Waiting for the pieces to come together was the hardest part of any op. The one part I wasn't great at. I stuck my cell phone in my pocket and looked at Des. "Your choice. Work in the garden? Hike up Foley's Knob?"

She woofed at both choices. "Maybe we better stick close to home right now."

She wagged her tail and raced through the door as soon as I opened it.

I was about halfway through weeding the garden when my phone rang. Sarah. "Miss you," I said.

"They're not here, Win."

"What's not where?"

"The transcripts from my office, they're not in storage. They should be here, but they're not."

"Glad you faced the boogeyman in the basement." I wiped my hands on my pants. "So who's in charge of the transcripts?"

"Me."

"Sarah, stop the panic and think. Who did the transcripts from your office?"

"John Morgan."

"Then ask him what he did with them. This is not complicated."

Silence. An exhale. "In my head, I know you're right. The pit of my stomach is saying something way different."

"Eat a cracker and talk to the detective. Now."

I clicked off. I was getting ticked. Then I remembered how scared I'd been freshman year in college. Wonderful freedom and terrifying consequences of openly identifying as gay. Walking hand in hand with Annie across campus. Feeling the stares, hearing the whispers. Trying to practice what Nathan called "duck medicine." Letting it roll off my back.

Sarah faced the same feelings in midlife. After I turned her life upside down. I thought about calling her back but decided to let my kick in the pants stand.

I'd almost finished my weeding task when the phone rang again. Sarah.

"You find them?" I asked.

"He never transcribed them because all the planning we did for the raids happened in the conference room. That was the evidence we were looking for. He gave me a copy of the recordings. Can I come over this afternoon? We can listen to them together."

"Need some hand holding, huh? I will be more than happy to provide a hand. Or two."

She snickered. "See you around three."

* * *

"You feel better?" I asked, after listening to Sarah's voice for a couple of hours. There'd been nothing "incriminating" on them. A little flirtation, but no clue who the recipient was.

"You're still pissed at me, aren't you?" she asked, wiping her hands on her jeans.

"Not pissed. Mildly ticked. I don't think it does you any good to panic, Sarah. You don't panic at work, even when you're facing a killer. Why get so twisted up over this?"

"I know." She leaned back on the couch. "It's totally irrational."

I watched her breasts as she crooked her hands behind her head. Lovely. "You've always fenced off your private life—at least since you've been a cop. I wasn't home when Hugh was killed. But I don't imagine you showed your grief publicly."

"No, I couldn't."

"Why not?"

Sarah stretched. "You've been hanging around Em too much."

"Maybe you should hang around her more." I wanted to unbutton Sarah's shirt. Free those beautiful breasts. Stay on topic, Win. "Think about it, Sarah. Why couldn't you show your grief? Did you think you had to live up to some image? Or couldn't you share the grief?"

She reached out to me. "I don't want to go where I'll hurt you, but did you show grief when Azar died?"

"Show it? I lived it. Wept. Wailed. Did everything but tear out my hair. I would've done that, but my hair was too short to get a good grip." I entwined our fingers. "But the people of the village understood. Even if they didn't know we were lovers. In their eyes, Azar and I were friends. So an expression of my grief was normal."

"You're saying it's cultural?" Sarah asked as she squeezed my hand.

"Nope. Or maybe part of it is. All of those straight women, sneaking around with the gray shades books. Embarrassed if they're discovered, loving every moment of the read. We've got a wide Puritan streak we've never lost."

"Like a skunk, it stinks, but it ain't gonna change. You'd think frontier living would've taken the starch out of that crap. But all it did was reinforce it."

"In the end, it doesn't matter. You know that, don't you, Sarah?"

She nodded and leaned her head against my shoulder.

"Sarah, we're married." I raised her hand and kissed it. "This isn't going to go away because you don't think about it."

"I keep going around in circles."

"You go round long enough in the same place, you create ruts. If all the marriage equality challenges end up in the Supreme Court and they decide in our favor, we can file a joint tax return. You'll be able to share my benefits, though it may take the military a bit longer."

"Hell, I hadn't even been thinking about that." She ran a hand through her hair. "Can we do that even if we don't live together?"

"Don't know. We'll have to ask my lawyer. All I'm saying is, we've made a commitment. We made it in the shadows. That doesn't make it less real. But shining a little light on it lets it sparkle." I ran the back of my hand over her cheek. "You want to go out to dinner?"

"All the way to Bloomington? I don't know, Win, I've got the early shift tomorrow."

"We could go into Greenglen." She stiffened. "Take that look off your face. I wasn't suggesting we fuck atop a table at the French Kitchen. Just have a nice dinner."

"Would McDonald's drive-through work?"

I laughed. "I'd rather starve. How about we skip dinner for now?" I leaned over and kissed her. Slow. Light. Teasing. She didn't let me get away with that for long.

* * *

Sarah had spent most of the night, left right before sunrise. She'd be cranky today. Or energized. I stretched as the coffee perked. I could smell Sarah's scent on my body, bringing moments to life again. What a woman. I only hoped she wasn't using sex to ignore the problems she faced. We faced.

Nathan called while I was finishing breakfast. "Sorry this Bassir thing is taking me so long, but there's a lot of contrary data out there. I thought if we could meet, you could tell me what's probable and what to ignore."

"Other than sounding like Mr. Data, I have no idea what you're talking about. It's early, Nathan. How about if I come over around noon?"

Nathan cleared his throat. Or was disguising a laugh. "See you then."

I went back to bed for a nap. Didn't shower, didn't change the sheets. Dreamed of Sarah. Awoke feeling warm and loved.

As I got ready to leave, I remembered the statistical analysis Paige had mentioned months ago. Attitudes toward gays in McCrumb County. As a fellow faculty member, she'd promised me a copy. I called Paige and asked her about the paper.

"Terry gave me hard copy, and I've been meaning to drop it in the mail to you. I'll do it in the morning. Promise."

"You have plans for later this afternoon? I could meet you at Ruby's. I'd like to talk to you anyway."

"What time?"

"I've got an appointment at noon. Could I call you when I leave for Ruby's?"

"Not a problem."

When I got to Nathan's, I could begin to see what he was talking about. Contrary reports of sightings of Bassir from Damascus to Berlin.

"Shit. Well, let's go through them, one by one."

Two hours later, Nathan said, "Let me check something." He began pulling up different sites. "I could check the passenger manifests if we knew what name he was traveling under."

"It'd be too dangerous for him to try to fly under another name."

"Unless he squirreled away another identity for a time like this." He brought up a facial recognition program and began running images. He swiveled his chair. "I'm running West Coast airports. This may take time, like hours. No use you hanging around if you have something else to do."

"Okay, I'll take off, but it's not what you think. Meeting in Bloomington. Would you collate all this stuff, send it to me? Maybe I can tap some contacts for verification."

"Will do."

"Anything on Bassir's early life?"

"Nothing. I'm still working on it, but somebody's done a great job of obliterating his past. I thought I'd found a trail, but it dead-ended. Keep working?"

"Please, as long as you have time."

As I drove to Bloomington, I thought of the bowl of spaghetti we'd found. From what we figured out, Bassir had made it out of Syria. Across the Turkish border, the most permeable one. From there, he'd gone to Istanbul. A flight out to Berlin. There, the more or less reliable route ended.

I had big questions. Why, if he had information the Assad government wanted hidden, didn't he release it as soon as he was out of Syria? Why Berlin? If he'd made it to this country, why was he still invisible?

I realized I was making ruts. Getting nowhere and digging myself in deeper. I needed more intel, better intel. I crossed my fingers that Nathan's homemade program was sophisticated enough to whisk Bassir's image from millions of others. Somehow, I thought it might be.

As I walked to the patio at Ruby's, I stopped to chat with a couple of people I knew. It felt good to be known by the community. To feel women at my back.

I spotted Paige at a table, sat down next to her. "Good to see you. Been awhile."

She laughed. "I'll bet I've seen you and Sarah a dozen times. Somehow you seem to only have eyes for Sarah and she for you. Still in the honeymoon stage, eh?"

My only response was a satisfied smile.

"So what else do you want from me besides the report?" She slid a manila envelope across the table.

"Could I have a summary of it first?"

"Bottom line is that the majority of people in McCrumb County believe homosexuality is wrong and there's no further reason for discussing marriage equality." She raised a hand. "But by a much thinner margin than ever before. It indicates a change in thinking."

"They hate us, but they're thinking about it?"

"Back to my question. What else is bothering you?"

I sighed. Tried to organize my thoughts. "This is going to sound crude. Prurient. But I don't mean it that way."

"Granted, I don't have to answer."

"When you were coming out, didn't want to think about it, did you hide behind sex? I mean…"

"I understand perfectly what you mean. Yes, Vi and I had a veritable orgy of positions and toys. She's very inventive. I loved every minute, and it helped me very much from thinking too much. Sarah's still not willing to face the question?"

I sighed again. "She vacillates. If she weren't sheriff, I think it'd be a lot easier for her. Sometimes I think it comes down to the job versus us."

"Hate to tell you, Win, but she's already made the choice." Paige tapped my wedding ring. "Does she wear her band on the job?"

"I gave her a chain because I knew she couldn't. She wears it around her neck."

"Couldn't or wouldn't?" Paige said. "I understand the complexity of the situation. God knows I was confused. I didn't think I was lesbian at first, but when I began noticing other women here at Ruby's—you know, breasts and curves, and wondering how they'd be in bed—I figured it was time to say yes. But I talked it over with Vi. Asked her if that meant I was lesbian. She started laughing and couldn't stop. Now we share our, um, observations. We both would love to see you naked. If you're ever interested in a three-way…"

"Ah shit, Paige. That isn't helping."

"I bet you've had plenty of three-ways."

"Plus four through eight. But that has nothing to do with what I'm asking."

"Eight? My, that must have been confusing." She sipped an iced tea and looked me up and down. "What are you asking?"

"How can I help Sarah? I don't want to push her into a mistake that she'll regret."

"It's beginning to make you crazy, eh? Vi wasn't nearly as patient as you." She tapped her fingers on the table. "Is Sarah seeing a therapist?"

"We've done some couples' counseling with my shrink. I found Emily because I needed help when I came back home from duty. She also does after-action work with the sheriff's department. Conflict of interest since I'm her client, so she'll only do couples' work with us."

"Maybe it's time for a session, Win. Seriously, I faced no job repercussions, and I'm not sure it would've mattered if I had. I can always find another position. How much a part of Sarah's identity is involved with her job?"

"Her dad once said she had the McCrumb County sheriff's gene. Micah was sheriff, *his* father was sheriff. It's a hell of a large part of her identity. Of who she is."

"Then the push-pull between office and marriage is very real. She may not come out as lesbian or married to a woman until some threat from the outside pushes her out. That's a dangerous situation."

CHAPTER SIX

Sarah

I left the county commissioners' meeting royally pissed. The county's economic picture, while not rosy, was no longer in the dire circumstances that had reduced my budget for the past few years. I'd had to fight to maintain our current funding because they cited our success with federal grants. Didn't they know federal grants were drying up faster than streams in drought? Plans for a water park were proceeding on the thin promise of more tourist dollars. As Dad would say, "Pah!"

Maybe the next election cycle, I'd run for the county commission instead of sheriff. Nah, I couldn't see myself in any other role, nor could I see myself presenting rational arguments to the bunch of old farts.

Before I drove to Win's, I put my wedding band on my hand and the chain in my pocket. Des greeted me like a long-lost friend and I found Win working in the garden.

"You're early," she said, mud all over her jeans and boots. "Something wrong?"

"The only thing that's wrong is the stupidity of a bunch of old white fogies who run this county like a fiefdom." Mud or not, I melted into her arms. I stood quietly and let her wrap me in her warmth. She kissed me on the forehead, took my hand and led me into the house after kicking off her boots on the back stoop.

"I need to shower," she said. "Want to help?"

I didn't need a second invitation, and the combination of streaming water and Win's hands let me forget everything outside the small steaming cubicle. I took her to bed and returned the passion, stroke by stroke.

We lay enwrapped in one another's arms and legs, and I felt safe.

Win ran her hand over my belly and I was ready to go again. "Whoa, Sarah, this is just me enjoying the feel of your body."

I pulled her close and kissed her. Her touch, even featherlight, made me want to open my legs and push her hand down to my center. "I think I'm addicted. Every touch of yours makes me liquid."

She propped herself up and scanned my face. "Remember what you said when we first got together?"

"That I was a middle-aged woman who'd been mostly celibate since Hugh died? That the times I'd had sex were worth skipping? Yeah, I remember it and how embarrassed I was saying it."

"You've gotten over the embarrassment stage," she said with a grin. "I don't know what's going on with you. Maybe you're filling up an empty well."

I remembered the Cris Williamson song and it began running through my mind. I was more than willing to begin filling up again.

"On the other hand, I've seen military members addicted to all sort of things," Win said. "I think I was addicted to sex without ties for a lot of years. My way of running away from an ache for closeness. You want to talk with Emily about it?"

"I thought she cut you loose."

"She kept the door open for me if I need it—and couples' counseling. I can call and make an appointment. If you want."

I looked into her eyes and saw concern echoed back at me. "Why am I making such a mess of our love?"

"It's not a mess," she said, stroking my chin. "Not now. It could become a real tension between us at some point." She kissed me softly. "I was listening to NPR this morning, and I heard a quote I liked. 'Curiosity is a great antidote for fear.' Maybe you just need to switch your curiosity from our physical bodies to what's inside your head. A bit."

I knew what she said was true, both curiosity about my thoughts and Emily. I didn't want to know what was going on inside my head. Why not? I sighed. "Call Emily. But before you call, will you do me again?"

* * *

Em couldn't fit us in until the end of the week, so I got to enjoy Tuesday without introspection. Win got a call as we were preparing dinner. She walked to her desk, settled down at the computer and scanned some files. "This is all?"

She nodded at the answer. "Anything on Kemat's missing years?" She nodded again. "I'll see what I can get from my sources. Thanks Nathan."

She disconnected as she walked toward the kitchen. "Trying to fulfill Kemat's request is a real bitch. We're missing too much data to do a thorough job."

"What's missing?"

She watched me throw pasta into the steam of the boiling water. "A good portion of Kemat's past. Why Bassir is back in this country."

"Why's her background important to finding this guy?"

"Because it's bothered me since I first looked her up. I need to have some handle on why she's asking me to find Bassir."

"You don't trust her?" I asked as I stirred the dancing pasta.

"It's not that." She walked behind me and kneaded my butt while she kissed the back of my neck.

"That's not going to work this time," I said. "If you trust her, why do you need her background?"

She gave my butt a light slap. "I don't like working in the dark. I like all my data laid out in front of me so I can move pieces around until the puzzle snaps into place."

I tasted the pasta and it was perfect. I ran it through the colander, mixed it into the sauce Win had prepared and plated it up. As I carried the plates to the table, Win finished with the salad. She was distracted while we ate. I could see her pushing the puzzle pieces around.

"Okay, what *do* you know about Kemat?" I asked.

She gave me a basic outline. "It's the period from when her family left Egypt to when she arrived in this country that's missing. They arrived legally."

"Where from?"

"Don't know. The only way I can get it is to ask Nathan to hack the State Department. I'm not going to land him in jail."

"I'm surprised he hasn't done it already." I glanced at Win. "He has an adventurous nature, and no, he doesn't hack for the department or me. You know anybody in ICE?"

She shook her head. "Besides, that'd send the wrong message. I don't want Kemat questioned. I just want to fill in the gap."

"Why don't you just ask her?"

"Not polite. She needs to trust me too." She put her fork down. Her plate was empty. "I'm sorry. I didn't mean to be distant. I couldn't let it go. Felt like something was going to click. It didn't."

We cleared the table and dumped the dishes into the sink to soak. Win turned to me, kissed me. "What would you like to do? Watch a DVD? Listen to some music and dance?"

"Hot movie, one that'll show me something new that'll crisp my toes."

Win laughed and smothered my face with kisses. "We got an offer to join another couple for some friendly sex. That something you're interested in?"

"*No*." I lifted up her T-shirt and kissed her chest, beginning with the space between her breasts. "Who asked?"

"I'll never tell unless you say yes."

I took a step back. "You think we should?"

She drew me back. "No. I have no intention of sharing you with anyone. Not until we're on Social Security ten years or so. Too stiff to do much swinging."

"I have to wait thirty years?" I grinned. "You have any movies that show what I'm missing?"

"Incorrigible. Utterly and infinitely incorrigible."

* * *

I'd only been in the office an hour when the call came in, not enough time to catch up with patrol logs or any other paperwork. I grabbed my cap and headed for the Alert State Wildlife Area. The streams were full, wildflowers coming into bloom and everything in the landscape showed shades of green. An hour later, I drove into the entrance to the remote protected land. The deputy who'd called it in walked me down a twisting path to the scene, which she'd rimmed with crime scene tape. It was too beautiful an early summer day to dwell in death and decay.

I put on booties and moved carefully toward the shallow grave. This would be a good dumpsite, isolated but accessible by the path we'd followed in. There weren't enough neighbors in the area to do a canvass, but we'd have to do one anyway. We needed a time frame first.

I stared at the jumble of brown bones. Could be old bones, although with the peat content in this swampy area, it was hard to tell. We'd have to call Dr. Elspeth Mackintosh, the forensic anthropology expert at IU. I didn't envy Elie's job, but personally, I'd rather look at a skeleton than a decomposing body.

I turned to the deputy. "How was it found?"

"Guy running field trials with his hound. Dog got distracted, did the digging."

"You get a statement?"

"Yes ma'am. He wrote it out and signed it. I let him go on home."

"Good work, Patty. Get hold of dispatch and get the cadaver dogs up here. Then extend the crime tape." I pointed out the perimeter I wanted.

Under her tan, she paled. "You think there are more?"

"No idea, but we need to check. Ask the trainer to get them up here quickly. I'm going to call Dr. Mackintosh, and I want them to sniff around before she gets here. She doesn't like dogs 'mucking up her scene.'"

The deputy nodded and got on her radio.

I punched in Elie's number. "Elie? I got bones and I'm pretty sure they're human. I saw part of what I think's the skull. We're at the Alert State Wildlife Area, and the bones are close to a boggy area. When can you be here?"

"Give me a couple of hours to round up my team and equipment. We should be there by four. Anyplace close for us to stay?"

"I'll arrange it. Thanks Elie."

As I closed my phone, Patty approached.

"Dogs are on their way, ETA twenty minutes."

"Great. That should give them plenty of time before Elie shoos them away."

"Gives me the spooks that there might be more," she said, looking over the clearing. "Or you think this might be a pioneer cemetery?"

I shrugged. "That's Elie's bailiwick. There are a lot of them in the county that have never been discovered. Will you stay until Elie gets here?"

"Yes ma'am. Here or at the entrance?"

"Entrance. There's not much traffic down here, so I think it'll be okay until I can dispatch somebody to help you. What's the name of the new DNR agent?"

"Jack Kindler."

"I'll see if I can track him down. They've sponsored educational programs here, but with the budget cuts, I'm not sure if they still do. I wonder if they do a regular patrol." I gave the clearing a last look. "If you need anything, give me a call."

I walked back to my cruiser, trying to get rid of the smell of old bones.

CHAPTER SEVEN

Win

I intercepted Kemat as she came out of the high school.

Her eyes widened when she saw me. She hurried over. "You have news? Yes?"

"You have time for lunch?"

She examined my face, finally nodded.

Though it would cost me this month's pension, I took her to the French Kitchen. Quiet. Few fellow diners. Perfect for a complicated conversation.

After we'd ordered, she stared at me. The intensity of her gaze reminded me of Taliban I'd interrogated. Single-minded. Passionate to the point of strapping on a suicide vest.

"Well?" she asked.

I put the surveillance photo Nathan had found on the table. "Is this Bassir?"

She grabbed it, examined it with the same intensity. "Yes, yes, yes! Where is he?"

"This was taken at LAX three days ago."

"He's safe! Praise Allah!" She caressed the photo. "Where is he now?"

"I've no idea. What name is he traveling under?"

She continued staring at the photo.

"Kemat, I can't do more without information from you. Nothing. It's a small miracle we were able to find this—thanks to a local genius, not my contacts." I switched to Tajik. I wanted to listen to her accent and phrasing. Perhaps it would tell me more about her background. Plus, it's difficult to lie in Tajik. Unlike English. "You have great fondness for Bassir. That's clear. What is his relationship to you?"

"I do not want to speak of this now," she said. In English.

I persisted in Tajik. "What was he covering in Syria? Not a standard story. Was it?"

"Win, I appreciate your concern but—"

"You asked my help. Now I'm asking yours in return."

She seized her napkin, snapped it open. Put it on her lap. "I will tell you what I can. No more."

"Tell me about your life after you left Egypt."

Her eyebrows lifted just a tad. She hadn't been expecting that. Good.

"My father was an archaeologist. When I was young, we traveled with him to his digs. We spent several summers in Afghanistan. My family moved to Diyarbakir when I was still doing my undergraduate degree, but of course I spent vacations with them. A few years later, we were caught between one devil and another. I came to the United States."

"Who were the devils?"

"Mubarak and the PKK."

Interesting. Mubarak's rise had been heralded by the jailing of intellectuals. Early 1980s. Nineteen eighty-four saw the rise of the PKK in Turkey and if I remembered rightly, a flood of refugees into Diyarbakir.

"Where did you meet your husband?"

"In England, where I was taking an advanced degree. Rory was…wonderful. We married and came to the United States."

Wonderful about what? It had that sound. Our luncheon banquet came then, and I had no more chances to ask questions.

As I drove her back to her car, I asked the question she'd evaded. "Who is Bassir to you?"

"Family."

I could tell by the set of her jaw she wasn't going to say any more. She had implied extended family. But who knew? "And you know nothing about the story Bassir was working on?"

She didn't answer. We were almost at the school's parking lot. I was running out of options. "What name was he traveling under?"

"His family name." Her jaw clamped shut again.

I pulled into the lot, parked next to her Lexus. "Can I assume you no longer need my help?"

"It is important to know where he is now."

I turned to her. "I can't search without a name, Kemat."

"Let me think about it." She got out. Before she closed the door, she said, "I will call you tonight."

* * *

"Win's accused me of ruts," Sarah said with the ghost of a smile.

"Ruts?" Emily asked, shifting in her chair to face me.

"When you go round and round over the same issue, you make ruts," I explained. "The more you fiddle with it, the deeper the ruts. It was an observation. Not a criticism or an accusation."

Emily returned her gaze to Sarah. I realized how much I'd missed my sessions with Emily. She'd clarified so much for me. Pushed me to face my fears. Forced me to say what was the tumult I'd felt when I'd returned home.

"You don't wear your wedding ring, Sarah," Emily said. "Does that bother you?"

"I do wear it, but not always on my finger. When it's not on my finger, I wear it on the chain Win gave me, expressly for that purpose."

"What do you feel when you put it on the chain?"

"Guilt." Sarah stared at her hands.

"What do you feel, Win?"

"I understand—"

"*Feel*, Win."

I took a deep breath. I didn't want to hurt Sarah, but this was the time for honesty. "Frustration. We're married—something I'd never even dreamed of. Even with Azar. Yet, I'm still in the shadow life. I can't go to the station for a visit just to see Sarah. Can't embrace her. Kiss her. If we pass on the street, it's as friends. Maybe acquaintances."

Sarah stared at me. Tears welled up. "I'm so sorry, Win."

I wanted to take her in my arms. Tell her everything would be okay. Take her to bed and wipe the words away.

"So," Emily said after a long moment. "We have guilt and resentment. Wonderful foundation for a marriage."

"That's not fair, Emily—"

"Yes it is, Win. You called it 'frustration,' but what you described was resentment." Emily crossed her legs. "Let me recap. Sarah's in a rut, searching for a solution that honors both you and her job. You, Win Kirkland, are in just as deep of a rut trying to stop the resentment you feel. So what are you both going to do to shake things up?"

Sarah and I exchanged a glance. She looked panicked. I felt the same thing. The silence stretched. I felt trapped because I had an answer. I wanted Sarah to move in with me. Come home to me every day after work. It's what I dreamed about on the nights I slept alone. Thought about when I ate my dinner alone. When I craved her touch. Her skin on mine.

Sarah cleared her throat. "Win thinks I hide behind sex so I don't have to think or talk about this."

"Is she right?" Emily asked.

"Probably. I don't know. I know every time I think about her, I get, uh, aroused. I've never felt a range of feelings and sensations as when we make love. And there's not a moment in the day when I don't want to make love with her."

"Interesting shift, Sarah," Emily said. "From 'sex' to 'making love.' Care to comment?"

Sarah sighed. Closed her eyes. Finally she said, "I can't separate the two. What I feel physically is what I feel emotionally. I want us to be…together."

"Then why don't you move in with Win?" Emily asked.

Panic flitted over Sarah's face.

"You're taking time to calculate the risk, aren't you?" Emily asked.

Sarah nodded. Tears began to cascade down her face.

"Sarah, you've got to take a step yourself, not wait for outside events to control your actions. Try living with Win for a week and then examine how exposed you feel. If it feels like too much, move back to your dad's. Perhaps you could make chunks of the week to stay at Win's. But if it feels all right, try it for another week. Set time limits, stop, reassess. Does that sound doable? Or does it terrify you?"

"Both."

Emily shook her head. "How's work? Anything that's stressing you?"

"We found a skeleton. Then more. Elie's processed seven so far and we think there's more."

"A serial killer?" Emily asked.

Sarah shifted in her chair. "I think so, but we won't know for sure until Elie works on them in the lab. If it's a serial killer, then he's been operating in the county for a lot of years, and I don't understand how that could be. It's going to be a hell of a case."

"And you, Win?" Emily turned to me. "Any stressors?"

I told her about Kemat and what she'd asked me to do. "She was supposed to call last night to give me more intel—that is, if she decided she wanted me to proceed. But I didn't hear from her. Until I do, I'm at a dead end."

Emily wrote a few notes, closed her file. "Think about what I've suggested, and if it's too much, come up with something else. I'll see you next week, same time, same station."

As we walked to our trucks, I wanted to hold Sarah. Rock her in my arms. But we walked carefully, a foot away from each other.

"I'll call you tonight," she said. "Maybe we could take a short trial run this weekend."

"It's fine with me. More than fine." I stopped beside my truck. "I didn't want to lay a guilt trip on you. But I think Emily was right—there's a seed of resentment in what I feel. I promise I'll keep it in check."

"I can't say it enough, Win. I am so sorry. I never meant—"

I touched her shoulder. "I went into this with my eyes wide open. Probably more than you did. You weren't thinking ahead. I couldn't stop from thinking ahead."

"You tried to warn me, and I just pushed it aside. I was falling in love, and that's all I could absorb. I'll come over tonight with a couple of changes of clothes. Baby steps okay?"

"I've always said 'an inch at a time,' Sarah. I'm not changing my tune now."

* * *

Sarah arrived with clothes and dinner in tow. Des danced around. I wasn't sure if it was for Sarah or the food. I knew which I was dancing for. I'd made room for her stuff and I thought she got a bit teary when she saw.

She sat on the bed. "I told Dad, you know, what Emily said. And he said, 'Somebody has to tell you what you should be doin' anyways? Git, Sarah Anne.'"

I shook my head. "God, I don't know how you pulled your parents from the gene pool, but you sure as hell hit the jackpot." I held her close. Thanking all the Powers Who Be for the whole chain of events that led us here. "I love you, Sarah. So much."

We kissed. I felt her tremble.

"I'm going to test my addiction," she said. "Let's eat first."

I kissed her again, harder. Moved my hands to her butt and pulled her closer yet.

She groaned. "No fair."

I let go of her, stepped back. "Maybe it's not addiction, just damn good sex."

We breached some kind of barrier that night. I began to see this place as our home as Sarah moved around with confidence. Belonging here, us belonging together. Our lovemaking that night reflected all the complexities of our love. Fierce, tender. Protective, risky. Receptive, aggressive. Sliding the scale between us.

We'd finished breakfast and Sarah was getting ready for work when my phone rang. I didn't recognize the number. "Kirkland."

"Win? This is Anam Daoud, Dr. Fitzgerald's assistant. She is missing, I cannot find her. Do you know where she is?"

"Slow down, Anam," I said, getting paper and pencil. "What makes you think she's missing?"

"She is not here!"

"She missed an appointment?"

"Yes. Many."

"When?"

"She never came in yesterday, and she had meetings all day. She is not answering her cell phone. She would warn me if she had other commitments, tell me to cancel the meetings or give her apologies."

"Have you checked her home?"

"I drove past last night, and there were no lights on. The last talk we had was when she left the high school."

"What time?"

"A little after noontime."

"I invited her to lunch, Anam. We didn't get back to her car until after two." I made doodles on the pad. "You need to ask the Bloomington police to do a public safety check. They'll check the house. I'll take the route from Greenglen to Bloomington. She may have run out of gas or got a flat." I didn't say accident, but it was on my mind. "Stay in touch, Anam. If I find her, I'll let you know right away."

"Why did she not call? She had her cell phone. I know this because she called me from Greenglen. Why?"

"Battery died, or it just could be the patchy cell service in the county."

"But—"

I could've told her not to worry, but that was a waste of breath. "You work your end, I'll work this one. Contact the Bloomington police right now."

She disconnected about the time Sarah walked in.

"What's wrong?" she asked.

"Kemat seems to be missing. She evidently never got back to Bloomington Wednesday."

"You think—"

"Too early to think anything," I said. "But yeah, I have a bad feeling about this. I'm going to follow the route she would've taken. See if I can spot the car."

"You want us to put out a BOLO?"

I didn't want impose on our relationship. For all I knew, Kemat had simply taken off. A tryst with a lover. Or a meeting with Bassir. But extra eyes would make the job easier to eliminate possibilities. "Yeah, please."

"I'm off to work." She kissed me, lined my bottom lip with her tongue. "See you tonight."

CHAPTER EIGHT

Sarah

I knew Win was worried about Kemat Fitzgerald. I thought Win looked up to her, not only as a remarkable woman, but a real mover and shaker. I didn't know what was being moved, but Win knew. I suspected it was far more than being a leading Arabic scholar.

I drove to the berm a little way down the road, pulled up Kemat's information from the BMV and issued the BOLO with a directive to report immediately. I hadn't driven more than a mile when my phone pinged. Dispatch. I pulled over again. "What's up?"

"I'm patchin' you through to Caleb, Sarah."

Caleb's voice came on. "We've got your Lexus. Rolled off the road and landed at the bottom of a small ravine."

"Driver?"

"We can't see any movement, but we just got here."

"Where?"

"SR 47, going northeast, right before that new hog farm."

"I'm swinging by Win's. Kemat was her boss and people at IU were getting worried. ETA, thirty minutes."

I disconnected, called Win and turned around.

"Is she okay?" Win asked as she got in.

"Caleb had just gotten there. Car's off the road, driver wasn't visible. If you want to call him..."

"I won't interrupt his work, just step on it, Sarah."

We arrived in twenty minutes. As we got out, I could see two cruisers. Caleb was working his way up the ravine, while another deputy took photographs.

"Hi Win," he said as he gained the pavement. "Not good news—the driver's deceased. I'm sorry."

Win looked as if she'd been hit in the gut. Hard. "Are you sure it's Kemat?"

Caleb handed her a pair of gloves, then a wallet. He motioned me aside, out of Win's earshot. "I called Vincente and Leslie. The driver was shot, one to the left temple." He pointed to skid marks. "My guess on this is that someone stepped onto the road, she hit the brakes. Another person could've been hiding along the side, stepped out and shot her."

"What makes you think there were two people?"

"The transmission's in neutral and no sign anyone rigged the accelerator. That Lexus is heavy, would've taken two to push it. But all of this is guesswork until we get forensics."

I nodded. I glanced at Win. She closed the wallet, walked over to us and handed it to Caleb. "Can I go down? Give an ID?"

Caleb stepped back.

"Nope," I said. "Only departmental personnel allowed. Why don't I take you to the office? We can wait for news there. There's no use standing around here, getting in the way of investigating officers."

She drew a deep breath, then nodded.

When we were in the truck, she asked, "What aren't you telling me?"

"She was shot, Win. Caleb thinks the car was rolled off the road."

"Shit." She lapsed into silence, her gaze unfocused. "Why don't you drop me at home? I've got files I've been putting together. On Kemat and her search for Bassir."

"You think this is related?"

She shrugged. "I can't think of anything else that would get a language professor murdered."

"We'll stop by and pick them up. Remember, I'm coming home tonight."

* * *

"I wish a couple of our detectives kept case files like this," I said as I closed the last folder she'd given me. I sat back in my office chair and rubbed my face.

"Well taught. Mostly by the MPs because we had to document everything. But I found it came in handy. Even in the field." She shifted in her chair. "You see anything I missed?"

"No. But I think Kemat must've had some sort of network in the Middle East, or maybe in this country with connections overseas. Possible?"

"Factual. She'd mentioned friends all over. West Coast to East. Egypt to Tajikistan. An informal network I think, but that was how she knew Bassir had gotten out of Syria." She scrubbed her face with both hands. "I suspect she had CIA ties, but I've never heard anything concrete. Maybe it's time to call Bill. She can't object now."

"Bill's fine but not the feds. If this had been a carjacking, we could investigate by ourselves. But this looks like an assassination with overseas connections. I have no idea how to approach it except follow the leads we turn up. You will help us?"

"Of course. But don't put me on the payroll in any way. Let me work this one in the shadows."

"Too many shadows in your life, Win. Are you sure?"

"I'm used to the life. I can tell the difference between a hundred shades of gray."

"Okay." I thought a moment. "Did Kemat ever say what her relationship to Bassir was?"

"All I could get out of her was 'family.' I don't know if she meant immediate family or extended. She was hiding something, I know that. I'll put out feelers, see what chatter I can pick up. But call Bill. He's got official channels he has access to."

Mike tapped on the door. "Got initial findings. You want to see them?"

I motioned him in. "Win, this is the head of our Fatal Accident Crash Team, Mike Bryer. He's a master of reconstructing crash scenes. Win was a friend of the deceased."

He slid the report across the desk. "I think Caleb hit it right on the nose. The only thing he missed was another set of skids—only these were from quick acceleration."

"The getaway car? Any idea what it was?"

"We have the size of the wheelbase, but no useable tread prints. I'll put all of this together in a report, but I thought you'd like early confirmation."

"Thanks Mike. I appreciate the quick work."

I watched him walk back to his desk. Before he reached it, my phone rang. "Sheriff Pitt."

"Elie here. Sarah, I haven't had a lot of time to work on the bones in the lab because we're still unearthing more graves. But I'm convinced this isn't a pioneer cemetery or some such nonsense. The oldest burial we've found so far is in the twenty- to thirty-year range. The one the dog found is probably the newest and is a double."

"Double? Two bodies?"

"Yes, though some of the bones are missing. Probably animals, so I think it's fairly recent."

"How recent?"

"I'm not going to try and guess until I get some lab time, Sarah."

"Do we have a serial killer?"

"Lab time and I'll have answers for you," Elie said.

"Stop being so damn conservative and take a wild guess! How much longer can I leave this on the back burner? If this killer is still in the county, we may have more killings which'll be on my head."

After a moment, she asked, "Are you finished with your temper tantrum?"

"Sorry. No excuse for the attitude. I know you can't dig faster and do the kind of work we need. Can I ask a question?"

"Apology accepted. What?"

"How many skeletons so far?"

"Nine and indications there are four more."

I groaned. "Thanks Elie. Let me know when you have more data."

I hung up, leaned back in my chair and closed my eyes. "An assassin and a serial killer. Welcome to McCrumb County."

"This is when I'd like to take you in my arms and kiss away the worry," Win said.

"All I can do now is wait for the data, so let's go home."

* * *

As soon as Win closed her front door, she swept me into her arms and held on tight. Kiss away the worry? Totally. We lay in bed, legs still entwined, engulfed in a languor that was peaceful.

"Before we got together, Em asked me what I did to lose the job stress and all I had was a lame answer about reading. I wish she'd ask me again." I wrapped an arm around Win and snuggled into her chest.

She rubbed my arm. "I understand the stress, Sarah. Kemat's murder is going to take a lot of deputy's hours without good odds of an arrest. Meanwhile, you've got a serial killer free to find more victims. Can I offer a suggestion? Or would you rather I just ravish you again?"

"Ravish away, wife." I moved her hand to my breast, leaned over to kiss hers.

"I better tell you what I was thinking—before I forget." She moved her hand to my hip. "What if you give Caleb Kemat's case? I can assist, unofficially. You and your head detective can work on the burial grounds. We can split the detectives according to need."

I thought about it for a moment. "Agreed. I'll make the assignments tomorrow."

Win grinned at me, took hold of my hip and pulled me over. "Straddle me, Sarah. We can gallop off into the sunset, stress be damned."

When we finally sat down to dinner, it was dark outside and we both were starving. Even though Win ate steadily, I could see she was thinking something through. I didn't want to interrupt her, but she should realize she was married to an inquisitive law enforcement officer. "So what are you thinking?"

She looked up and grinned at me. "Do I get no privacy?"

"Hmpf."

"I didn't call Bill. Did you?"

"After Elie's call, I forgot. I'm sorry. I'll do it as soon as we finish eating."

"No, don't. I'll pick up a couple of burn phones for us to use. I'll call him when I activate them."

"Why? Who do you think's going to eavesdrop?"

"I wouldn't put it past the CIA." She pushed her plate away. "They're not a nice group to deal with. I say that from firsthand experience."

"But they have no jurisdiction here. They're not allowed to operate on US soil."

"Yeah, right. Let's just play it safe, Sarah." She picked up my empty plate, put it on hers and pushed away from the table. "I have a couple of leads. As soon as Bill's on board, I'll get Nathan to work them from his end."

"What leads?" I asked as I followed her into the kitchen with the rest of the dishes.

"You really want to know? Or would you rather concentrate on the other case?"

"You're going to cut me out of my own investigation?" I dumped the dishes in the sink.

Win laughed. "God, you're such a control freak." She began to run water.

She was right. *My* department, *my* case. Since I bore the ultimate responsibility, was that wrong? I thought about that as she passed dishes for me to dry. Maybe I was too hands-on. Did it bug Caleb and John? They'd never told me to buzz off. But then, that wasn't the style of either man. I finished the last one and put it in the cupboard. When I turned to hang up the dishtowel, I saw Win studying me.

"You really think I'm a control freak?"

She laughed and embraced me. "Well, we know how to remedy control issues, don't we?"

* * *

We'd just finished a really early breakfast. I'd opened my laptop to scan recent news on the *Sentinel* site. Recent news meaning how the local press was treating the Alert case.

"Does this mean we're married?" I asked as I turned my laptop so Win could read the headline: "Seventh Circuit Rules for Marriage Equality."

"We damn well are married." She smothered an expletive as she read the headline. "In Vermont."

"I mean *here*." I turned the laptop around again. "I know I should've been following Indiana's marriage equality struggle, but with so much happening…"

"Who knows?" She shrugged. "These cases will wind their way through the courts until they hit SCOTUS. It's inevitable. Whether we're a married couple will rest in the hands of nine human beings. Scary proposition."

"Better than in the general populace, at least in Indiana. Look what happened in California."

"I'm not so sure about that. Some people will feel like these decisions have been crammed down their throats. Get more angry than they already are."

"How closely have you been following this?"

"When *Windsor* first came up, I called my lawyer for clarification. About where we may stand."

"So where do we stand?"

"Who the hell knows? Today yes, we're married here. The attorney general will file an appeal for a stay or something. Then we won't be legal in Indiana. Clear?"

"Don't you dare shrug at me again." I ran both hands through my hair. "Sorry, but this is so bizarre. What normal couple doesn't know if they're legally married?"

"Normal? You mean straight." I could feel her anger blaze up before she tamped it down. "I know so many couples who've been together twenty or thirty years. They've never had the rights straight couple have. I want us all to be recognized as real, loving couples, but I'm scared about the backlash."

"Well, if we're legal…"

"How many lawbreakers are there? If there were none, you'd be out of a job. Even if the laws change, there are still a lot of ways to discriminate against same-sex couples. We'll revisit all of the ramifications for years. It's not only about laws, it's about hearts."

I closed the laptop, moved around the island to her. "Who the hell has a right to attack what's in our hearts?"

"Haters. People who are afraid, self-anoint."

"And we're supposed to change those hearts? How?"

She shook her head. "No idea. Demonstrate we're another loving couple? Like all the other couples who are legal?"

"That means I'd have to come out."

"Is there another way? I don't have an answer to that either." She pulled me close. "But only when you're really ready, Sarah."

"Hell, Win. You're half of this couple." I stepped back. "I'd better get to work."

CHAPTER NINE

Win

Sarah and I sat in her office, waiting for Caleb and John. We'd left home shortly after dawn with Sarah pushing me out the front door. Anxious to put into action some things we'd talked about last night. Maybe to ignore our conversation about our marital status. I sipped my coffee, tried to get into the flow of law enforcement. Hard when Sarah was two strides away, fingering her lips as she studied the overnight log.

My attention was caught by a tall figure entering the front door. An argument with the counter sergeant. "Uh-oh, trouble's coming."

Sarah looked up, then through her window. "You know him?"

"Nope. I know his walk. Equal mix of arrogance and authority. Bet you ten bucks he's some kind of federal agent."

"No bet, I smell a fed too. But his hair's too long for FBI."

The man opened the office door without knocking, flashed a badge and said, "We're taking over the Fitzgerald case, and I'd like your files now."

Des growled from under Sarah's desk. Sarah raised an eyebrow. "She's an attack dog. Since I don't know your name, I can't make the proper introduction, so she might take it upon herself to tear you apart."

He paled. "Agent—"

Sarah held out her hand. "Credentials."

He handed her his credential case. She whipped out her phone, took a photo of him and of his credentials. "I hope you don't mind if I get confirmation of this, Agent Westin."

"Good luck with that, Sheriff." His lip curled in a lousy imitation of Elvis.

Sarah tossed me the case. Agent Brandon Westin. CIA. Well, fuck.

He stared at me. "Win Kirkland, if I'm not mistaken. Formerly MCIA. We have a lot in common, Ms. Kirkland."

"We have *nothing* in common, Mr. Westin. MCIA doesn't commandeer other intelligence units or hire mercenaries to do its dirty work or operate clandestine renditions. Shall I continue with a list of how different we are?"

Caleb walked into the office, his scowl showing he was aware of the tension.

Sarah nodded at her chief deputy. "Would you please escort this man to I2?"

Westin rose with enough force to kick the chair back. "You can't arrest me, you fucking fag dyke."

Sarah's eyes opened wide. Her face colored. She nodded to Caleb. "Get him out of here," she said in a low voice.

Caleb grabbed Westin, forced his arm behind him and marched him out of the office.

Sarah's face was a study in controlled fury. She slammed the desk with her fist.

She should've known she'd hear that sooner or later. I'd made a stop at the Flying J by the interstate this morning. Not as safe as Wally World, but I'd worn a plain ball cap, kept my head down, paid cash. Just another trucker. I took my new cell phone from my pocket, put in Bill's number. My text was short: *Call.* I signed it *Homa* and sent it.

Sarah was still in the crimson state. She wouldn't respond to reason. Probably wouldn't even hear what I said. I didn't know if her anger stemmed from being called a fag dyke or from his challenge of her authority. I wondered at the arrogance of the man to walk into a cop shop and demand files. McCrumb County was rural. Did he assume he'd be dealing with a country bumpkin? "Never assume" was Bill's number one rule. Gather intel until you *know*.

My phone buzzed. Bill. "We have a situation." I stood up, left the office. I filled him in as I exited the building by the back entrance. "You know Brandon Westin?"

"Christ. That bloody ass kisser?"

"He walked into Sarah's office and demanded files on a homicide she's working." I didn't want to break the news to him like this, but I told him about Kemat. "What should we do with him?"

"Hold him until I get there. I'll catch a flight down from Camp. Any charges Sarah can file?"

"I'm sure she can think of something, but if he's charged, he'll lawyer up. I'll check with Sarah. There's stuff we should talk about when you get here."

"Give me an hour. Pick me up at the airport?"

"You mean the one short strip with a windsock that crop dusters use?"

"That's the place."

He disconnected and I walked back in the building. I could tell from Sarah's glance that she'd cooled off some. Some. I motioned for her to take a walk with me. When we got outside, she examined my face. "What?"

"Bill left one of the bug scanners here, didn't he?"

Sarah nodded.

"You might want to sweep the building. That guy didn't just waltz in."

"Oh hell. I don't know if I can go through another spy drama, Win."

"Bill's on his way. He said an hour. He knows Westin, called him an ass kisser. Maybe he can handle the drama end." I cupped her chin. "How are you?"

She took my hand in hers. "Shocked. I never thought I'd hear those ugly words hurled at me, not in my own office. Don't say it. I know you warned me. I just never believed it."

I wrapped her in my arms, damn the consequences. A brief embrace. I stepped back. I didn't want to ask the question, but it had to be said. "Question is, why? Did he pick up on the county gossip? Or does he know about us for sure?"

Tears formed in her eyes. "Why the hell can't we simply love one another without all this constant crap? I love coming home to you. I love living with you, even if it's for a few days at a time. I take a step toward you and all hell breaks loose. Is it Azar? Testing to see if I'm strong enough for you?"

"She was love embodied. She would never hurt you. Or me." This is what happens when you don't heed solid advice. When you push it away. "Think of it as a reality check, Sarah."

"Hell and damnation."

"I'm going to pick up Bill. You okay to take the reins again?"

"Yeah. Will I ever get used to it?"

"Not the hate. Never the hate."

* * *

"How do you manage to get in the middle of these situations, Win?" Bill asked as he climbed into my truck.

"Seemingly without any effort on my part. What's going on? Was Kemat working for you?"

"No."

"Come on, Bill. Westin waltzed in, wanted to take over the murder case. Called Sarah a dyke. Kemat was my friend, and Sarah's my wife. This is personal, and I won't back off."

He fastened his seat belt. "Let's go, I'll tell you what I know as we drive."

I put the truck in drive, took off with a spray of gravel. "If she wasn't working for you, was she a CIA agent?"

"Damn, Win, you know how secretive those idiots are. Even when we ran ops with them, we only had the part of the story they wanted us to have." He crossed his arms. "Kemat had an extensive network, but it was her own, doing what she wanted it to do. Protect women in the Middle East, raise money for that and get women out of brothels, away from child brides…"

"She ran Sacred Woman?"

"She founded it and steered it for a lot of years. Created safe houses for the women staffed by widows and other outcasts. You know it?"

"I've donated for years, helped with a couple of their ops. She changed a lot of women's lives."

"If there was any connection between Kemat and the CIA, I think it was on her terms."

"Then why are they trying to take over the case?"

"Maybe to discover who was in her network. Maybe because they had a joint ops going with her. I don't know yet. But I've got people digging."

"What makes them think they can do this domestically? It's Sarah's jurisdiction."

"Pure idiotic bravado. MCIA has jurisdiction both abroad and domestically, and I'm sure they know we've got links with Sarah and McCrumb County. Either they're really desperate or they've got another agenda. Let me interrogate Westin."

"He's not going to sit still for that, Bill."

"Oh, I think he will. Either he talks to me now or he goes to Camp Atterbury's brig. And from there? He could just disappear."

"Would you really do that?"

"I sure can threaten it, Win."

We drove in silence. Rendition isn't a pretty word. An act that led to the dark and ugly side of humanity. MCIA didn't subscribe to the practice. Nor to torture. Not now, not in its past.

As I pulled into the sheriff's parking lot, I asked Bill a question that I should've asked at the beginning of our travel. "Can you get clearance for Nathan to do some snooping?"

"What trail are you following?"

"Nothing specific, not without some electronic help. Clearance?"

"I'll put it in writing. But don't keep secrets. Keep me in the loop. You know we can work together, and I sure as hell don't need a cowboy screwing up my ops."

"*Your* ops?"

"Sarah's ops, okay?"

When he walked into Sarah's office, he swept her into a bear hug. "Congratulations Sarah." He set her back down. "Where's your ring?"

She blushed. "Around my neck where it's safer for me."

He frowned. "Sorry, I thought Win was just cheap." He grinned at me. "Really, I'm sorry you two have to hide. If this county only knew what a damn potent law enforcement pair they had. Sorry you had to hear those words from an asshole."

"Maybe I needed to hear it, Bill." She gave him a half smile. "Our guest is in Interrogation Room Two, yelling for his rights. Caleb had a run at him, but zeroed out. He's all yours."

"It will be my pleasure, Sarah."

* * *

Bill worked Westin all day, going at him with seemingly unrelated questions, then leaving the room. He got a continuous stream of intel from his operatives between interrogations. He didn't share. At four thirty, he transferred Westin to the back of a troop transport under marine guard. By that time, Westin was a sliver of the arrogant bastard who'd walked into Sarah's office that morning.

Bill watched the transfer with a scowl. He turned to Sarah. "I'll give you a full report as soon as I get it together. Promise. It may take a day or two, so don't fret. If someone comes asking after Westin, tell them you told him to scram—under threat of calling the federal prosecutor for this district. He left, and you haven't seen him since."

"I should've thought of making that call," Sarah said.

"I'm glad you didn't. We'll be able to find out what's going on."

"Not something…rough."

"We don't do that crap, Sarah. Ever."

"Just threaten it," I added. I shook his hand. "Thanks Bill."

"Both of you stay safe." He climbed aboard and let the canvas flap down.

We watched the truck pull out. I turned to Sarah. "You ready to go home?"

"Hell yes."

When we got home, I let Des run around since she'd been confined to Sarah's office most of the day. When I got inside, Sarah was sprawled on the couch, staring at the ceiling. I helped her up, took her into the bedroom. "Strip and lay down on your stomach."

"Win, I don't feel like—"

I held her for a moment. "I know. I want you to think about what Micah said a long time ago. That kind of corrosive comment can eat into you until it kills the love. You have to let it go, Sarah." I kissed her forehead. "Now, get your clothes off, please."

I rummaged around in the bathroom cupboard. I found my oil warmer and an essence of sage and lavender massage oil. When I walked back into the bedroom, Sarah lay on the bed, naked and worried. It took every ounce of control I had not to begin kissing her body until she was as intoxicated as I was. I set the warmer up on the nightstand, put some oil in it.

Sarah's eyes were wide. "Is this some new kind of…adventure?"

I couldn't hide the smile that crept over my face. "Um, not the kind you're thinking about. Just a massage. No love play. There's a Chinese proverb that says something like, 'Tension is who you think you should be. Relaxation is who you are.' Would you like your masseuse clothed or naked as you?"

"Uh…"

"Okay, clothed. Now turn over on your stomach." I placed a small pillow under her forehead, two pillows on either side of her head. Tested the oil.

I straddled her, dribbled a few drops on her back. I began with the small of her back and worked the oil into her skin upward. Didn't touch her butt, though I would've loved to kiss her lovely cheeks. I kneaded her tight muscles, ran my thumbs up her spine. Then down, butt, thighs, calves. All without touching her inner thighs or what lay between. When my hands were fairly oil free, I began work on her neck and the back of her head.

I could feel her relax under my hands. She made little groans when I hit a knotty area. Moans as she surrendered to the process. Forty minutes later, I turned off the warmer.

She turned her head. "You can do my front now."

I shook my head. "I'm going to fix dinner. You nap. I'll send Des in to wake you up."

"A woman couldn't ask for a better wife."

As we ate, Sarah asked, "Would you teach me how to give you a massage like that? I mean, how you know what to knead, how to use thumbs, all of the mechanics? And how to keep my libido out of it."

"Sure—but no promises about your libido."

"I want to take care of you too. Be a wife to you." She sighed. "I think oil is a good antidote for corrosive words. You're right. I've needed to deal with the ugly side, and I've ignored it. What Westin said felt like a sucker punch."

"That's what it was meant to be, Sarah. It's bait. Something to get you off-balance. Angry. Ready to strike out."

"He succeeded." She put her fork on her empty plate. "I realize I can't let that happen because it cuts off the flow of blood to my brain. I'm liable to react in a way that could cost me my job. Excessive force isn't something I tolerate in my deputies."

"So now you know what it feels like. Easier the second time, a breeze by the fourth."

"Hell."

We cleared the table, did the dishes. My eyelids were beginning to droop.

"Now, will you finish it?"

"Finish what?"

"My massage." She opened her robe. "You still have my front to do."

I wasn't sleepy anymore. "You want me to use oil?"

"No," she said, her voice husky.

CHAPTER TEN

Sarah

We'd had our morning briefing for both task forces and were waiting for additional information from Bill. Nathan, with an official "go," was working on a couple of leads Win wasn't ready to talk about yet.

John Morgan, my head detective, had talked to the new DNR agent, Jack Kindler. Kindler didn't know squat, but willingly turned over twenty-five years of patrol reports. Detectives were going over them now, but without specific dates, they felt a bit overwhelmed.

I walked upstairs to the detectives' office. "Hey guys. Could you use some extra help?"

They responded with applause and a couple of whoops.

I turned to John. "What would you think about some help from Dad? He's got more county history in his head than all of us combined. Maybe he can remember something if he goes over the records. Up to you, John."

"Micah would be a godsend, Sarah," John said. "We've got a couple of patrol out canvassing, but what do they ask? Nobody lives that close to actually have seen anything—even if we knew when they were supposed to be looking."

"We'll get more specific timing from Elie when she knows it," I said. "Just don't hold your breath. In the meantime, let's try working from the other end. Go over the missing persons reports."

"For the past twenty-five years?"

I nodded. "I think Dory loaded the end of that information in our database last month. At least you won't have to go through moldy files."

I went back downstairs and called Dad. "How would you like to come to work?"

"If it means I get to see more of you, tell me where to report."

A severe guilt pang hit my heart. "I'm sorry, Dad, I—"

"Don't go all serious on me, Sarah Anne. If you can't tell when I'm joshing you by now, you best turn in your badge, 'cause you ain't got no detectin' skills."

"I miss you, Dad."

"I'm enjoyin' havin' the house to myself. First time since... Well, I never been by myself in it. Kinda nice. How's it goin' with Win?"

"Good. She's amazing, utterly and forever amazing. But I do miss you."

"Now, what kind of a job you have for me? Is it about the bones?"

"Yep. We're going over DNR patrol records, checking missing persons reports. But we need the 'stuff between.' Maybe a rumor, or a minor incident that meant nothing at the time. Interested?"

"Of course, daughter. Want me in today or can I start tomorrow mornin'?"

"You have plans today?"

He chuckled. "See you in the mornin', Sheriff."

I drove out to the dig at Alert. They were still busy, which made my heart sink. I spied Elie, or rather, her short-cropped white hair, in the middle of a group of students. I waited until she had finished issuing orders.

She spotted me as the group dispersed and walked over. "Getting impatient, Sarah?"

"No," I said without hesitation. "Waiting, without complaint and with grace, I hope."

She grunted. "I can tell you two things. All of the skeletons we've raised were women, and they were all murdered. I'll lay it out in a report, but it'll take some time. I only have one lab assistant I trust with this work."

"How many more graves?"

"We're working out from the center of the grid. I suspect from the GPR readings, we may have two more. We'll see."

I looked over the killing ground, shivered as if there was a cold fog surrounding it. A slight rise of land in a boggy area that harbored all sorts of wildlife. A refuge—if you didn't know what lay below the ground.

* * *

I beat Win home and was fixing dinner when I heard her truck in the drive. Des barked and was at the front door before the engine shut off. I watched Win stretch, loving the arch of her body. I wondered how long this would last, this heat I felt just watching her.

She came in the front door, stashed her backpack and walked into the kitchen. She gave me a Ward peck and sniffed. "Smells good. Think we'll ever get enough summer weather so we can eat light?"

"You're complaining about my cooking?"

"Never. But I'm gaining weight. Guess I need more exercise." She wrapped her arms around me and gave me a long, lovely kiss. "You don't know what a gift it is to come home and find you here, Sarah."

"Yes I do. It's a miracle to come home to you, every day." I set the timer. "How'd it go today? Nathan make much progress?"

"He's amazing." She took two beers out of the fridge. "Tell me something—he's married, right?"

"Was. They divorced long time ago, and Susan took the kids back to Idaho. She missed the mountains and her people. He's married to this land. It wasn't a bitter thing, just admitting that it wouldn't work the way it was. He's wired the kids, and they video chat every night."

"Damn, I had no idea. I'm glad I didn't ask. Guess that's what I get for being gone so long. Somehow I missed all that." She looked into my eyes. "Missed Hugh's death too."

"Nathan's okay about it, and so am I. You were off fighting for all of us." I stroked her hair. "Now—progress?"

She handed me a beer and settled on a stool by the island. "We've pretty well reconstructed Kemat's network. About two hundred people all over the world. What I was interested in was who isn't on the network."

"Why?"

"Hard to give a good answer. Gut feeling." She closed her eyes a moment. "I was working from the notion that network people wouldn't kill her."

"Makes sense. But surely there are millions of people who aren't."

"I was looking for people in the area—at IU, in Bloomington. Or even in Indy." She took a sip. "I went into Bloomington today, took Kemat's assistant to lunch. Thought I'd run a few names by her."

"Does this story have a punch line?"

"Shit, you're an impatient wench." She took another sip.

"What don't you want to tell me?"

"A smart wench, to boot. Remember I told you about that Kashmiri woman who came on to me? Well, Noor isn't in the network, and she's somebody I thought would be. She saw us leaving the restaurant, intercepted us."

"And?"

"I have a coffee date with her Friday afternoon." She took another quick drink.

"We have Em on Friday, and we can't cancel again. She'll fire us." I ran a towel over the counter. "What's this flirt's full name?"

"Who? Oh. Noor Bhatti. I thought we'd see Emily, you go back to work, I go into Bloomington." She was peeling the label off her bottle.

"Win, what are you going to do with her?"

She glanced at me, then examined my face. "I'm not going to sleep with her to get intel, if that's what you're worried about."

"Have you ever? Slept with someone just for information?"

"No."

"Okay." I hung up the towel. "How far would you go, if you thought she knew something?"

"Sarah! What is it with you?"

"You said she was a stunner. Makes me feel…mousy."

"She is stunning, Sarah. Huge, dark eyes. Long hair the color of ebony and just as lustrous. Looks as good loose as wrapped at the nape of her neck. Large, high-set breasts. Ass also high and juicy. Walks like—"

"Stop, Win!"

She was around the island in two strides, and I found myself in her tight embrace.

"Fuck it, Sarah." She kissed me, hard and insistent. A bit breathless, she said, "I can admire her body without wanting to take her to bed. I can talk to her without wanting to take her to bed. I can flirt with her without wanting to take her to bed. I could even kiss her without wanting to take it one step further." She stepped back a tad. "I don't trust her. I don't love her. I don't want to come home to her."

I pressed against her. "Sometimes I just wonder why…"

"Because you're beautiful, Sarah," she said, brushing back my hair. "Inside and out. It's your spirit that I fell in love with—though I think the exterior wrapping is spectacular too." She cupped my butt. "Your ass is high and juicy, and I love looking at it. Almost as much as I like it in my hands. Or kissing it. Or any number of other things."

I could feel myself blushing. "Win, I'm so…I inherited Dad's nose."

"I can't convince you how beautiful you are, but I can show you." She slipped my sweatpants down while she kissed my neck. "Sarah, I don't want any woman but you. I want you so much. Now. Tomorrow. Forever. That's what I promised you."

* * *

I told Em about being called a fag dyke, how it felt, but not how Win had eased my disquiet. She didn't need to know everything.

"How did Win help you regain balance?" Em asked.

Win laughed. "Shit, Sarah, you should know better by now."

"With an old Chinese proverb," I said, turning to Win.

"'Tension is who you think you should be. Relaxation is who you are,'" Win said. "What she didn't mention is that I gave her a massage to go with the quote. No sex, just unknotting muscles."

"Good job, Win. Write that proverb down for me before you leave, please?" Em turned to me. "So, you have any idea what's coming next? What this CIA agent has planned?"

"None. But if he somehow manages to make it public, I'm ready to step out."

"You're sure, Sarah?"

"Yes. I'm tired of taking my ring off and hiding it. I'm tired of pretending I'm living at Dad's."

"You've moved in with Win?"

"Not everything, but clothes, yeah. I started out thinking maybe it'd be a couple of days, but I haven't left. It's so good to come home to her."

"Well, you two certainly are painting a rosy picture," Em said. "When the shit hits—and it will, Sarah—some people will call you things a lot worse than fag or a dyke. Some people will shun you. Some will try to hurt you or Win. I just want you to be prepared to take a lot of abuse."

"We'll take it together, Emily," Win said.

Em examined her with that funny half stare. "All right. If it happens, call me. I can at least share strategy. Anything else?"

"Sarah's jealous," Win said.

I groaned.

"I have to interrogate a smokin' hot babe," Win said. "Sarah thinks she can't measure up, so I'll get distracted."

Em raised her eyebrows. "I'm surprised with you, Sarah. You're about the last person I'd suspect would worry about appearance. You make a stunning couple on the dance floor."

I could feel my face turn red. "That's because Win's breathtaking. I wasn't jealous, just a bit uncomfortable. Win had talked about her before, and then she started describing this woman, breasts and butt. I'm not a hottie. Not with a nose like a hawk's beak."

Em shook her head. "Sarah, if you and Win broke up, you'd have a long line of women standing in line to capture your attention. So would Win. So who's the suspect? Do I know her?"

"She's not a suspect," Win said. "I need to figure out where she fits in the puzzle I'm trying to solve. Her name's Noor Bhatti. She's either lesbian or used to giving a good performance. Ever see her at Ruby's?"

"The name doesn't ring a bell," Em said. "What's she look like?"

I groaned again.

"Petite. Maybe five foot two. Long black hair. Bollywood face like Deepika Padukone. Stacked."

"That's not exactly the description I heard," I said. "Maybe you should go in with Win, check her out. Any information about her movements could help solve the problem."

It was Win's turn to groan. "I don't need to have my shrink chaperone me, Sarah."

"I've got the afternoon off, and anyway, I was going into Bloomington to meet Marty," Em said. "I won't have to drive in. Pick me up at the house?"

CHAPTER ELEVEN

Win

"I'm not checking up on you, Win," Emily said as we drove toward Bloomington. "But I've been hearing about an Indian woman who's tearing through the community. Seems to take great pleasure in breaking up couples and then dumping the one she hooked."

"Wow, that's cold. But Noor isn't Indian, she's Kashmiri."

"Would most of the women around here know the difference?"

I shook my head. "Is she just a troublemaker? Gets off on other women's pain? Or is there some kind of pattern to what she's doing?"

"I don't know. But that's why I wanted to come along. I'd like to sit close enough to hear what she says, if that's okay."

"Sure. Despite Sarah's fears, I find Noor too pushy. Manipulative. She's hot, but she knows it."

"You weren't even tempted?" Emily asked, rolling up her window.

"I enjoyed the view—from a distance. If I were in a whorehouse in Islamabad, I might've sampled the wares."

"She's a prostitute?"

"I don't know for sure she has that background. But I wouldn't be surprised. Her moves are too similar, her eyes way too cold, too experienced. Now she's a visiting scholar in Indo/Pakistani culture."

"This is going to be an interesting time."

I let Emily go into the coffee shop first, waited five minutes. I got my double latte and sat at a table close to her. I'd brought a dense paper on recent Afghani events, figuring Noor would be at least ten minutes late.

"Well, hello Win."

I checked my watch. Fifteen minutes. I closed the report, glanced up at her. Oh, yeah. Full smoking mode. Sheer material, hijab barely on her head. "Hi, Noor. How are classes going?"

She shrugged. Sat down. "How are you?"

"Trying to get ready for the intensive."

Her hand snaked across the table. Slithered onto mine. "I could help you prepare. Perhaps we could go to my apartment and I will show how my culture…operates. Is that the right word?"

"What's up with you, Noor? I'm obviously not interested. Why the pursuit?"

"Not interested? Are you sure?"

I held up my left hand, fingered my wedding ring. "There are plenty of single women at Ruby's. Why aren't you hunting there?"

"Hunting? You make me sound so…"

"Predatory? Good English word, put it in your vocabulary. What is it you want from me?"

"I have heard you are a wonderful lover. Many women say so. When I go back home, I will be without lovers again. I need to fill up with wonderful experiences so that the winter will not be so cold." She watched me from beneath long lashes. Leaned toward me. "You could help me stay warm."

Unless she talked to Julie, the women in the area hadn't sampled my skills. So who had she been talking to? I smelled her perfume, the same familiar scent I'd picked up from Kemat a couple of times. What the hell was it? Complex, with touches of spices and citrus. It stirred around the edges of my memory. I couldn't nudge it to center stage.

"So what are you teaching for the intensive?" I asked.

She sighed, a long, plaintive exhalation. "Am I not attractive to you at all?"

"You're very beautiful, Noor. I can introduce you to several women who'd keep you warm during a long winter. They'd welcome you to their beds."

She waved her hand dismissively. "I am not interested in them. They think that with their little toys, they are so experienced. They are children." She leaned toward me again, her nipples erect through the thin material. "But you, Win, have had true experience. I can see it in your eyes. In your wondrous body and the way you move. I know those muscles have memories I could rekindle."

"Noor, I appreciate your words, but—"

"I can take you to the mountaintop, a slow magical climb to the top of the world. Let me show you, Win." She kissed my palm, never taking her gaze from my eyes.

I withdrew my hand. Pushed my chair back. "I'm sorry, Noor. Just not interested. I'm perfectly happy to climb the mountain with my partner. We don't need a guide."

I sat in my truck a good fifteen minutes, trying to sort through my impressions, before Emily joined me.

"Noor gave quite a performance, Win. I'm amazed you could walk away from an offer like that." She dropped her tote on the floor of the passenger side.

"It wasn't hard. I found her cheap."

"Are you up to joining Marty and me for dinner? I'd like to run a few ideas past you."

"I want to go home. Shower."

Emily shifted in her seat so that she could watch me. "What memories has this woman stirred in you?"

I closed my eyes. "A very expensive whorehouse in Islamabad. The madam used an expensive, distinctive perfume. Gave it to her women who had special clients." I opened my eyes. "Don't look so shocked, Emily. A lot of the women who work in places like that love women. Once a moon, they'd close to men and invite dykes to party."

"I had no idea. You know Noor was a prostitute?"

"That phrase—'take you to the mountaintop'—was used in the Palace of All Delights. The question is, how did a young whore get to be a visiting scholar in the US?" Had Kemat known? Shared the same kind of past? "I'd love to hear your thoughts, but not tonight. Could we meet tomorrow?"

"I don't go into the office on weekends, Win."

"Why don't you come over to my house? Sarah's working the early shift. She'll be home by three."

"You want her to hear about Noor?"

"Yes—because I have nothing to hide."

* * *

When I got home, I kissed Sarah and headed for the shower. Declined her offer to join me. When I got out, she was waiting for me in the bedroom.

"What happened?" she asked, worry pulling her face into a frown.

"Expensive perfume and cheap memories," I said as I slid her into an embrace. "I didn't fuck her, Sarah. If that's what you're worried about. I found her repulsive. Cloying, like her perfume."

I told her what I'd remembered. "I never connected Kemat with the Palace, but she must've spent time there. Or with Noor."

"On the basis of a perfume? She could've found it anywhere."

"No. The madam—can't remember her name—had it made exclusively for her by a Paris perfumer. Fatima—that was the madam's name. I never heard a last name and I doubt that was her real name anyway. She was very picky about her clientele. About her 'girls.' Most were young. Poor. She trained the promising ones as courtesans."

"You went there?" Sarah asked. She stepped out of my embrace. "Patronized a house of prostitution?"

"I never paid for sex. But I'd find out what stuff the women wanted, found a way to get it to them. I suppose—"

"Damn straight it is. Paying for sex."

I turned to her, my towel slipping. I refastened it. "Those women at the Palace were relatively safe. The sex trade all over Asia and the Middle East is a living horror. Conditions for girls and women are unimaginable. I tried to help where I could. Stealing girls away and getting them into safe places. Helped get them an education. I guess I thought of the Palace the same way. Helping."

Sarah turned away.

"You think I'm delusional? Maybe I was. But every time I went to the Palace, it was my respite from the bullets and bombs and blood. I could lay in their arms and forget. If I had nightmares, they comforted me. Be glad I didn't start drinking. Or doing drugs."

"Let me have time to process—okay?"

I faced her. My hands clenched. "No. I've killed people, maimed them. There were times when I thought I could never wash the blood off. So I turned to women who provided solace? So fucking what? How is it different that picking up a woman in a bar here in the states? Don't you judge me, Sarah. Don't you dare fucking judge me."

Des had come to the bedroom door. Whined. I grabbed clothes and went back in the bathroom to dress. I took Des for a walk. A long walk. It was dead-on night when I got back, exhausted. All the old ghosts seemed to await me in the shadows. A single light shone from the living room. Beckoned me inside.

I felt fear in the pit of my stomach. Sharp. Piercing. Had I screwed everything up? I couldn't retract my words. Wouldn't. What I'd said was true. I'd done what I did to survive. To stand, intact as I could be, in front of my own door.

It opened. Des galloped by me and into the house. Sarah stood as a silhouette, backlit. I could feel my heart pumping wildly, hear it in my ears. She opened her arms.

I moved into them. She was crying, soaking the shoulder of my T-shirt.

"I'm sorry, Win. I'm so sorry. I never meant to hurt you. I'm so, so sorry."

I held her tight. We rocked gently to her sobs. I drew back. Raised her head in my cupped hands. "I can't change my past, Sarah. It's part of me. Maybe I should've told you about my escapades before we married. I thought I didn't need to."

"You didn't. Don't." She touched my cheek. "I'm a provincial, stupid, good girl, always following the rules. My reaction to prostitutes is to arrest them, not see them as women. Johns are so much dreg." She took a deep breath. "I'm so sorry, Win. I was judging you—and I have no right. Hold me and tell me I haven't screwed everything up."

I ran my hands down her back, wrenched her to me. "These are the same lips that kissed whores. My cunt, the same one that welcomed them. All the pleasures they brought. A lot of other women. Can you deal with that?"

Her eyes searched mine. "Yes. But I don't think I'll ever like it."

* * *

"Elie thinks all the bodies are out," Sarah said, hanging up her duty belt after what looked like a long day for her. "God, I hope so."

"Anything from the patrol logs you've been going over?" I asked.

"Yeah. Dad said the DNR are lousy record keepers." She sank onto the couch. Rubbed her face with both hands. "I'm worn out, Win."

No wonder. We'd made love with urgency last night. Then talked. Sarah gently probed. When her questions weren't comfortable, I'd said no. And then, we'd make love again. It had been a repeating loop most of the night.

"You want to take a nap? I'll wake you when Emily gets here."

"No, just let me stretch out here."

I kissed her forehead and went into the kitchen. We'd passed another milestone last night. Our first fight. Then been able to talk about it. My world hadn't been black and white since my first tour. Sarah, on the other hand, had to operate according to the black and white of law statutes. Although, I thought she saw more. Responded to more.

I heard Emily's old Jeep climbing the drive. The Jeep needed a tune-up. I walked outside with Des at my side, her ears pricked forward. She caught Emily's scent, wagged her tail. Emily climbed out, dressed in jeans and a T-shirt rather than her office wear. Appealing figure.

"Nice location, Win," she said, taking in the clearing. "Great house. Where's Sarah?"

"Taking a nap on the couch." I told her about our milestone fight and the words that had been spoken.

"You seem to be okay," she said, her eyes narrowed.

"I was terrified I'd screwed up everything. She felt the same way. She knew I had a past, I never thought I'd have to explain it."

"You don't." She started walking toward the porch. "That's a pact Marty and I made when we first got together. Past is baggage that we don't share unless it directly touches on our present relationship."

"Like what?"

Her eyebrows flew up. "Really?"

"I didn't mean…I meant how do you draw boundaries?"

"Carefully. There are things in my past I'll never tell Marty. If she asks me why I've acted a certain way, or said something, I take the time to look in my past. I usually can find the trigger, and I'll tell her the trigger, but not the event."

"Clever."

"The purpose is to figure me out so I can change my behavior. It works the other way too."

I stopped walking. "My anger scared me, Emily. It was red-hot and building when I left."

She scanned my face. "You think it was your PTSD?"

"I don't know. Maybe."

"Remember, Win, you walked away. You knew you were coming to a dangerous boil and made the decision to go cool off. Did you get physical? Beat a wall? Throw things?"

"No. Balled up my fists, I think."

"Come in this week. We'll take a good look. Figure out a strategy—this isn't the last time you're going to get angry with Sarah."

I opened the front door for Emily. Des sneaked past us and jumped on the couch. Sarah was awake now.

Emily sat in a side chair as Sarah rubbed her eyes and stretched.

Sarah gave her a groggy smile, ran her hands through her hair. "We had our first fight last night and survived it, but I needed a nap."

Emily returned the smile but didn't say anything.

"So, what insights into Noor did you come up with?" I asked.

"Is she really as hot as Win said?" Sarah asked.

Emily shifted her gaze to Sarah. "Yes. Reminds me of one of the new Bollywood stars. Beautiful face and very shapely figure." She took out her phone, thumbed through some images. She handed it to Sarah.

I watched Sarah deflate. "Oh my God. She's gorgeous."

I took the phone from her limp hand and sent the image to my phone. "I need to find out who she is, and this'll make it easier. Thanks Emily."

Emily took the phone back. "Win wasn't interested in this woman. Let me make it clear for you, Sarah. That woman used every move she had, and all she did was turn Win off."

Sarah took my hand. "I know I'm being silly, but allow me a bit of silliness now and then?"

I put my arm around her shoulders. "A rare now and then. How about we get down to business?"

Emily crossed her legs, ran a finger down the seam of her jeans. "She was desperate to succeed with you. Now granted, you're a beautiful woman. But every time you said you weren't interested, she tried harder. I got the impression she *had* to seduce you."

"Jesus, Win," Sarah said. "What'd you put in her drink?"

"She's been that way since I first met her which was at the last Sherry Hour of the semester. Said she'd seen me on campus and wanted to meet me." I rubbed Sarah's shoulder. "The thing is, I'm on campus so little. Go to class, teach, leave. I thought it was bullshit at the time."

"Well, I think you were her target, Win. She made a call right after you left," Emily said. "Reported her failure, and then she got yelled at."

"Why didn't you tell me this at our debriefing?"

"First, I didn't know it was a debriefing because I'm not a spy. Second, my concern was you, not Noor. Now do you want me to finish this?"

"Yeah, go ahead."

"They began the conversation in English, but switched after the first few sentences. I couldn't understand the language, but I got the tone. He was very angry with her."

"He?"

"I could hear him from the receiver. He was that loud. She called him Mohan and was definitely familiar with him. He wasn't pleased."

"She's working for someone?" Sarah asked.

"Sounded that way to me. She was properly in her place by the time she hung up. Also, very upset."

"I wonder what the hell's going on—and what Kemat had to do with it."

"Be careful, Win. Noor is a desperate young woman," Emily said. "I don't think you've seen the last of her. She's dangerous."

CHAPTER TWELVE

Sarah

I walked Em out to her car.

"So you survived your first fight—how does it feel?"

"Hell, Em. I was terrified I'd blown the whole relationship over things that happened when Win was in the service. She was furious with me for judging her. She walked out, and I was afraid she'd never come back."

"It's her house, Sarah. You knew she'd be back." Emily stopped at the car. "But it's a really important step for her. She expressed anger. I think if she didn't love you so much, she would've shrugged, never let you see the anger or her vulnerability. You both have baggage. Put it in the attic and lock the door. It's not something you can change. Live with it."

"I thought we were supposed to be aware of the baggage, be ready to unpack it."

"You take care of your own baggage, not Win's."

I hugged her. "Thanks for shepherding Win through the really rough times. For what you've done for both of us. Continue to do."

She gazed at me with her half-mast stare. "What do you want?"

"Are you always so suspicious?"

"Yes."

I sighed. "I'm afraid of that woman—Noor. I had no idea she was so flat-out gorgeous."

"Are you afraid Win will slip into her clutches, succumb to her charms?"

I nodded, unable to force words out.

"Then you're not the woman I've always thought you were. Strong, honest, capable," Emily said as she opened the door and climbed in. "If you saw the way Win reacted to Noor's advances, you'd know you have nothing to worry about. Looked like she'd sucked on something really bitter, not a tit."

What a way with words. "You're saying don't borrow trouble."

She started the Jeep. "You better believe it, Sarah. As lesbians, we already have enough."

I watched her disappear down the drive. I heard the front door open, felt Win's arms go around me. "It's time for a real nap, Sarah. You've got two more duty days. Come on in, crash on the couch and I'll start on dinner."

I leaned into her. I wanted to ask her if she could really forgive me, but I was afraid I'd start something again. I should just let it go.

She turned me around. "What?"

"How do you know there's something?"

"Your abs got tight. Now what's up?"

"Can you really forgive me for being such an asshole?"

"Yeah—if you promise to do the same for me." She tightened her arms around me. "Neither of us is perfect. We make mistakes. Dumb decisions. But, if we're in this for the long haul, we need to let the water flow under the bridge. Not dam it up or pretend there's no river."

Tears slipped down my cheeks, and I touched her face. Felt her smooth skin, got lost in her light blue eyes that had been so icy last night. I rested my head on her chest. "I'm so tired, Win. I'm wiped out."

She guided me inside and onto the couch. As soon as my eyes closed, I was asleep.

* * *

Since the "bones" task force was so small, we'd met in my office. I felt frustrated because we'd made so little progress. No easy identification on the remains and no witnesses. Hell.

"Think we oughta go an' talk to Nathan's uncle, mebbe he's a great-uncle, can't rightly remember," Dad said at our morning meeting. "Ethan Ravensong's his name. He was the progenitor of the Wildlife Area an' I'm thinkin' knows the area as well as any man alive. I believe he still spends time out there."

"Good idea, Dad. I don't know why I didn't think of it."

"Ain't seen him in awhiles. Reckon we can ask after him with Nathan."

"Would you do that? And get directions to his place. I don't know where he lives. John, anything new?"

"Damn little. Elie said all the bodies are out, no more graves. She'll have a preliminary report for us this week. She's damn close-mouthed about it, but I think she's formed some definite opinions."

"She won't share until she knows beyond the shadow of scientific doubt. Lloyd's kept a pretty tight lid on this, but there's a lot of speculation out there. As soon as we get something from Elie, I think we should let him run with the story."

"Bring them pesky reporters down from Indy," Dad said, his voice holding a warning.

"Worth the bother if we can get a lead from the general public here in the county. Somebody's got to have noticed women going missing."

We broke up soon after to follow each of our leads. I stared out the window of my office, wondering what I'd missed. The time span not only counted my tenure as sheriff, but Mac's and Dad's. Mac wouldn't have noticed a serial killer if the guy wore a sign around his neck and turned himself in. Dad was a totally different matter. He'd always had his fingers on the pulse of the county. Why hadn't he heard anything about missing women? Missing persons report had yielded nothing. Women disappeared, and no one noticed. How could that be?

Women who passed through the county, but didn't live here? Migrant farm workers? Those families were close-knit and would surely have reported any missing family members. I couldn't think of any other groups. Women alone? Hookers? Always a possibility, but I had no idea how to track them down. Some worked the truck stops by the interstate, some moved on with the truckers. Finding them was nigh on impossible. I made a note to talk to Wade McCormick, retired pimp. Maybe Vince Forrester, who'd headed up the Vice Squad during Dad's time in office. I'd heard he was in a nursing home and not doing well. Maybe Dad would have more luck with him.

"You wanna go talk with Ethan Ravensong now?" Dad asked. "You got time?"

"I'm not getting much else done, so let's go."

Dad drove his battered old Ford truck up a trace not far from the Alert State Wildlife Area. Evenly spaced potholes rocked the truck like a lullaby. Smoke rose in a thin, white stream from the stovepipe that protruded from the roof. The only sound was a creek flowing nearby, and I could see sunlight dancing on it through the trees. We pulled into the clearing, Dad shut off the engine and we waited. An old man opened the cabin's door and waved us in.

The cabin furnishings were as spartan as the old man with his faded flannel shirt and buzz cut. Ethan shook Dad's hand. "Good to see you, old friend. And this must be the daughter you are so proud of, all grown up and following in your footsteps. Coffee?"

"Please," Dad said and sat at the table.

I followed, and after Ethan served us, he joined us. "I am guessing this is not a social call. What can I do for you folks?"

I glanced at Dad, raised my eyebrows. He was going to do the talking.

"You heard 'bout all them skeletons they been diggin' up at Alert?"

Several emotions tagged across his face, too deep in his psyche for me to read.

"No," he said. "Nathan has threatened to 'wire me up,' but so far, I have managed to resist my nephew's efforts. I like living at peace with my surroundings. Are they ancient burials?"

"No," I answered. "We think these women died in the past twenty, twenty-five years."

"Women? How many?"

"Thirteen."

He made a garbled sound. I thought he was having a heart attack. He pushed away from the table, walked to a plank attached to the log wall. He ran his finger down a row of spiral-bound notebooks.

He returned to the table. "I have been keeping a journal on that land since I learned to write."

He opened the notebook. "I knew something was wrong, long time ago. I tried to get that DNR agent to investigate, but he seemed incapable of expending any energy."

He flipped through it. "Yes, seventh of September, ninety-two. First one I found."

"You found a grave?"

"Perhaps, but I did not think so at the time. It looked more like a trench that had been backfilled. Covered with leaves and forest debris. I would not have noticed except I stepped on it. First, I thought it was gophers. Then I started removing debris."

"You'd never found any before ninety-two?"

"No. But I found trenches like that on through the nineties."

"Every year?"

"Ninety-two through ninety-nine. Like the seasons change, every September."

"Nothing after ninety-nine?"

"Not for years, but they started again in two thousand and eight. Always a shallow trench, maybe ten to twelve feet long, no more than two feet wide. I thought somebody was taking soil samples for a school project."

"You never reported them to Dad?"

"I pointed them out to Fred Bauman, asked him if he knew why they were there for the first few years or so. He said he would check, but I do not think he ever did."

"We have all the DNR logs. We can check. Do you have a record of the other dates?"

Ethan rose wearily. "I feel responsible. I felt evil there and tried to chase it away with the old ceremonies—instead of finding its source."

Dad shook his head. "Don't go blamin' yourself, Ethan. Bauman always was a lazy sonofabutt. You done what you could with the evidence you had."

"I should have brought it to you, Micah. I knew Fred Bauman thought I was just a crazy old Indian. You would have taken me seriously."

"Can't go back, Ethan. We can't never go back."

* * *

When we returned to the station, we began collating the DNR records with Ethan's notebook dates. Not one time had a DNR agent been in the vicinity on the dates, or a week before or after. I couldn't blame the agents. They had an enormous territory to cover and most of their work wasn't patrolling for criminals.

The question my mind was forming: accidental timing? Or was our killer watching?

I glanced at my watch. "Damn." It was already past five. I called Win. "I'm running late. Sorry."

"Must mean progress on your case," she said. "Wish I could say the same. Could you pick up a pizza on the way home? Didn't get to the grocery today."

"Sure. Miss you."

"Get going, Sarah. I'm starving."

"For what?" I heard her laughing as she disconnected.

We ate sitting on the couch, the pizza box on the coffee table between us. Until I'd smelled it, I hadn't realized how hungry I was. It was a race for the last piece.

"No luck with tracing Noor?" I asked as I closed the box. I'd been generous and given Win the last slice, probably out of guilt from being late.

"No. We couldn't find her listed with any cell phone carrier. Probably uses a burn phone. But I called Bill. He suggested we work from the other end."

"Other end? Pakistan?"

"Yeah. He's got an agent who can look there. Who's due in this area soon. Her name's Pan." She took a deep breath. "We have a history, Sarah. Before she was my bodyguard here."

"I don't want to know," I said, not looking at her. "Em said we both have to deal with our own baggage. Pan is yours."

"I just…oh, shit." She threw her napkin at the box. "Be prepared for a flashy, oversexed woman who'd like to lay any female she comes in contact with."

"What?"

"My baggage. Just be prepared."

"She's coming here?" I motioned to the room. "*Here*?"

"No, not to our home." She leaned back and crossed her arms. "But you'll probably meet her. Task force and all."

Win looked miserable. More of a story here than ancient history. "She's the agent Bill sent to be your bodyguard? But you'd known her before that?"

"Yeah."

Had Win slept with her? Before her visit? During it? We were already together, weren't we? I couldn't remember. Maybe it was during the time Win stayed away from me and had been all business. Maybe. Looking back, falling in love with Win was such a blur to me.

I took a deep breath, scooted over beside her and rubbed her thigh. "Is she as beautiful as Noor?"

Win expelled her breath and grabbed my hand. "Yes. Better figure too."

"Oh hell."

Win put her arm around me and leaned over to kiss me. She paused. "We're married. I'm not going to wander. I gave you my word, Sarah."

"I know that, in my heart I know that. But I feel like I can't compete with these gorgeous, exotic women who seem to flock to you."

"They come with agendas. You don't have one. That makes it safe for me to love you."

"Oh, I have an agenda," I said as I unbuckled her belt and untucked her shirt. She watched as I unbuttoned her shirt, pushed it aside.

When I started to undo her bra, she stopped me and trapped my hands in hers. "Don't hide from your doubts with sex. Please."

"I'm not hiding. You slept with Pan, you've said so yourself. I can't say I don't care, but it's past. You succumb to her charms now, and there'll be hell to pay, Win. And I mean that from the bottom of my being."

She kept looking into my eyes. She unfastened her bra, took it and her shirt off and then began unbuttoning mine. She untucked it, took it off. Her eyes never wavered from mine. My bra followed. She pulled me close, breasts meeting breasts, flesh forming the only barrier between us. Her eyes closed as she kissed me.

CHAPTER THIRTEEN

Win

I disconnected. Turned to Sarah. "That was Bill. Pan's flying in to his headquarters today. He wants me there."

She drank her coffee, didn't look at me. "I meant what I said."

"Why don't you come with me?" I moved around her, massaged her shoulders. "You've always said Mondays are slow for you. Plus, you'll get an idea of what Pan's like."

"A lesbian nymphomaniac."

"Who will put the moves on you the minute she lays eyes on you."

"Fat chance."

I turned her around to face me. "Is that what you're afraid of? That you're too ugly for someone you just described as a lesbian nymphomaniac?"

"Not ugly. Plain."

I kissed her, hard and long. Felt her breasts under her uniform shirt press into me. "Plain, my love, you're not. Where the hell did you get your self-image?"

She ran her hands along my thighs to my butt. "I never had any problem with self-image until all your bimbos started showing up."

I laughed, gave her a peck on her forehead. "Come with?"

"Caleb should go—he's your partner on this."

"If I'm not mistaken, this is his day off." I held her at arm's length. "Are you scared of her?"

She started putting our breakfast dishes in the sink. "No. I'm afraid of the comparison, standing side by side. When you see that, you'll realize I'm the country mouse and utterly boring."

"A what? Do you remember last night? What is wrong with you?"

She ran water. "I never had these feelings with Hugh. Never worried if I could keep his interest." She turned the water off and then faced me. "I think it's because I'm so new to the life. Unsure about who I am in a new world." She shrugged. "That's lame, I know. But I can't imagine life without you. I couldn't bear it."

"Shit, let's stop worrying so much about losing one another through infidelity. You know I've felt the same thing. Worried you'd get tired of me. Want to sample other pastures. I'm willing to put those feelings away." I walked to her. "Can we simply enjoy the loving? Keep talking about issues? But not dwell in doubt?"

She wrapped her arms around me. Leaned into me. "Swear, I'll try."

"When you feel insecure, remember what happens when you touch me. I know you can feel it. Hold onto those memories while we make more." I kissed her. "Now—are you coming with me?"

"How soon do we have to be there?"

* * *

Sarah went into work a little late. I picked her up at two and we headed for Camp Atterbury. To Pan. Shit, what had I gotten us into?

Once we were on the road, Sarah took her ring off the chain and put it on her finger. Talk about life in the shadows. I knew what she was feeling. All my years in the Corps, I'd hated the hiding. But with one difference: I'd never had a relationship to protect. Nothing but fleeting hookups. No home and hearth involved. I'd lived a different life. I had to admit I didn't know how to guide Sarah through the forest of conflicts I'd pushed her into. Well, maybe not pushed. Maybe she'd chosen.

When we walked into Bill's office, Pan rested her butt against the edge of his desk. Dressed in a black silk blouse—unbuttoned enough she showed her cleavage—and a short black skirt, she brought back memories I should forget. When she saw me, her eyes lit up and she swished her hips to me. Shit, what a walk.

"Win, sweetie, been so long when I see you." She started to put her arms around me. Face turned up, lips parted.

I stepped back. Held up my left hand. "I'd like you to meet my wife, Sarah Pitt." I reached for Sarah's hand, brought her to my side.

Pan looked her up and down. Smiled that provocative smile that let me know exactly what was on her mind.

"I wager you are not stodgy married couple, are you?" She smiled at Sarah. "Congratulations, Sarah. Women all over world try to salt Win's tail and all of us miss. Though we share some… interesting times, didn't we, Win? Do you share games we play with your new bride?"

Sarah was blushing like mad. Bill wasn't far behind.

"Um, ladies, I think we'd better get down to business," he said.

Pan let her gaze linger on Sarah's breasts. "Yes, I love to do that."

"We're debriefing here, Pan," Bill said, a little more forcefully. He motioned to a conference table. "Pan's dug up some interesting intel on Noor Bhatti. Let's get going."

Pan oozed into a chair, her attention still fastened on Sarah. She switched her gaze to me. An offer of all the pleasure in the world was apparent in her eyes. "You have a good memory for scents, Win."

"Stop it, Pan," Bill said. "Report."

Pan slid her long fingered hand along the table's surface. Such promises it made. "I simply mean, Win correct. Noor sold to the Palace as a girl. She tutored in all the graces those women possess. She very successful. She left only few years ago, sold again. To a wealthy Kashmiri, Mohan Shamsi. He is on the look-for list, yes?"

"Watch list. Yes," Bill answered. "How'd she get her academic credentials?"

"She studied for them, so do not underestimate her. She had been taught to study, to learn, for many years. She is intelligent woman. It would have been a piece of soap for her."

"Soap?" Bill asked.

"Cake," I said. "Do you have any idea why she was sent here?"

Pan shrugged, a luxurious movement. "That would take more investigation. I do not like Kashmir."

"Do you know how she got Dr. Kemat Fitzgerald to hire her?"

"Good sex, I can imagine."

"Pan, quit. Stop the games. I never caught a whiff that Kemat was anything but straight." Although I'd smelled Noor's perfume on her a couple of times. "There's got to be some connection, some pressure point Shamsi used." I turned to Bill. "He's an international arms dealer, right?"

Bill nodded. "He might've been looking for an in with Intelligence officers who are studying at CELI. We'll have to work on that angle. You think he killed Kemat?"

My turn to shrug. "If she were in league with him, no. No reason. But if she discovered what Noor was up to, it's possible."

"It was an execution," Sarah said in a gruff voice. "A left-handed shooter who put a .38 to her temple and angled it down so it went through her brainstem. That says he was either sending a message to others or was willing to risk getting caught because she was too dangerous to him."

Pan sent a smoldering glance at Sarah. "I love smart women in uniform, don't I, Win?"

Bill ignored her comment. "Which do you think is the case, Pan?"

"I will require more search. I was hoping to spend a few days here…resting. I can find out where to begin with computer. Can you put me on, Win?"

"Put you up. No."

Pan pouted like the super flirt she was. I never knew where the act stopped and the real woman began. Perhaps she'd been playing these games so long, she'd forgotten a line even existed.

"We'll give you base housing, Pan," Bill said. "But you cannot cut a swath through the women on this base. I hear about hijinks, you're on the first plane out. To Kashmir."

Pan rose, the view of her breasts flashed at Sarah, along with a very sexy smile.

* * *

We drove halfway back to Greenglen before I couldn't stand Sarah's silence anymore. "So, what do you think of Pan?" I finally asked her.

"She's a little overwhelming," she said, her color heightening. "She's like a Eurasian version of Marilyn Monroe on estrogen."

I grinned. Apt description.

"How did you meet her?"

"R&R somewhere. Singapore, I think. At a bar."

Sarah was silent as she watched the landscape go by. "You slept with her more than once?"

"I think we're getting into baggage territory, Sarah." I took a hand off the steering wheel and groped for hers. I squeezed it. "We had sex when we found ourselves in the same town with downtime." I waited for Sarah to squeeze back.

"The 'games' you played with her—do we do the same things?"

I withdrew my hand.

"I didn't mean…I just have visions of the two of you together and…"

"Live with your imagination, Sarah. I'm not helping you. You want to go back to your office?"

She was silent. I could feel her examining me. "I have to pick up my truck."

I took the turnoff for Greenglen. Pulled in next to her car twenty minutes later. "I'll see you when you get home. Don't forget to take your ring off."

She turned the shiny band on her left hand. "Is this fight number two?"

"No. A continuation of the first one. I've told you I have a past. Too many women to count. Pan is one of them. She helped me forget. She helped me survive. I will not apologize for any of that. Or for Pan."

Sarah wiped her cheeks. Nodded. Got out and walked in the back door of the station. As I drove home, I began to realize what an unexpected pressure Pan exerted on Sarah. She'd seen couples dancing together, kissing a bit. But not the open, bare-ass sexuality of a woman like Pan. I thought Pan scared her. And, perhaps, intrigued her. I hoped to God Bill didn't let her off the base.

It was dark when Sarah finally made it home. I'd been reading, sprawled out on the couch. I watched her as she got rid of her duty trappings. She paused before she turned around. "Truce?" she asked when she faced me.

"I'd rather sign a treaty, Sarah. This is the last time I'm going to say this: Pan is in my past, and that's where she'll stay."

Sarah walked slowly to the couch, sat on the end of it. Touched my leg. "I'm letting my insecurities run away with me, aren't I?"

"Yeah."

"She scared me, Win. Such raw sexuality—I've seen it directed at men by other women, but never from a woman to you."

"From a woman to two women, Sarah. She came on to you too. Flashed her boobs at you good." I put the book on the table, sat up. "That's part of who Pan is—unbridled enthusiasm for sex. The other part is one of the best intelligence agents our government has. She'll ferret out Noor's connections to Kemat."

"I don't doubt she's effective, but hell, I've never had any woman flirt with me like that. I felt like my breasts were already in her hands."

"Another few minutes and they would've been."

"No."

"I saw your expression when she flashed her cleavage at you."

"I…it surprised me. I…"

"You wanted to explore the invitation." I swung my legs onto the floor. Took her hand. "If you want to get turned on by someone like that, okay. Make it a fantasy. But be damn careful what you fantasize with Pan."

"While we make love, are you fantasizing about other women?"

"I have no ability to go beyond the moment with you. No fantasies but you." I kissed her, rubbed her thigh. "Never hesitate to ask for any kind of experimentation, Sarah. Just don't ask how I learned my skills. Deal?"

She nodded. "Sometimes I get so confused. Feel stuff I've never felt before."

"She turned you on, didn't she?"

Sarah turned bright red. "Yes."

"Would you have fucked her?"

"Win!"

"Welcome to the life. I don't know a lesbian who wouldn't be turned on by Pan." I put my arms around her. Rubbed the back of her neck. "Stay away from her, Sarah. She's the dangerous kind of sex."

"You're not?" She tugged me closer, kissed me with fire. Straddled me.

Her breath was coming faster. Her hands ranged over my body. Her lips followed.

Pan be damned.

* * *

I leaned my head back and closed my eyes. I hadn't even looked at Emily's Zen sandbox. I was in a state of pleasant exhaustion. We'd spent most of Tuesday in bed. Or doing bed things all over the house. I'd tried my best to give Sarah pleasure. Show her she had nothing to fear from women like Noor and Pan. She'd explored new ways. A couple of times, she'd turned me inside-out and left me wanting more. Immediately.

"Win—you ready?"

Emily stood back from her door. I walked in. Sat in my usual chair. Maybe I should've canceled. Things seem to have righted themselves.

"You look awfully satisfied, Win. You make up with Sarah?"

"Yeah." I told her about Sarah meeting Pan, her confusion with the attraction she'd experienced. "If Pan had appeared at my house instead of Bill's office, we might've had a three-way."

"Really?"

I shrugged. "Pan turned her on. But then, Pan can turn any woman on."

"Pan's the woman in the skimpy bikini on some beach? The woman you cheated with?"

"I hadn't promised forever at that point." I shifted in my chair. This wasn't going where I thought it would.

"Does Sarah know?"

"I think she suspects, but I never told her."

Emily nodded. "Do you still find Pan attractive?"

"Of course. I enjoy looking at beautiful women. You don't?"

"Do you fantasize having sex with Pan? Or other beautiful women?"

"No. When I'm in Bloomington and alone, I fantasize about making love with Sarah."

Emily smiled. "Just be sure. How would you react if Sarah strayed?"

"You mean fantasize or do the deed?"

"Take your pick," Emily said as she jotted notes.

"Fantasy is just that. If she slept with someone else, I'd be devastated." I shifted again. "Should I be worried?"

"I shouldn't think so. You two have a strong bond, one of the strongest I've seen with a new couple. Just remember, she's new to the life. If she should experiment a bit, it's not necessarily the end of the relationship." She squinted at me. "It isn't, Win. Now, let's talk about the anger."

Jerk me around much, Emily? Back to our first fight. "I recognized how angry I was getting. I left. Went for a walk."

"Was it the kind of blind rage you experienced when you first came home?"

I thought. Closed my eyes. "It would've been. But I was aware the rage was coming."

"Good." She leaned toward me, handed me a paper. "I've outlined some strategies you should practice. They're pretty standard, but I have tailored a couple of them for you."

I scanned the list. "Makes sense."

"You're generally way slower to anger than you used to be. Just don't let it sneak up on you. And never, *never* strike out physically. It'll bring a whole cascade of memories. Do anything to get away from that impulse. The resulting self-incrimination could sink you, Win."

"I thought you're supposed to make me feel better," I said as I rubbed the chair's nubby fabric.

"You've come so far. I know it hasn't been an easy journey—especially since you fell in love with Sarah. I'm trying to keep you on the path."

"So tell me, don't you ever get turned on watching other women?"

"I told you," Emily said with a grin. "You and Sarah are a stunning couple."

CHAPTER FOURTEEN

Sarah

I hated going to work, leaving our warm bed, going back to work a case that had little chance for a good resolution. I found my attention drifting from the stack of paperwork in front of me to yesterday. Hell, this morning. I wiggled in my chair and tried to switch my focus back to the log.

Caleb tapped on the door. "Win coming in this morning for the briefing?"

"She's got an appointment, then I think she's going back to Atterbury to interview an agent. Is it time already?" I glanced at my watch. They must be waiting for me.

"She get any intel?" Caleb asked. "You should've called me. I could've gone up. Saved you the trip." He grinned. "Oh, never mind."

"It was your day off." I grabbed my notebook. "Win made notes for you." I opened my notebook and handed it to him. "Read fast."

John Morgan hadn't come up with anything new, but since we'd given him specific dates, he was running all the records. Even misdemeanors like speeding tickets. Boring as hell, but it was detail work that caught killers.

"Elie called this morning, and she's got preliminary data for us," I said. "I'm going in this afternoon. Let's hope the killer left something behind."

"On bones that've been in the ground that long?" Caleb asked.

"It's not long in Elie years because old for her is measured in centuries." I turned to John. "Think about thirteen women who disappeared and no one missed them. Who are they?"

"I've been thinking, Sarah. The only group I've come up with is hookers. Maybe their pimp killed them. Or some evangelizing bastard."

"Take that idea and run with it. See if any of the jurisdictions around here are aware of missing prostitutes. Concentrate on the most recent date. Be sure to check with Indianapolis Metropolitan PD. They probably have more prostitutes per square mile than any other place in the state. Problem is, so many of them don't have anyone who'd report them missing."

That afternoon, I drove to Bloomington with half an eye on the weather and the rest of my mind wandering around in my feelings about Pan. The weather had warmed up enough that severe thunderstorm warnings were out. A radical cold front passing through could level a cornfield or flatten a town, but it cleared out the sticky air mass. I wished a cold front would pass through my mind.

Would you have fucked her? That question built in my mind like the heavy cloud banks to the northwest. I hadn't answered the question. In fact, I'd been so shocked to hear it, I hadn't said anything but Win's name. Fuck was an ugly word. I tried to push away the image of Win and Pan together. Win's beautiful body open to Pan's explorations, Pan's voluptuous breasts rubbing against Win's body. Emily had given me a book when Win and I had first gotten together. Did they do the things in the book that Win and I never had? Was Win as open with Pan as she was with me?

The question still echoed in my mind. Would I? Was I simply jealous of Win's past lovers? Or had Pan found an ember in me that could blow into a full flame? How could I even think that?

Pushing those thoughts aside, I found Elie in her cramped office, head bent over a bone. I tapped on the open door.

"I've got everything set up in the lab," Elie said with a nod.

I followed her down a corridor and sucked in my breath when I saw the skulls in a line on a counter.

"I know, Sarah. It's one thing to know there are burials, another to see the skulls of women who were murdered." She motioned me to a stool. "The dates you sent me helped order their burials—all confirmed by evidence of deterioration."

"Still no identifications?"

"I sent dental records to every dentist in the county, then the southern half of the state. Now I've posted them on a national database. But don't hold your breath."

"You think they may be transients? Prostitutes, maybe? Or something like migrant farm workers?"

"From the stress on their musculature, I'd say farm workers is more likely." She pulled up a couple of slides. "I won't give you the science lecture, but these women were used to lifting heavy objects. There's also a lot of wear on the spinal column that confirms it. Could be farm laborers, or women working in a warehouse or with a trucker."

"Most farm laborers who move through the county are Hispanic—tight-knit families who'd miss thirteen women."

"And report it? If they're undocumented?"

"I pray to God they would. We're not ICE and this isn't Arizona or Alabama. Vincente's asking around, but he's coming up with nada so far."

She walked over to the skulls. "This makes you realize the full extent of the madness, doesn't it?" Elie sighed. "The wound on each of the skulls is in the exact same place on all the skulls."

"The cause of death?"

"Yes. Not only is the location the same, but the same exact size. I'm sure the weapon is the same, but I don't know what it is."

"Not a gunshot wound?"

"No. No exit wound, no bullet within the skull. Not a gunshot."

"With your database of weapons—"

"There's nothing close in the database. Somebody got inventive. I've sent the wound pattern and measurements to the FBI, but nothing from them so far." Elie leaned against the counter and crossed her arms. "So here's my scenario. The perpetrator uses enough pressure on the throat to render the victim unconscious. Then uses the unknown weapon to kill."

"At roughly the same time?"

"Can't tell."

"So he could transport the unconscious woman from the place of original abduction to the burial ground, kill her there and bury her."

Elie nodded. "Or takes her to a third location, kills her there and transports the body to the burial ground. That seems unlikely since we haven't found anything indicating torture. But you should keep it in mind."

"Hell, I hate this—families out there who are missing someone." I extended my hand toward the skulls, but couldn't touch them. Women with lives ahead of them. "Have you done any facial reconstructions?"

"Computer generated images, but I find them very flat. They're in the packet I'm giving you. But I'm sending them to a forensic artist I know." She handed me a thumb drive. "All of the report's on this."

The lives and deaths of thirteen women, boiled down to scientific data on a thumb drive. "Thanks Elie. Keep in touch."

* * *

My thoughts on the drive home tried to fill in some of the missing pieces of thirteen deaths. I kept circling around the lack of missing persons reports. How the hell could that be? Runaway girls disappeared every day, some to never surface again. Ditto prostitutes. But neither would've shown the wear and tear of consistent heavy lifting. That returned me back to the circle: migrant farm workers, maybe warehouse workers or truckers. But how many women worked either of those jobs in McCrumb County? Besides, somebody would've reported them missing.

I called John. "Have you thought about widening our search to national databases?"

"Tried it, but without more definite information, it'll take us a couple of years to get through. A lot of missing people, Sarah."

"Try looking for long-haul truckers. Elie said the ages of the women are from about twenty-five to fifty-five. That should narrow parameters some."

"Are you coming back to the office?"

"It'll be after five when I'm close, so I thought I'd go home. Something I should look at?"

"No, but your dad's still here. He won't go home as long as there's some kind of lead to follow. He got here at six this morning."

"Thanks for the concern, John. Is he close to the phone?"

"Yeah, hold on." Some clacks on the other end, then Dad's voice.

"Why don't you come over tonight for dinner?"

"Well, that'd be a right nice treat. Would be much obliged. Ain't as much fun, cookin' for one."

"Uh, watch what you say, Dad."

"Phooey. What time?"

"Finish up and come—no, on second thought, just come. Meet you at Win's in half an hour."

"I'll be there. You just make it safe an' sound."

As soon as he hung up, I called Win. "Are you home yet?"

"Just pulling in."

"I invited Dad over to dinner. Do we have anything to eat, or should I pick up a pizza on the way home?"

"Reckon I kin rustle up somethin', Sarah Anne."

"Oh, Sweet Jesus, you sound exactly like him—too much, way too much." I checked my side mirror and pulled onto the highway. "You get anything new at Atterbury today?"

"Tell you when you get home. Hurry up. Storm's coming fast."

We disconnected, and I looked in the rearview mirror. Black clouds roiled behind me. I stepped on the accelerator. I should've asked Win if it was okay to invite him. After all, it was an auspicious occasion. He'd been to Win's before, but not since I'd moved in. I was inviting him into our home. Auspicious, and I should've called Win first.

My thoughts returned to thirteen skulls who'd never gotten to go home. We were missing something, but hell if I knew what. I went back over the list of possible occupations. What the hell was I missing? Letter carriers? Weight wouldn't have been evenly distributed. But maybe FedEx employees or one of the other box carriers. Amazon employees? They had a distribution center farther south, but it was fairly new. But with all of these, wouldn't someone have reported these women missing?

Fuck it all. I stomped on the accelerator and flew down the road. I turned on my light bar. I had no reason to speed other than

utter frustration. I saw the first forks of lightning snake from the clouds.

Would you have fucked her?

"I don't know, Win, but I'm coming home to you."

* * *

The big splashy drops began as I ran toward the front door. I pelted in and found Win lounging on the couch. I stooped to greet Des, gave her a kiss on her muzzle. "Where's Dad?" I sniffed. "Where's dinner?"

"He called right after you hung up, said he was bringing it." She walked toward me. "Said he—do you want a direct quote?"

"Paraphrase, please."

She put her arms around me. "He didn't want to make it into a big deal. Said we could cook for him some other time."

I leaned against her. "It is a big deal, Win. First time he's been here for dinner since I've moved in. It's a big step for both of us. I should've asked you first."

"I think he wants you to believe it's the natural progression of events. Of our love."

I kissed her, ran my hands under her T-shirt.

"I don't think we have time for this, but I've got a rain check, right?"

I heard Dad's truck coming up the drive. Kissed her again as a promise. Des ran to the door, tail wagging. It opened as a sharp peal of thunder shook the house.

Dad gave me a peck on the cheek, shook the water from his ball cap and beckoned to Win. He kissed her on the cheek. "Hi, Other Daughter. Real gully-whomper out there." He handed Win a couple of bags, greeted Des, put his arm around me and walked us to the kitchen. "Stopped at that new Italian place over to the interstate, got a coupla stromboli an' calzones. Just need to heat 'em up."

"A salad too," Win said, unpacking the bags. "Extra sauce. You get my vote."

The storm raged outside with strike after strike of lightning, too close together to tell them apart. But I felt safe with the two people in the world I loved most. Dad had chosen well. The food

was good and conversation general. When dinner was finished, I called the station to check on damage while Dad and Win cleared the table.

"So how's the county?" Dad asked as I sat next to Win on the couch.

"Faring well, no major damage reported other than some trees down. But streams and creeks are up. We'll end up with some flooding, but not until later. I don't have to go to work."

I could see Win smile out of the corner of my eye.

Dad stretched his long legs out, slouched in the chair. "Elie got anythin' new?"

I outlined everything Elie had said. Showed him the photos of the skulls. Then explained why she thought the women had been involved in an occupation that required heavy lifting.

Dad shook his head. "Let me think on it, Sarah. I reckon we're missin' somethin' 'cause them folks what work those jobs are gonna be reported missin'."

"I kept going around and around on the drive back and couldn't come up with anything else. Frustrating as hell."

"Home health aides," Win said. "I hired a service for Mom. They'd get her up and out of bed, help her into the wheelchair. A lot of lifting. There weren't many businesses back then that provided those services."

"Good idea, Win," Dad said. "I know a coupla folk what used to run them. Somethin' to start on tomorrow. An' speakin' of that, it's getting late an' I better get home. See if that ole roof is still attached to the house."

We walked him to the door. "You got a wonderful home, Win, an' I'm glad you're sharin' it with Sarah." He hugged us both and walked to his truck.

After his taillights disappeared down the drive, Win closed the door and opened her arms. "Time for me to collect my rain check."

I moved into her arms. I kissed her long and hard, desire springing up like an ember to flame. I again slipped my hands under her T-shirt, and this time met with a full response. I was home.

CHAPTER FIFTEEN

Win

I propped myself up. Looked at Sarah's body next to me. Thought I was the luckiest dyke in the world. "I never in my whole life imagined being married."

"Not even when you were a kid? The white gown, cottage with the white picket fence?" Sarah asked, sleep still marking her voice.

"Did I ever talk about weddings with you? No. Though I think I did have daydreams about running away with Joan Jett."

Sarah snickered. "Damn, Win."

"What about you? Picket fence and all?"

"No. I fantasized about being sheriff. Guess we have to be careful what we wish for."

"I couldn't have wished for anything better than you." I traced her nipple with a featherlight touch.

She covered my hand with hers, pressed into it. "Does it hurt you that I don't wear my wedding ring all the time?"

"I understand. You wear it when we're places that are important to us. You know, Ruby's and with friends. For now, that's enough."

"That's not what I asked you." She gently rubbed my fingers. "Does it hurt you?"

I looked at her hand covering mine. The ring I'd given her when we'd married. "I don't feel pain. Wistfulness. But I know if we'd married when I was in the service, I would've been wearing it around my neck too. Even that might've been too risky."

"I think it hurts me."

"Think?"

"Hell, we've both been hanging around Em too much. I'm aware of resenting not being able to wear it all the time. Not having you recognized as my partner in life. The small stuff seems to grate, and the big stuff like that CIA agent makes me boil over."

I took her hand, kissed it. She hadn't asked me about my meeting with Pan yesterday. Maybe she wanted to avoid the whole issue. Refuse to admit she'd been turned on by Pan and her offer for an extraordinary experience. Maybe I should let Sarah work the issue for now. Wait for her to bring it up. I ran my hand down her body, kissed her breast. Felt her sharp intake of breath when my fingers began to explore even lower.

* * *

It was barely dawn. She was pouring coffee into a travel mug when I walked into the kitchen, still towel-drying my hair. "Save me some."

"I thought you'd been wide awake for quite some time," she said with a coy smile. "You get anything new yesterday?"

No mention of Pan. "Some. We're filling in Noor's background. And Kemat's. I think they knew one another before Noor ever arrived. We're trying to figure out how and when." I picked up the carafe and emptied it into my cup. "This kind of thing takes time, Sarah."

She took a sip of my coffee. "Work it as hard as you and Caleb can. I may be investigating thirteen deaths, but they're an old trail. Kemat's murder is new, but we'll lose that trail if we don't get something solid soon."

"Ma'am, yes ma'am." I pulled her into my arms. "I love you so much. I really am the luckiest dyke in the world." We kissed and I felt desire rising. I pulled back. Took her hand. "Don't forget to change your ring before you get to the station."

She took a deep breath. Nodded. "See you at nine. You are coming in for the briefing, aren't you?"

"I'd much rather come in for a debriefing with you."

* * *

"Hell of a frustrating week," Sarah said as she entered the house and hung her duty belt on its peg. "Dad's been poring over the old logs, trying to figure out when he saw a complaint against a home health provider."

"He should be able to pull up those records real easy," I said. "Didn't you say all your records were computerized? Or is Micah allergic to computer records?"

"He used to be—allergic, that is. But when he retired, he learned with Nathan's tutoring. Said he never had time before." She walked over and leaned against me. "The logs were never computerized. We were short-staffed and did the best we could. So now he's in the records room, covered in dust and sneezing every five minutes. I get so tired of trying to swim upstream during a constant flood season."

I hugged her. "Maybe, when this case is over, I can spend some time entering data."

"That's a good waste of your time. If we just had enough in the budget to hire a civilian clerk, everything would run smoother." She pulled back. "I want to get out of this uniform."

"Can I help?"

She laughed, kissed me lightly. "Can we go dancing tonight?"

"Love to. There's a—"

The phone rang. My burner. I didn't recognize the caller's number. "Yo."

"And 'yo' to you too," Pan said in her smoky voice. "I want you at Ruby Slippers tonight. Is possible?"

"We're planning to. What's going on?"

"I have interesting date. Might need backdown."

"Backup. What's going on?"

"Come early, find dark corner. Stay off dancing floor."

"But that's what we're coming in for—" She'd hung up. I sighed. Things were never easy with Pan. I told Sarah. "You still want to go?"

"Why not? I can watch you squirm." She walked down the hall toward the bathroom, shedding garments.

We ate on the way in, found an appropriate dark corner. Waited. The show had already started when Pan made her entrance in a smoldering tunic cut down to her navel. Well, almost. Her date was dressed more conservatively in black trousers and an intricately patterned blouse. Pan met my gaze, guided the other woman to a table in front of us. As the woman hung her purse on the back of her chair, I saw her profile. Noor. What the hell was Pan up to?

"Is that—"

"Pan and Noor."

"My worst nightmare. Ever." Sarah snuggled into my shoulder.

"Or great entertainment."

The rest of the set was an X-rated movie, playing right in front of us. When the singer took a break, Pan excused herself. I ducked into Sarah's shoulder, thinking I should've worn a hat tonight. Sarah murmured in my ear. "I think Pan wants me to follow her."

"Be careful, Sarah. Don't let her back you into a corner."

"Literally?"

"Any kind of corner." I watched her thread her way through the tables. I put my arms on the table. Rested my head on them. I didn't even have sunglasses with me. Shit. Pan should've warned me, but that would've spoiled her fun.

I wondered that Noor hadn't followed. A stall would've given a relatively private place to complete their performance. But Pan had always been a tease.

I felt Sarah slide back into her seat. Put an arm around me. "Stay put. Noor's still looking around. Okay. Pan's back. Hell, don't they realize this is a public place?"

I raised my head. Sat back into Sarah's arm. Bumped my head. "What the hell is that?"

"A hat I borrowed from the bartender. Think it looks good on me?"

"You look like a raider of the lost dykes," I said with a lift of an eyebrow. "Completely swashbuckling."

She grinned and plopped it on my head.

I tilted it slightly. "So what did Pan say?"

Sarah handed me a slip of paper. Too dark to read with accuracy, but they looked like phone numbers. "What's this?"

"Off Noor's phone. Don't ask me how she got them because she didn't say."

I sighed. "I can imagine."

"Don't." She slapped my shoulder. "Anyway, she said Noor's had a couple of calls that she left the room to take. Pan thinks there's an ongoing op of some kind that Noor's involved in. She couldn't hear much, and evidently Noor didn't say much."

The singer walked onstage and began the set with an up-tempo number. Pan led Noor to the dance floor. Shit, that woman could move. Noor? Not so much, but she tried to ape Pan's moves. "Noor'll get eaten alive if she doesn't show some originality."

"On all levels?"

"Oh yeah." I remembered the first time I'd danced with Pan. Dirty dancing. Some smoky bar crowded with women's bodies. I'd fought her all the way, didn't let her touch me. Changed moves as soon as she caught on to mine. I knew instinctively I couldn't let her lead.

"They are beautiful women, Win. Beyond gorgeous. And the way Pan moves…" She slipped her hand to my thigh.

I examined her face. Gaze fastened on Pan, lips slightly parted. Completely turned on. What the hell had Pan unleashed? Sarah would have to deal with it because I wasn't about to seduce her in a public place. Even if the lights were low.

The song ended and the exotic couple returned to their table. I ducked my head and kissed Sarah. Not gently. Moved my hand to her stomach. She responded by pulling me closer, moving her hand to my thigh. I enjoyed the moment.

Then I shifted back a tad. "Are they sitting?"

She smiled. "They left. Now, can we dance?"

* * *

I'd found our lovemaking frenetic that night after we got home, not that I'd objected. Maybe it was like watching porn for Sarah, got the juices flowing and your partner benefitted. But when I thought about it, I realized it wasn't just Pan's flirtatious eyes or sensual hands. Not the overt sexuality that had gotten to Sarah. It was her exoticism. Like an alien lily growing in Indiana soil amid sturdy plants. There wasn't a damn thing I could do about that. Except ride the plow.

Sarah called Sunday afternoon, just about the time she should've been leaving for home. "Dad finally found the complaint. We're going down to Seymour to interview the owner."

"Of the home health care provider?"

"Yeah. I called Elie and asked if that occupation would fit her profile. She said a resounding yes. Plus, there's a lot of movement by those women—they *are* mostly women. They don't stay in one place for a long time. Good lead, Win."

"Any idea when you'll be home?" I asked, trying not to sound like a clingy wife.

"Should be there for a late dinner. How about I pick something up? You liked those calzones, didn't you?"

"Fine by me. See you when you get here."

I took Des for a walk. I was glad Sarah might've found a break with her case, but I wasn't sure I'd made any progress on Kemat's murder. I'd spent the morning with Nathan and Bill, tracing phone numbers, calls and locations. It turned out Shamsi was closer than we'd anticipated. In Chicago. At a very expensive and exclusive hotel.

What the hell was he selling or buying that Kemat posed a threat to? I was convinced Kemat had posed some kind of threat. Was eliminated because of it.

Bill had been unusually tight-lipped. Maybe because we were working with Nathan. Maybe not. He still hadn't tracked down Kemat's missing years, and I couldn't help but feel those years held a key to this case. He hadn't directly heard from Pan since she'd left the base. I told him not to worry. If Noor had any information, Pan would get to the bottom of it. Perhaps that held too much of a literal meaning for him, because he didn't say anything else. I could tell he was worried. Why wasn't he sharing?

Des nuzzled my hand. Barked. She was not pleased with my lack of concentration on her walk. I snorted at her. She snorted back. I surrendered, pushed everything out of my mind. Jogged down the drive and headed for a slow run.

Des grinned and kicked up her heels.

CHAPTER SIXTEEN

Sarah

We found Laurie Highsmith at her daughter's house. She couldn't remember the details of the complaint, just how unreasonable the complainant had been. But she said we were welcome to the records stored in the basement.

"I'm sorry I can't tell you more," she said. "But my memory isn't what it used to be. Too much damn television. Take the records with you. Don't have any need for them. Should've thrown 'em out a long time ago."

"I'm glad you didn't." Dad and I went to the basement and found a wall of banker's boxes neatly stacked against the rear wall.

"Wonder how long my knees is gonna hold out," Dad said. "You wanna just take the nineteen-ninety boxes?"

"Maybe we can form a line. You bring them over, put them on the highest stair you can reach, and I'll take them out."

"You are either a fool or figurin' you need to lose weight. Win don't care."

Mrs. Highsmith sent her son-in-law down with a dolly to help us. It still took forty minutes, but then we were headed out with a bunch of records that might not have anything to do with catching a killer. I was getting hungry. We stopped on the way into Greenglen to pick up dinner for me and Win.

When we got back to the station, I rallied everyone there and within fifteen minutes all the boxes were in the detectives' den. Dad kissed me on the forehead. I thought he was going to say something, but he turned and climbed into his wreck of a truck. He rolled the window down after the engine caught. "Get yourself home, Sarah. Leave them boxes 'til tomorrow. They ain't goin' nowheres and neither are them victims."

I waved. I was almost as dusty as Dad had been the other day, but I wanted to get home. I was hungry for dinner and for Win. I was afraid she'd seen how turned on I'd gotten watching Pan on the dance floor. When we'd gotten home, I'd lavished everything I'd learned from Win on her and her body. Wanting to assure her she was every bit as exciting as Pan. At least, that's what I'd told myself at the time. Yet, there'd been flashes of Pan's body as we'd come to climax.

I hoped to the heavens she hadn't noticed.

Damn, double damn and to hell with it. Weren't things complicated enough without adding Pan to the mix? Night was coming on, the sunset sending its last gasps heavenward in a gold and crimson cry. Surrendering to the inevitable.

I pulled up Win's drive and transferred my ring to my hand. I remembered the inscription she'd had engraved inside, the same one Dad had placed in Mom's. *I will love you forever. Promise.*

I gathered up the bags for dinner and walked to the porch. The door opened and Des almost knocked me over. I couldn't tell if she'd missed me or just wanted the food I carried.

"Des," Win commanded.

Des sat.

Maybe we should work on commands for me. I kissed Win and held up the bags. "Dinner is served."

She gave me a questioning glance, then opened the door wide. She put the calzones in the oven to warm while I went and showered. When I walked back into the kitchen in gym shorts and T-shirt, she got a silly smile on her face.

"Smells wonderful in here. Is it ready?"

"Um." She took them out of the oven, set them on a trivet on the counter. She removed her oven mitts, took hold of me and slid her hands down the back of my shorts. "You're very distracting to the cook. Your skin feels so..."

I could feel her take a deep breath. "Let's eat first," she said in a shaky voice.

"Eat what?"

"Dinner, Sarah. Dinner first. Then I'll show you what appetite is."

* * *

I set the morning task force meeting for eleven thirty to give John and the detectives enough time to work through some of the boxes I'd brought in. Caleb's part in Kemat's murder seemed to be at a standstill, so he'd gone upstairs to help the other task force. I walked over to Beans aBrewing to stretch my legs and clear my head. Progress on both cases was so damn slow. Win had another meeting with Pan this afternoon and I was glad I didn't have to attend. I'd never get those images of Pan on the dance floor out of my head. Her movements had been an open invitation to every woman in the room for one hell of an exciting experience.

The muggy air had arrived with the southeasterly winds, the heat spread from the west. Crops would be happy, and their caretakers, but for the rest of us, the soggy air mass wrapped around us like a sauna set on high.

I reached the door at the same time as Zoe McClanahan, the *Sentinel*'s lone reporter. We ordered and sat at a table where I could watch the street.

"Any progress on the Alert murders?" she asked.

"A little, I think. Remember, this is an ongoing investigation, Zoe. There's a lot I can't talk about on the record."

"I know, and I don't want to screw up the investigation, but Sarah, people are uneasy—wondering if this guy is still walking around the county, scoping out new victims."

I sipped my mocha. "Would you do me a favor? Go through the *Sentinel*'s records and check for old stories on home health care workers. Complaints, dust-ups or general coverage."

"You think the victims were aides?"

"It's a possibility—goes to Elie's findings and an old complaint Dad remembered. I've got a faint memory of a spread Lloyd did about the industry. At this point, anything might help solve this, though I realize I may be grasping at straws."

"Be glad to give you all the straws you need," Zoe said with a grin. "Any more on that professor's death?"

"That one's proving just as murky as the Alert case." I could feel the victim's swampy fingers wrapping around me, begging me to push further. "About all we really know is what I released at first." That and an international arms dealer might be involved.

"You want us to publish another call for witnesses to step forward?"

"It can't hurt, but that road is so lightly traveled that time of day, I really doubt if anyone saw anything."

I left Zoe as frustrated as I was. We needed a break in both cases. I'd meant what I'd said to Win—the colder the trail became for Kemat's killer, the harder it'd be to prosecute anyone. We'd lost our golden forty-eight hours a long time ago.

I wondered what had happened to the good old days of county sheriffs going after rumrunners, brawlers and an occasional murder done in anger before witnesses. Our naming of the meth-making RV as the Gray Ghost wasn't an accident. My grandad went after a Gray Ghost too—a bootlegger running booze. Different time, different crime. Even in Dad's early tenure as sheriff, he hadn't had to deal with the tsunami of drugs and all the grief they brought. Much less foreign intelligence officers and serial killers. God only knew what was coming down the pike.

I walked into the conference room at eleven twenty to find Dad waiting for me.

"Elie called, said she was on her way," Dad said. "Sounded real excited. Woman's amazin', what she can put together outta a few old bones."

"She didn't say what she'd found?"

He shook his head. "You know she won't give a peep 'til she can lay out the evidence in a wrapped-up, neat package."

Caleb, dressed in civvies, stuck his head around the doorjamb. "I'm going to the meet with Win. Got nothing to report, so can I go ahead and leave?"

"This is your day off, remember?"

"I'll put in for comp time, promise. But it's kinda exciting to meet a real spy."

Just wait until he met this one. "Get out of here."

"Lotta excitement for a hometown guy. Let him enjoy it, Sarah," Dad said after Caleb had left.

Elie walked in, her stride full of energy. "We've caught a real break." She held up a thumb drive. "Got somewhere I can plug this in?"

By the time we had her set up, John and another detective were seated and waiting.

Elie opened a file and the photo of the thirteen victims slashed across the screen. "These skulls are Caucasoid, but I noticed a consistent unusual trait. I won't give you all the scientific terms. They're in my report, but our victims were probably from a sub-group. Related, but not direct family. I'd gotten as far as I could, so I sent queries to colleagues in this country and Europe."

She flashed another photo. "This came in from Florida. Same characteristic. And this one from Romania. Both skulls belong to Romany victims."

"Romany? Gypsies?"

Elie nodded. "There are a number of clans in the US. Almost all have legitimate businesses, but a very few still practice the old traveler way. Whatever the lifestyle, they handle crime against their community themselves."

"No missing person report?" I asked.

"No. We've had Romany transversing this state for ages."

"When I was a kid, they'd pass through ever year in them wagons," Dad said. "Like in the movies, they were—real fancy-painted wagons with rubber tires and pulled by horses. Took back roads, asked farmers for permission to camp. Good folk, for the most, but not open to outsiders."

"Were the wagons still rolling during your time as sheriff?" I asked.

"Purt near petered out by then. Changed to vans or station wagons, those of them still roamin'. Heard one of the big families settled in Indianapolis. Might want to call Dick Schiff, IMPD. 'Member hearin' him talk 'bout them at a meetin'."

"Will do. Elie, the skull from Florida—the same kind of wound you've been working with?"

"I got close-up photos and it's identical in size and location. They found the body in 2013." She handed me a slip of paper. "I told Dr. Riley to expect a call from you."

I could've hugged her, except Elie wasn't a hugger. "You've gone beyond and above. Thank you."

"There is no above and beyond duty when we're dealing with murder victims."

"The date fits with the others. This is part of the missing years for murders here. Maybe our killer took a vacation down south."

"Then why is this the only victim in eight years down there?" John asked.

"Maybe because they haven't been looking for the rest," I answered.

CHAPTER SEVENTEEN

Win

I picked up Caleb at the sheriff's department and filled him in on what we'd found with the phone numbers.

"You should've called me in, Win," he said. "After all, this is a county investigation."

"Sorry, but I had to clear it with Bill. National security. If I want to keep my nose in this, I have to adhere to the rules. His rules."

"What—he thinks I'm going to leak his intel and escape to a Russian airport?"

"I can't give any good reason, Caleb. I think we should share intel among agencies, especially local. But I'm not in command."

Caleb nodded, transferred his gaze to the rolling landscape. "Gonna be a good year for crops, long as we don't get hailstorms and all that shit."

We hadn't gotten two miles farther down the road when he cleared his throat. "I guess you and Sarah got married over vacation time in January."

I didn't answer.

"I mean, you're wearing a ring, and I've seen Sarah's wearing one around her neck."

"How did you see that?"

"She bent over and it slipped out. We were lifting the same thing, so I wasn't leering or nothing." He brushed his mustache. "Look, Win, we've got Sarah's back. It's no-never-thing if she's gay or not. She's the best damn cop I know. The department feels the same way."

"You know that for a fact?"

"Yes, ma'am, I do." He crossed his arms. "I understand why she don't come out, but just tell her she don't have to hide it from us."

I grinned. "Uh, no. That's something you have to tell her firsthand."

"That's what I was afraid you'd say. Anyway, congratulations." He looked at me. "I mean it. You're the best thing that's happened to Sarah in a very long time. Every time she sees you, or thinks of you, her eyes just light right up. That hasn't happened since Hugh was murdered."

"Thanks. I worry I'm the worst thing in the world to hit McCrumb County in years."

"Why?"

"First David Paria, then General Scott Lester. Now Dr. Kemat Fitzgerald. Nice to know I've got your vote in spite of all that."

"You weren't the bad guy, Win. In any of that."

Bill had set the meet at the Brownstown library. I didn't see his truck in the parking lot, but God only knew what he was driving today. As we walked in, I spotted him perusing a magazine at a table closest to the door.

He glanced up, nodded and walked toward a side meeting room. Pan was waiting. Even dressed in her flight uniform, she looked voluptuous and ready to dance. Buttons unbuttoned on her blouse so a lot of cleavage was visible. I heard Caleb's sharp intake of breath as he followed me into the room. Bill introduced them. She gave Caleb one hell of a seductive smile. Even though she only slept with women, she flirted with everyone. Maybe I should've warned Caleb. Naw, more fun to watch his reactions.

Bill sat down. "I hope you'll tell Sarah we're working as fast as we can. Searching data is important, but intel that comes from the ground is better. That's holding us up."

I understood, but it didn't help my sense of frustration. We weren't making the progress we needed. "Are you working on Kemat's background? The missing years?"

"As much as we can."

I turned to Pan. "Has Noor said anything about Kemat?"

"I asked her where she and Kemat met."

"You *what*? Shit, Pan."

She waved my objection away. "Noor has photo of them together, sits on her bureau. They were much younger, Noor just a young teen. I told her I saw professor's picture in the news."

"She bought that?"

"She was not paying much attention to my questions, Win. You understand?"

Bill cut in. "What'd she say? About knowing Kemat?"

Pan kept her gaze on me. Raised an eyebrow. Smiled. "She said Kemat was a woman of strong purpose."

"That's all?" Bill asked.

Pan nodded, her gaze still on me.

"What do you think she meant?" I asked. "What's the meaning behind the words?"

"I had impression she saved Noor somehow."

"But Noor was purchased from the Palace by Shamsi. How does Kemat fit in?"

Pan shrugged. "Perhaps Kemat behind purchase. Perhaps no purchase. We move on to other things." She smiled seductively. Raised her damn eyebrow again.

"In case you've forgotten, you're here to get intel, not for pleasure," Bill said. "Look this list over and see if you recognize any of the names." He shoved a paper across the table. Then another sheet and a pen. "Write down the names and what you know about them."

She gave a heavy sigh. Went to work.

"We've got three possibilities who are living close enough they could've executed Kemat. I've put tails on each of them, and we're monitoring their communications. We've got a lot of dots, and we're trying our best to connect them." He shifted his gaze to Caleb. "If you're going to prosecute, you need hard evidence. That's what we're trying to get for you."

Pan pushed the papers back to Bill. "Great hope this will help."

He glanced at what she'd written. Nodded. "Anything else, people?" When no one responded, he said, "I'll get this info to Sarah ASAP with some additional information."

He put everything back in his briefcase and started for the door. I shooed Caleb out. Turned to Pan.

"I have a lot of respect for you. We've shared good times."

"But?"

"Stay away from Sarah. And from me. Sarah's new to the life. Your charms can be overwhelming."

"For you too?"

"Yes." I looked away for a moment. How much could I trust her? Turned back. "I don't want to fuck this up. Sarah's the center of my life. I don't want to cause her pain or any more confusion than she's already feeling. Are we clear?"

Pan stared at me for a long moment. No flirting. No seduction in her eyes. "I always care for you, Win. Do now. I will not play with Sarah or you. Those adventures over and no future between us. Feel sad to place you in memory." She smiled, the seductive curve back on her mouth. "Glad we fuck good when opportunity came."

* * *

Caleb had no more gotten in the cab of my truck than he said, "Is that woman gay too?"

"Oh, yeah. Thoroughly."

"Thank God." He fanned himself with his notebook. "One hot mama—or shouldn't I say that? I mean, I don't want to be disrespectful."

"Uh, she *is* hot, Caleb. But if you made a move on her, she'd cut you off at the knees. With a machete." I turned onto the highway. "Kemat's got family. A brother and I think a couple of sisters. I'm going to sic Nathan onto tracking them down—if that's okay with you?"

"Fine by me." He glanced at me. "You don't think Kemat was behind Noor's sale. Jesus! I can't believe I said that. Sale. I thought slavery ended a long time ago."

"Those kinds of sales go on all over the world. Poor people sometimes have no choice. Combined with how women are viewed. Treated. It's surprising there are any wives, but the men need heirs." I picked up speed as we left town. "That's what surprises me. Kemat's known for fighting for women's rights. I can't imagine her facilitating a sale."

I hit five miles over the limit and held steady. Caleb was brushing his mustache, looking out the window. Contemplating the mysteries of lesbians? Ha! If only he knew.

When we pulled into the sheriff's parking lot, I put the truck in neutral. "Think about picking up Noor for questioning."

Caleb's eyebrows shot up. "Ask her what? On what grounds?"

"Material witness. I think with some good questioning, she'll expose a lot more than she should. It's one of the few leads we can follow on our own."

"Run it by Sarah. She okays it, I'm on board."

I nodded. Watched him walk in the back door. Wished I could follow him. See Sarah. Embrace her. Make love on her desk. Ah well, shit.

She didn't get home until dark, greeted me with a peck. Headed directly for the shower. I wondered what was up. Ten minutes later she walked into the living room, her hair wet and slicked back. Looked like Rudolph Valentino with blue eyes. She sat down beside me on the couch.

"Hard day?" I asked.

"Long day," she said. "Things are beginning to break on the Alert murders. Elie's a genius. You want to hear about it?"

"Later? I'd like to put an arm around you, just snuggle a bit."

She leaned into me. "Deal." She jerked back. "You smell like Pan. I picked up on her perfume the other night."

I put my arm around her, pulled her closer. "So do Bill and Caleb. It was a small room, Sarah." I grinned. "She had Caleb drooling."

"Caleb?" She nestled into me. "I shouldn't take tomorrow off, but I am. If anything breaks, I'll go in."

"I like your hair like that. Kind of super-dyke."

She laughed. "How about a buzz cut?"

I shook my head. Ran my hand down her bare thigh. "I love you in shorts. Good thing you don't wear them at work."

She nuzzled my neck. "Compliments will get you everywhere you want to go."

I kissed her. Lightly. I still had something on my mind and didn't want to get too involved. I leaned my head against hers.

"What?"

I turned to look her in the eyes. "I think you should talk to Caleb. Tell him we're married."

"What'd he say? What'd he tell you, Win?"

I shook my head. "Talk to him. You owe him. He's always had your back. If you don't tell him something important like this, you're undermining his trust."

"What did he say to you?"

I got up. "You want something to eat? Salad?"

"Win!"

"No. It's a trust issue between you and your chief deputy. You can get mad at me all you want. It's not going to help you with Caleb."

She took a deep breath. Another. "I'm sorry I put you in the middle of this."

"I'm your wife. We share the burdens."

Sarah looked up at me. "Did your unit know about Azar?"

"Yes. We were a unit. Four people, operating together in enemy territory. Trust was the basis for getting out alive." I turned toward the kitchen. "But I did ask her permission first."

She followed me into the kitchen.

"Are you hungry?" I asked.

"I'm so damn tired of this crap. I'd like to resign and move to Vermont with you."

"What's going on? Coming out to people close to you is always hard. But, shit, Sarah. You've been so fortunate. No one's turned their back to you."

"Your mom came around?"

"Yeah. Took a lot of years for her. Painful years. My brothers never did. You already know Caleb's not going to do that."

"I'll talk to him on Wednesday." She took my hands, kissed my palms. Fastened them behind her back. "I've been thinking about Pan. Not thinking, exactly…"

"Fantasizing?"

She ducked her head.

"Nothing wrong with fantasizing. Acting on the fantasies is something else. Pan's seductive. She loves every minute of the dance. Caleb thought she was 'one hot mama.' That's Pan. She entices dreams. Fantasies. One-hundred percent erotic. Exotic. I know. I've been there."

"How do you end the fantasies?"

"By replacing them with real experiences." I slipped my hands under her shorts, began moving them in a slow rhythm over her bare skin. Tongued my favorite place on her neck. I felt her hands move to my breasts, playing the same rhythm.

We were well on our way to erasing fantasies.

CHAPTER EIGHTEEN

Sarah

I called the office Tuesday morning, just checking in for developments. When I called around noon, Caleb told me it was my day off. "I'll call if there's any news," he said. "Why don't you go swimming?"

"Get off your back? Sorry, Caleb, I'm really sorry."

Win had spent the morning on either her computer or her burn phone. I felt out of the loop on both cases, and that made me restless. It was too hot and muggy to enjoy a walk, even though I'd done a short one with Des earlier. Now, Des was asleep on the cool tiles of the entryway, dreaming away, paws flexing and eyelids fluttering. I wondered if she ever dreamed about her missions.

With nothing else to do, I stretched out on the couch and my mind wandered toward Pan. I felt it was dangerous territory, not just because her charms churned up my fantasies, but because I was aware Pan had unleashed Win's prophesy. I was noticing women at Ruby's in a different way, watching how they moved. Not at the grocery, at work, or at meetings at the high school. Just where I knew the women were lesbian. Maybe all that woman awareness had registered with me before and I'd had no idea what to do with it—except ignore it. It struck me that I was struggling with my identity as a woman. As a lesbian. I thought it might be time to say, "Yes, I am."

Win would laugh at that. She'd known far longer than I, with a surety I still hadn't come to. Or I wouldn't be lying on a couch in my wife's home, thinking about the most exotic woman I'd ever seen and deciding if I was lesbian. Screw it all.

"Are you ready for lunch?" I asked as I sat up.

"Sure." Win's eyes were glued to her monitor. "Salad maybe?"

I walked into the kitchen and began assembling veggies and greens. Win had been wrong about one thing. My desire for her hadn't lessened one bit. I'd watched her working all morning, and fought the impulse to walk behind her, wrap my arms around her and fondle her breasts until I had her full attention.

"What?" she said as she walked into the kitchen and picked an olive from the bowl.

"I thought you said the honeymoon phase would pass, especially since I moved in."

She threw her head back and laughed. "Shit, what do I know?"

"What about you and Annie? As I remember it, when you first got together, you two couldn't keep your hands off one another. How long did that last?"

Win leaned against the counter and crossed her arms. She stared at me.

"Okay, baggage," I said. "I'll butt out."

"Actually, that's not what I'm thinking. Annie had a complicated background and after the first flush of having sex with a woman, I got uneasy."

I stopped chopping and looked at her. "You? Uneasy with sex?"

She laughed, a short bitter bark. "Annie was something else. She'd been brought out by a relative or family friend. Never did find out which. I'm not talking about a cousin or someone she went to school with. An adult woman."

"You said 'brought out by'—what does that mean?"

"Seduced." She shook her head. "Not that Annie wasn't ripe for it. But it was just wrong on so many levels. Besides that, I think the woman was some kind of dungeon dominatrix." Win shrugged. "I was a kid off the farm. What the hell did I know about bondage and discipline? None of that stuff was in the novels I'd managed to find."

A naive, corn-fed kid. "It must've been overwhelming, Win."

"It confused me." She rubbed her face. "There was stuff I didn't want to do. She called me a provincial wimp. Promised when I went to visit New York that summer, she'd open my eyes good and proper. Gay clubs, lesbian parties."

I remembered Win's father's massive heart attack and death shortly before the spring semester ended that had ended so many of her plans. "Are you sorry you never went?"

She shook her head. "It would've been way too much way too early. I understand the scene a lot better now. Still don't want to participate. I think if I'd experienced all that stuff then, I might've fled to some man's arms."

"Really?"

She grinned. "Probably not."

I started chopping again. "The stuff we've done, you know, where did—oh, crap. That's none of my business, is it?"

"No. Let's just say I learned from a woman who was very skilled. Who was willing to show me how. Without demanding I reciprocate." She walked to me, took the cleaver out of my hand. "You're the first woman I've ever allowed to tie me up—even if it was bondage lite."

"I'd better be the only one."

"Promise." She touched the wedding band I wore. "We both promised."

* * *

I got into my office early on Wednesday, plowed through the paperwork and was waiting in the conference room as the task forces filed in. I wanted to be back in the loop.

John came in smiling. "Elie's work has unlocked a lot of leads to work. Not to mention Micah's connection to IMPD. We're getting there, Sarah."

"We may be on our way too," Caleb said, thumping a fat file on the table and sitting.

"Man, I should take more time off," I said. I waited for somebody to say no.

Win and Dad came in together, grinning at one another. They were getting way too close, and I wouldn't have any secrets left.

"Who wants to go first?" I asked.

John actually raised his hand. "First, Elie sent along the computer-generated images of the victim's faces and then the sketches the artist had finished. We've started running them through the state database. No hits yet, but we also sent the files to the FBI.

"Second, we sent Martin to see Mrs. Highsmith with the pics. She tentatively identified two of them—though she can't remember their names."

"Hell, that doesn't sound like progress," Caleb said.

John didn't miss a beat. "Third, we've contacted the Dade County Sheriff, and he's reopening the investigation on the murdered woman. He also sent his file on her. I told him what we'd found and the time period our killer wasn't here. He said the area they'd found the woman in looked a lot like ours. I told him to look for slot trenches. I also asked him to send the single victim's bones to Elie and they're on the way."

"Any connection to the home health industry?" I asked.

"He's going to look into it, but without an ID, it's impossible to know. At least he's digging up records of businesses that were open then. He'll send queries. Guess they had a lot more than we did."

"Retirement center of the world," Dad said. "Never could see why sensible folk wanted to live in the swamps an' wait for a hurricane."

"Fourth, I contacted Micah's friend in IMPD, Dick Schiff. He's still in contact with the Indianapolis Romany family and has offered to take the photos to the patriarch. I also sent him the modeling Dade County had done. We should hear later this afternoon."

"Think he'll get the gypsies to open up to a cop?" Caleb asked.

"Only one way to know," John replied.

"A lot of progress," I said. "I've might've hit some pay dirt too. I've been thinking about the murder weapon. Elie's reconstruction of the wound looked like a bolt. I kept thinking about how a bolt could be propelled with enough power to break through a skull."

"A stun gun for cattle," Dad said with a grimace. "Why the devil didn't I think of that?"

"That's what I came up with, Dad. A penetrating captive bolt gun with a stainless steel bolt that recoils back into the gun so it can be reused. They aren't used so much anymore, not since the Mad Cow scare.

"I called Dr. Huff because he has a large animal practice. He had some skull exemplars and volunteered to take them to Elie's lab this morning. We should hear this afternoon."

"So this means what?" Caleb asked. "Guy worked at a slaughterhouse?"

"Mebbe," Dad said. "But folk 'round here with dairy herds had 'em too. Think the Feed & Grain used to sell 'em. Narrows down the possibilities, though. Killer had to know how to use it."

"Questions? Thoughts?" I asked. When the silence had extended to a point where I knew I could end it, I said, "Good work, really good work. Keep me up to speed." I turned to Caleb. "Progress?"

He looked at Win.

She cleared her throat. "We've got a couple of leads, but damned if I can talk about them. I'm flying out to Seattle at noon to interview some of Kemat's relatives. We need to fill in her past. Sounds lame, doesn't it?"

"Sometimes, progress don't seem like it. Gotta shake the facts 'round 'til they make sense," Dad told her.

"This isn't going to be another dirty bomb, is it?" John asked.

Caleb grimaced. "God, I hope not."

"Okay, let's go to work. Caleb, can I speak with you a second?"

He remained seated. "Safe trip, Win."

"With military transport? Almost guaranteed. Should see you tomorrow night."

After dinner last night, she'd told me about the trip. I wasn't particularly happy with the decision, but I knew her instincts were solid. Besides, I'd trusted her with Kemat's investigation and now was the time to let go of the reins. Before we'd left the house this morning, she'd also prodded me again to talk with Caleb.

When the room was empty, I turned to Caleb and took a deep breath. "Win and I have been in a relationship for a year. We made it official in January." I pulled the chain out, showed him the ring.

"So I finally get to say congratulations! Win's a great lady, and I sincerely wish you two the very best." He turned the file around. "You want me to quietly spread the word in the department?"

"Would I be viewed as a total chicken if I said yes?"

"People around here understand, Sarah. Still folk in the county who are rabid antigay and it could be bothersome for arrests or questioning. They'll keep their mouths shut. But they should know—especially since you're not living in sin." He grinned again, rose and shifted the file to me. "Win said you need to go through this. Personally, I think it's to keep you occupied while she's gone."

"Thank you so much, Caleb. You'll never know how much your support means to me, not until you're sheriff. I should've told you a long time ago. I've just been scared."

"Don't go sappy on me, Sarah." He turned to go, then stopped. "Win thinks we should bring in this Noor for questioning—it's in the file. But I think we should wait until Win gets back."

"I agree." He left and as I carried the files downstairs, I thought I was surrounded by a hell of a good group of people. I'd been at my desk for forty minutes before I realized I hadn't tucked the ring back inside my shirt.

CHAPTER NINETEEN

Win

Flights on a C-130 are not a place to read or write. Dark, cavernous. Strapped in so we wouldn't be thrown into crates filling the hold by air turbulence. I napped on the flight to Seattle.

I picked up a rental car, tried to follow Somera's directions to the University District. After a few wrong turns, I parked on a leafy, sloping street. Checked out a three-story apartment building, built with an art deco feeling and painted a muted yellow and brown. Or maybe the gray skies made the colors look so faded. People on the street ambled along. I couldn't spot anyone on surveillance. I walked up a flight of cement stairs, buzzed Somera's bell and waited for her response. Two seconds later, it came.

She received me graciously in her sleek, modern home, served tea to me and her two brothers. All my questions were answered honestly and with thought. Gravely. They'd started much earlier on their wandering than Kemat had indicated. Probably the late 1960s or early '70s. Their father had been accused—unjustly, as it turned out—of selling items from the Egyptian Museum. He'd been so outraged that the accusation had ever been considered, he took his family and left Cairo.

He'd worked digs in a number of countries. Sometimes taking his family with him, sometimes leaving them in Diyarbakir or sending them to the mountains in Afghanistan.

When that part of the story was told, Somera shooed her brothers from the room. She reminded me of Kemat, the same bone structure in her face, the same warm brown eyes. She, like Kemat, wore Western dress. In her case, flowing forest-green pants and a sea-green silk blouse. She wore a paisley scarf thrown over a shoulder, held a matching silk handkerchief.

As soon as her brothers were out of the apartment, she lifted her gaze to me.

"They will not speak of this to you, but I must. One summer in the mountains, Kemat and her younger sister, Nathifa, were abducted by a band of brigands. They were taken to Pakistan."

"For ransom?" I asked.

She merely looked at her clenched hands, shook her head.

"For the sex trade?"

I could see her barely nod. My stomach twisted, but I waited.

"Kemat managed to escape and found her way to an embassy. The family was reunited almost a year after they had been taken." She kneaded the silk handkerchief with hands that shook. "Kemat was pregnant."

Then I understood. "You're Kemat's daughter."

"Yes. As you know, Kemat would have suffered as a woman pregnant but unmarried. My grandparents raised me as their own."

"Bassir?"

"My twin brother."

No wonder Kemat didn't talk about this period of her life. "Do you know where he is?"

"No. He called me from Los Angeles and told me he was all right. That was all."

I sighed. "Kemat told me he was traveling with papers using his family name. Do you know what he called himself?"

"Of course. Ruairi Fitzgerald. He used the Irish spelling."

A lot became clear in that silent moment. "I cannot thank you enough, Somera. I will forever be in your debt. I understand what a painful story this is for you." I rose to leave. "Do you know what happened to Kemat's younger sister, Nathifa?"

She raised her gaze to me, her eyes filled with tears. "No. Kemat would never say."

On the flight back to Atterbury, my thoughts were jumbled. I leaned my head against the jump seat. I now knew the cause of Kemat's fight for women's rights, one that came from her own experience. She never would've participated in the sale of Noor, not even to get her out of the Palace. I wondered if Shamsi had begun his criminal dealing with the buying and selling of women. Had Kemat and her sister been his victims? Those were things I could check on when I got back.

What haunted me was the younger sister, Nathifa. If they'd been separated, Kemat would've have said that. That she didn't know where the girl had been taken. Something else had happened. Something awful. Unspoken.

I didn't want to think about the possibilities. I closed my eyes. Let the rumbling of the engines and the constant swaying lull me back to sleep.

* * *

I met with Bill as soon as I landed at Atterbury, gave him a complete report as we sat in his office.

"You think this is true—the abduction?" Bill asked. "I mean, she could've just had an unlucky affair."

I glared at him. "An affair wouldn't have caused trauma. The family would've solved the problem and moved on."

"Okay. I'll have Shamsi's early records examined carefully. See if we can dig up his connection to sex trafficking. If it's true, it means she hated him—but I wonder if he knew about her history?"

"What it means is that she was a fierce enemy. He had to know at least that much. You really need to dig deep on Noor. There's something hinky about her turning up. I think Kemat would've spotted a spy right away. I'd love to see that photograph of her and Kemat."

"You think she faked her history? Got close to Kemat to disassemble her network?"

"Possible, but I think there's more to the story. Kemat was a very bright woman. She'd have smelled an imposter a mile away." I looked out the window. All the military uniforms made me shiver. "Any word on the three stooges?"

"Stoo–oh, Shamsi's 'associates'? They're staying put, no phone chatter. They seem to have a fleet of cars and trucks, so we're trying to get that sorted out. I'll let you know as soon as we do."

"Okay if I pass Bassir's info to Nathan?"

Bill agreed.

I yawned. "Next time, you think you could afford a commercial flight?"

On the drive home, my mind kept going back to Kemat's story. That's why she'd asked me to find Bassir. She knew of the work I'd done—when I could. Never enough time with war raging. That's why she could trust me. The military turned a blind eye to the brothels and how women ended up in them. The women caught in the web of organized prostitution stretched across the region.

When I got home, Des and Sarah greeted me as if I'd been gone a month. Hell, a year. "Dinner's almost ready. You want to shower first?" Sarah asked. "Or a massage? You look tense."

"I would like to be held, preferably sitting down. Just held. No talking. No lovemaking. Let me lean a bit, Sarah, into you. Into silence."

She led me to the couch, put her arms around me. Didn't say a word. We didn't move until the timer dinged.

As we ate, I asked her for a progress report on the Alert case, and she explained all the leads that had opened up. "I've got to talk to Lloyd tomorrow. I want him to publish the sketches we've got and make a request for information. The patriarch in Indy has given us a couple of names and is working on more. I need to let those families know."

More women punished for being women. I felt tears form. Closed my eyes. Took a deep breath.

"Win? What's the matter? Did something happen?"

I shook my head. Fought for control. "Later." I kept my eyes on my plate. Took another bite. Concentrated on the little things. Chewing. Lifting the fork to my mouth. One bite at a time.

We finished, cleared the table, did the dishes. Sarah leaned against the counter and folded the dishtowel. "I'm going to take Des for a walk."

I nodded.

"You will tell me, won't you? Not cram it down?"

I nodded again. Made the "cross-my-heart" sign.

I stretched out on the couch, covered my eyes with my arm. I knew the pressure point. All the women who suffered. Every day. All over the world. Were murdered by johns or pimps or crazy men. Were tortured. Used. Discarded. Kemat had been one of them. But she'd escaped. Had not forgotten. Fought for other women. Became fierce. Became a warrior.

Now that I was home, I tried not to think of the women I'd left behind. I sent money to those I knew money would help. That seemed lame. So much fucking pain.

The front door opened. I heard Des's nails patter across the floor and Sarah's squeaky cross-trainers. "Win? You here?"

I raised my arm.

Des came around the couch, nuzzled my neck. I took her head in my hands and crooned to her.

Sarah followed her and sat by my knees. "Um…"

"I'm okay, just weary." I told her Kemat's story.

"I had no idea. On the few occasions when I met her, I never would've guessed. She seemed so strong, so determined."

"That strength came from pain." I held her hand. "Thinking about those graves, those unknown women, brought it all up for me."

"The women you rescued from the whorehouses?"

"The women who replaced them. It's a never-ending stream of misery and degradation and pain. So many end up dead, thrown in crude, unmarked graves."

"Like our Romany women." She rubbed my hand, massaged my fingers with her thumb. "I understand that and why you told me to stop when I got all judgmental. No, it's okay. You're right. I'm a provincial idiot who hasn't seen shit. I don't know what I can do to help, but if there's anything, holler."

I pulled her to me, kissed her. "I may have nightmares tonight."

"I'll be by your side, Win. I'll always be there."

CHAPTER TWENTY

Sarah

Win woke me four times during the night but had quieted at my voice and my touch. I couldn't even imagine what she'd seen in countries all over the world. I'd gotten all high and mighty because she visited these women for comfort. Comfort received, I thought, and comfort given. How could I have gone off on her?

As I made a late breakfast, I heard Win on the phone, talking to Em. Good. With Win's background, I felt so damn useless. I could hold her. I could listen, but I felt I was treading water when the nightmares came.

She walked into the kitchen with the phone. "Emily can slot us in Monday afternoon after your shift. Okay?"

Us? Maybe Em would throw me a plank to rest on, if not a raft. "Sure."

Win confirmed and clicked off. "Did you get any sleep last night?"

"Yeah, not to worry."

"This stuff blindsided me. Never came up before, and I'm not sure if the trigger is Kemat's murder or the graves of all those women here."

"Maybe both, or maybe their combination at the same time." I plated the scrambled eggs. "Are you coming in today?"

"I need to huddle with Nathan, see if we can pick up Bassir's trail." Win carried the plates to the table.

I followed with coffee. "You think Bassir's involved?"

"No. Not as a killer. I think he was the catalyst. Whatever story he uncovered in Syria must've set someone's alarm off. Maybe Shamsi's." She began to eat. "Among other things, Shamsi's an arms dealer. He's got to have his fat fingers in the Syrian pie. Way too lucrative to be threatened by a story in the press."

"Which side does he support?"

"Probably all."

"Well, hell. What do you want us to do about picking up Noor?" I asked.

Win raised her eyebrows. Grinned. "You want to do that?"

"Caleb said you wanted to bring her in for questioning. I would rather never see the woman again in my life."

"She shook you up good, huh?" She motioned with her fork. "I want to panic her a bit. Bill's put a tail on her, and I think he may use the shadow trick. One tail is in the shadows, one tail obvious. The shadow man sees what happens when the target notices the obvious one."

"More spy games. I'm just a simple sheriff in a simple county in a simple state. Ain't up to playin' no spy games."

Win laughed. "You're going to be late, Sheriff Simple. I'll get the dishes. Go on."

I kissed her.

She grabbed my hand. "Thanks for last night. I don't think I woke up, but I remember your arms and your voice. I knew I was safe. You didn't sign up for this."

"I signed up for you, Win." I took her hand into both of mine. "Last night, I wondered what images you saw in those nightmares. I've always thought I'd seen the underbelly of humanity in this job. But I haven't seen shit."

She took me into her arms, and we rocked to her rhythm for a moment.

"Besides, you've had to put up with my uncertainties, my fears that somebody might find out I'm lesbian," I said. "That's so damn feeble."

"No, it isn't. We're not in competition about the most gruesome sight we've seen or the most horrendous thing we've survived. What we feel in the moment is always the most important thing—and always equal."

"How'd you get so wise?"

"Emily." She kissed me. "Now go to work, Sarah, and let me get to my spy stuff."

* * *

I dropped in at the *Sentinel* office before I went to the department. I didn't see Lloyd, but Zoe was busy clacking away on her keyboard. I waited until she paused before I stepped through the low swinging gate. "Breaking news?"

Zoe looked up and grinned. "Trying to get all the names straight before I forget the faces—big story on the 4-H preparations for the county fair. Hot stuff. You have some breaking news for me? Please?"

"I've got a press release for you and some sketches." I laid the file on her desk. "With the help of IMPD and the Romany community in Indianapolis, we've identified two women."

"Wow. Gypsies? How the hell did you get onto gypsies?"

"Elie—Dr. Elspeth Mackintosh. Once this is over, you should interview her. She's one hell of an interesting character and one of the leading forensic anthropologists in the country." I pointed to the file. "I brought the sketches because I thought if you scanned them in, people would see sharper images. We really need the public's help—if they recognize the women, from where and when."

She started placing the sketches in the scanner. As she ran them, she read the press release. "Why home health aides?"

I explained and told her to contact Elie if she needed more detail. "If this doesn't sound self-serving, could you explain why cases like these are so hard to work and go so slowly. A witness may have noticed something odd twenty years ago but by now, it's long forgotten. Paperwork goes missing. People move."

"I know the lead detective in IMPD's cold case unit. I'll give him a call and do the interview as a sidebar. That okay?"

"That would be great. Thanks Zoe."

She returned the sketches to the folder and handed it to me. "I'll write it up and post all of it right away." She gave me a tight smile. "I know you can't release much in an ongoing investigation, but it's my job to push, Sarah. If I ever get really obnoxious, tell me."

"Deal."

I got to the task force meeting as the others were filing in. "The Kemat team are following a couple of leads, so this morning, we'll just concentrate on the Alert case."

"A lot of news," John said. "I've had four contacts with Detective Schiff since the last time we met. We've got names for all the women except two."

"Let Zoe know ASAP. She's running the story today."

"Will do. The Romany patriarch contacted his counterpart in Florida and guess what? They've got eight women missing. He told them to contact the Dade cops, and they will." He turned the page in his notebook. "All of the women identified worked as home health care aides—so Win's guess was a good one. We've contacted the companies they worked for, well, the ones that are still around and asked for their records. Those are coming in now."

"But how did the perp get by with it?" Detective Jay Thorn asked. "You'd think if the guy kept asking for aides and they never went back to work, somebody would've asked questions."

"Good point, Jay. Will you follow that line? Maybe our killer didn't use his own name or his home, and if not, how could he move around the locations?"

John nodded and took notes. "We'll be able to answer better when the records get here. But if he was using different addresses, he had to use empty homes. I wonder how he knew which ones were empty?"

"Another good question. Maybe the killer worked as a realtor, utilities meter reader, a landscape contractor—what else?"

"Mail carrier," Jay said.

"A local cop," John offered. "Although I don't know how we ask Greenglen PD if one of their guys is a serial killer."

"Don't. Ask if one of their people left in 2000 and returned to the area in '08. Tell them we're making the same query of other agencies in the area. Talk to Stas. We've worked a couple of cases with him, and he's solid."

"Has Micah found anything yet?" John asked.

"Not yet, but you know he won't quit until he does. He went down to talk to the deputy who was on desk duty a lot of those years. Thought he might remember a name or maybe a more specific time. He'll be back this afternoon. Grant's in a nursing home in Evansville."

John was looking at the whiteboard. "As much as I hate to say it, who better than a cop to hide a string of murders?"

CHAPTER TWENTY-ONE

Win

"Bassir's been careful, Win," Nathan said. "But I've got his phone located and his flight plans. It seems he's staying put for the moment."

"Where?"

"Tucson, Arizona."

"What the hell game is he playing?"

Nathan pulled up another page. "These are his Internet searches since he got there. My guess, for what it's worth, he's putting the story together. Getting documentation or verification."

"In other words, going on about his business." I started pacing. "I wonder if he knows his mother's dead?"

"Doubt it. I got his phone number through a call to his sister a few hours after he landed at LAX. Kemat was alive then."

"He didn't contact them again? Or try to get in touch with Kemat?"

"No phone calls, just Internet searches."

I stopped. "Could someone else find his number? Trace him?"

"No. I deleted the record of his call to his family right after I found it."

"Good work, Nathan. Really good. If Bill could recruit you, he would."

"Hmpf." He swiveled his chair around to face me. "Any way to contact Bassir? Warn him to stay put?"

"And tell him about his mother?" I sat on the arm of his couch. "He doesn't know me from Adam. Or Eve. Doesn't know his mother asked me to look for him. Any message I send him could be viewed as a trick. Might panic him into moving where Shamsi could find him. Let me think about it. In the meantime, monitor him. Let me know if he contacts anyone. Or starts to move."

"Are you going to let Bill know?"

"I don't know. I should. Bill could send agents to pick him up, provide protective custody."

"But?"

"We don't know where the eyes are—the guys who'd let Shamsi know if agents left for a pick-up."

"Get the duty roster at Atterbury, and I'll cross-check everyone against the numbers Shamsi's been using. Or should I just ask Bill?"

"Let me swing by and ask." I sure as hell wasn't making many decisions. I could see the question "Why not?" in Nathan's eyes. Because I felt Kemat had entrusted her son to my safekeeping. I didn't want to fail her. It was her last request of me. "Okay, go ahead and hack the base—civilian employees first. Do your cross-checking thing. If you don't come up with the eyes by tomorrow, I'll pick up Bassir myself."

He stared at me with his dark eyes. "Isn't that taking unnecessary risk?"

"I'll be careful. I have Sarah to come home to. But this is something I have to do. For Kemat." I gave him my burn phone number and asked him to track my location. He set up a "panic" app, the number seven plus pound sign that would alert him and the nearest cops if trouble appeared.

I called Bill on the way home. The three stooges were staying put. No contact with Shamsi. Everybody was waiting for the mouse to appear so the cats could tear him apart.

* * *

"How do you know Shamsi's got 'eyes' on Bill? Is it just a guess?" Sarah asked as we lounged on the garden swing after dinner. "Did Bill tell you?"

"He's been complaining about leaks. Little stuff, mostly. But all of it about weapons. Shipments. Cancellations." I slouched down, swung my feet up on the table. "I feel such a debt to Kemat. I want to protect her son since I couldn't protect her."

"That's irrational."

"I know."

Sarah gave a push with her foot, fidgeted with the hem of her T-shirt. "Maybe not."

"Maybe not what?"

"Maybe I'm wrong, and it's not irrational. Kemat was doing the work you'd been doing, and I think you feel guilty for not doing more now." She turned to me. "For not being there, stealing away girls and getting them to safety. That's pretty much what Kemat was doing with her network, wasn't it?"

"It looks like she did a lot of political organizing in all the Arab Spring countries." I leaned back, stared at the darkening sky. "But yeah, a big portion of the network was dedicated to rescuing girls and women from the sex trade."

"I think that's why you had the nightmares—your own subconscious prodding you to do more. I think finding Kemat's killer is about making up for your lack of current involvement with rescuing girls."

"Shit, Sarah. Stop hanging out with Emily."

She put an arm around me, pulled me close. "We're both complicated human beings. I've been so used to not thinking about stuff. You were right when you said I had head-in-the-sand syndrome, and I know my butt's been bitten because of it. I'm trying to learn to go deeper."

"Easier to diagnose somebody else, isn't it?" I snuggled into her.

"You better believe it." She stroked my shoulder. "Isn't there some other way to contact him beside going to Tucson? Through his sister, maybe?"

"Shamsi's crowd has to be checking Somera's phone calls."

"You think they're listening in?"

"Doubt it. That still takes a bug. I think they just want Bassir's number, then they can track him like Nathan did."

"Why don't you come into the office, call Somera and tell her what's going on? It's to be expected that the sheriff's office would contact the family." She laid her hand on my knee. "I want you to stay safe."

"You've got a weird notion of 'safe.' A woman who carries a weapon every day. You want *me* to be safe?" I slipped my hand under her T-shirt, felt the warmth of her skin as my thumb rubbed her breast. "Okay, I'll call her from your office. Satisfied?"

"You mean satisfied enough that we can get some loving going?" She leaned over, kissed me. "I do worry, and I know it's dumb. But when you stepped out in front of Scotty's truck, I couldn't breathe."

I sat up. "I'm careful. I don't take unnecessary chances. Otherwise, I never would've made it back home."

"We had Stop Sticks deployed. There was no need to put yourself in harm's way."

"I knew the way he operated. The minute he hit the Stop Sticks, he would've been on high alert. He would've shot the first soldiers he saw. But seeing me alone, he figured I'd dropped them. Thought he could deal with me without problems. I knew his arrogance."

"And counted on it."

"Right. I concentrated on finding the best solution. You, on the other hand, have a department to run. Your mind can be turning over thirteen problems at once. I've watched you. It terrifies me you're going to make some minor bust and not pay attention to a threat."

"You ran your unit," she said, eyebrows drawn into a frown.

"Four people in a limited area with one mission. Different. Please, let's not argue about this. Every day when you go to work, I have faith in your abilities. I need you to trust me in return."

I watched traces of anger, defiance and pain chase their way across her face.

"I do trust you, but just because I trust you, doesn't mean I can't worry," she said, searching my face.

"Keep it under control. Worry is a useless emotion."

She reached her hands behind my head, kissed me like a dam had broken. One had broken in me. I cupped her breasts, echoed the rhythm of her tongue. The rhythm that would take us up the mountain together.

CHAPTER TWENTY-TWO

Sarah

Dad was waiting for me when I walked into the conference room. He greeted me with a big smile.

"You found the log entry," I said.

"More 'n' that." He slid a file down the table. "Percy's body may be givin' out on him, but his memory works fine. He remembered a guy come in three times, early spring, June and last time in July. Same complaint. Women takin' care of his parents was beatin' up his dad. An' stealing. Last time he come in, he had pictures of his dad's bruises.

"First time he come in, Percy took down the information, sent it to FSSA who shoulda investigated. When the guy come in July, Percy called Adult Protective Services. Their field investigator was over in to Jennings County, never done nothing. In August, Percy wrote out a complete report, sent copies to FSSA and APS. Included copies of the photo. Sent 'nother copy of the file to our esteemed representative."

"So he didn't log it, he made a file."

"Yep. Shoulda done both, but he didn't. That file there is the original."

"Good work, Dad." I opened the file. The man who filed the complaint was Willard Steven Harrison. I called Doc Webster and asked him to look through the ME's files for deaths of Anne or Willard Harrison, the first. I clicked off. "God, at last we have a name."

"Mebbe not the right one, but I reckon we can check him out. See where he is."

John rushed in with apologies for being late. "We've been interviewing all the businesses, and the result is the same in each case. Someone called them, requested not only help with a parent, but said they'd heard so-and-so was very good from friends."

"And the women they requested?"

"Never showed up for work again," John said, opening a file and putting the list in front of me. "Thing is, each time he called, it was a different business. He called two twice, but years apart, so nobody put things together."

"His name?"

"Different name each time, different address," John said. "Your guess was right."

"They identified the women?" I asked.

"Yes. We've got their files and we're looking for relatives now."

"Call Detective Schiff, see if he can help. John, run a background check on Willard Steven Harrison. Call Nathan and ask him to do a deep background check. I'll get the warrant for you."

John looked stunned. "You found the killer?"

"Person of interest, thanks to Dad."

"Nope, thanks to Deputy Percy Grant, retired," Dad said. "He was on the desk back then an' took extra care of all who come in."

I handed John the file Dad brought, asked the two of them to put their heads together and send Dade County everything we had, including a photo of Harrison when it came in. "Still a lot of work to do. Let's nail this bastard."

* * *

My next stop was my office, where Win sat in my chair as she watched the phone. "You talk to Somera yet?"

"Yeah. She was reluctant to contact Bassir. Said he told her not to after that first call. I told her to use a phone line outside the house. She's got a dentist's appointment, thought she could use their phone." Win stretched. "Matter of waiting now."

"Seems like that's all we do. Wait for documents, wait for witness interviews, wait for some grace to fall from heaven."

Win got up and wandered over to the couch, briefly touching my hand. "Shit, you think I'd be used to waiting by now."

"It's never easy, Win. Especially when you need one more thing to figure out who the perpetrator is or to build a case for the prosecutor." I sat in my chair, swiveled around to look out the window. Another hot, muggy day, with an overcast sky and people walking Courthouse Square in slow motion. I thought even nature was waiting for the inevitable storms to slam through, sweep the air clean and flatten everything flimsy.

John tapped on the door, walked in and laid a file on my desk. "His state records, no red flags. Cop with Greenglen PD. But the interesting thing is that he moved out of state for eight years, the same time span that our killer stopped killing. Nathan's working on more."

"Is this address current?"

John nodded. "Been living there since early '09. Got a job as a security guard for the new car plant. Don't know why he didn't go back to Greenglen PD."

"Call the plant, John, and get a feel for his employment record." I tapped my pen on my notebook. "I think we ought to have our CSIs take a look at his parents' home. Was he living at home then?"

"For the last four years or so before his dad died. Then he moved his mom to Florida." He rubbed the back of his neck. "Other people live there now, and I can't believe any evidence might still remain."

"I agree, but we can't let one stone go unturned."

He nodded, looked at Win then back at me. "Congratulations, ladies."

Then he was gone.

"Score another one for the good guys," Win said, smiling at me.

"Yeah, yeah, yeah." I grinned at her. "Still feels funny."

"Get with the program, wife."

The phone rang and we both jumped. I motioned for Win to pick up.

"Kirkland." She glanced up at me. "Yeah, she's right here." She handed me the phone. "Nathan."

"Found a few interesting things," Nathan said. "Let me get them in order, and I'll send them to you. But I thought you should know that Harrison worked at a slaughterhouse while he was in college. Maybe he brought home a souvenir."

"Great news! That's one more nail in the coffin. Wish we could find the damn cattle gun, though. Maybe when we pick him up. Thanks Nathan."

I told Win the news, as well as the other leads we were investigating.

"I'm jealous," she said. "You're wrapping up your case, and Caleb and I are no further along than when we started."

"You've uncovered a lot, Win. Patience."

Another tap on my door, and I looked up to see Doc Webster. "Hey Doc. What's up?"

"John called me, asked me to see if I had any medical records for Anne and Will Harrison. I didn't bring the files, but Anne had early onset Alzheimer's. I think when Will Junior took her to Florida, he ended up putting her in a full-care facility."

I took rapid notes. "We can check. What about Will Senior?"

"ALS, fairly rapid progression."

"Lou Gehrig's disease?"

"Yep."

"When did he first show symptoms?"

Doc rubbed his chin with his knuckles. "Somewhere in the mideighties. It was beginning to get bad, but he fell down the stairs before he landed in a wheelchair."

"Was anyone home at the time?"

"His wife, but she couldn't remember what happened. You need anything else?"

"Not for now. Thanks Doc."

When he was gone, Win glanced at me. "If I ever end up with dementia, please take your Glock and put me out of my misery."

"Never. I could never do that, no matter what."

CHAPTER TWENTY-THREE

Win

I was getting restless. Cranky. We ordered lunch in and I couldn't even taste the sandwich Tillie had sent. Bassir should've called by now. Or Somera calling back to say he wouldn't talk to me. I thought about making an airline reservation but wondered whose eyes would see it. I could drive, but it was a hell of a long one. With no guarantee he wouldn't take off.

Shit, shit, shit.

"Please stop pacing," Sarah said. "You're making me dizzy. Find something to distract you until the call comes."

"Only one thing I can think of that would distract me." I raised an eyebrow.

"Win, pipe down. I have a job to do here and it wouldn't be…"

"Proper? Seemly?" I put my hands up. "Okay, I surrender. I'd go for a walk to discharge, but I can't because I might miss his call. Ditto the dojang. Ditto everything but pacing."

"What did you do when you were in-country?"

"I was making my own calls, Sarah, not waiting for one."

"Push-ups?"

I sat on the couch, crossed my ankles, crossed my arms.

"Shall I time how long this lasts?"

"Leave me alone or I'll ravish you on your desk."

Sarah blushed, laughed. "God help me. I'm about ready to call Bassir myself."

"No! You could spook him, Sarah, and then I'd never…" I realized she was pulling my leg. "Shit. It's a good thing I'm not armed."

"Stretch out, go to sleep, Win. I've got to get this warrant ready so the judge can sign it in the morning."

"For Harrison?"

Sarah nodded, head back down over the paperwork.

"How deep is your closet?"

"Uh…" She glanced at me. "What's on your mind?"

"If we play a little kissy-face, I might be able to settle down." I gave her my best smile.

She didn't even bother to answer.

The phone rang. "Sheriff Pitt. Yes, yes she is. Hold on."

She handed me the phone. "Kirkland here. Is this Bassir?"

"Yes. Is this line safe?"

"Yes. Do you know who I am?"

"My mother mentioned you several times since she hired you. She trusted you, Win Kirkland. Evidently, so does my sister. What is it I can do for you?"

"I need to talk with you. I'd like to do it face-to-face. Is that possible?"

"Why?"

Because I could tell if you're lying. Because I need to tell you about your mother's death.

He filled the silence. "Are you CIA?"

"No! I served with MCIA—Marine Corps Intelligence. I'm working with the sheriff's office to investigate…some things that've happened here. If I'm knee to knee with you, your reaction to a question could lead to other questions. On the phone, I can miss something too easily."

"Do you know where I am now?"

"The Borderland Motel."

"Are you sure you aren't CIA?"

"Positive. I think I can get a ride down to Tucson on a military flight, maybe pick up a car from them. I won't leave a trail, Bassir."

"Do you have a secure provider?" he asked after a long pause.

"Yes. Local. I've known Nathan since we were kids. He's how I found you. That's what began all of this. Your mother asked me to find you for her. I wouldn't have brought Nathan in if I thought it would endanger you."

"I will send him a document, but please, ask him not to open it yet. Give me, please, his address."

I complied.

"Call me at this number when you arrive," he said.

I pumped my fist. "I will. Thank you, Bassir." I put the phone back on its receiver. "He'll see me. I need to call Bill and set up transport. The waiting's over, Sarah. Now I can do something."

"You're going to Tucson?"

"This isn't hazardous duty. Relax. Everything's cool."

"Famous last words," she said.

"But you might want to put the appointment with Emily on hold."

* * *

We finally managed to get out of the station and head home. After I'd called Bill with my newest burn phone, he set up a ride for tomorrow morning.

"I'm sending a pic of your contact at Davis-Monthan AFB," he said. "She'll get you a car, probably want to ride along. That's up to you."

"Direct to Tucson, neat. Thanks Bill."

"Take care of yourself. The major will have a weapon waiting for you, so don't try to carry onto the plane."

When I told Sarah, she just wore her worry face. But she didn't say anything. Progress.

I made omelets when we got home and we ate without much conversation. Sarah's expression didn't change.

After cleaning up, I sat on the couch, pulled Sarah down on my lap. "You can't worry all the time, Sarah. Besides, this isn't an op. It's meeting someone who may be able to clarify the situation for your investigation. Quick in, quick out."

"That's what you'd say if you were going back to Afghanistan," Sarah said, stroking my cheek.

"No. I'm never going back. Not until I'm an old woman and the memories have faded. If they ever do." I kissed her. "Really, Sarah, I'm not expecting trouble."

"Then why were you talking about weapons?"

"It's simply routine. You always carry a sidearm, even when you're off duty. Speaking of which, I think we should talk to a lawyer."

Sarah stiffened. "You want a divorce already?"

"Why is it always the worst-case scenario with you? Besides, nobody can divorce anybody here. We'd have to establish residency in Vermont, and you'll never leave McCrumb County that long." I ran my hand along her thigh. "We need to work through all that marriage equality stuff with a lawyer. But more than that, we need wills, living wills, the whole kit and caboodle."

"God, I don't want to think about this," she said.

"In Indiana, if we'd applied for a marriage license, one of us would be guilty of a class D felony."

Sarah shook her head. "No, that can't be right, Win."

"Check the state statutes. On the application, there's a section for 'female' and one for 'male.' Period. If I filled out the 'male' section, I would've perjured myself. Or something weird. You'd have to arrest me."

"Not for filling out an application. I don't believe it. I'm checking the statutes first thing in the morning."

"Sarah, we have no rights here. We're not married as far as the state's concerned. If something happened to either one of us, we'd have shit. This house would go to my brothers."

"It's so damn unfair."

"Yeah. Welcome to reality." I raised her chin, kissed her so lightly our lips barely met. "You've had great responses by the people who know you. Your family. Your deputies. It's looking like everything's copacetic. But if you get shot again, in the hospital I have no right to even see you because I'm not family."

"But before, when I was in the hospital, you were there every day, Win."

"Because your dad told the hospital I was family. Micah okayed it, or I wouldn't have gotten to be with you those first few days. Nights. Nothing but a brief visit—along with half the county. I know you don't want to think about it." I took her hand. "You have a dangerous job, Sarah. You owe me peace of mind."

"Hell. You're an extortionist."

"Damn straight. Can I set up something? At least find out what our options are?"

Sarah hugged me. "Okay. But I can't stand thinking about something happening to you, which is what wills and all that stuff means."

"No. It means security for us. Not letting the bigots win." I rubbed the curve of her butt. "Think ahead. Maybe I'm in a nursing home—"

"I would never put you in a nursing home, Win."

"The decision wouldn't be yours. As things stand now, the legal power would go to my brothers. If we lived here for all those years together, you'd be out on your ass. My oldest brother is a real jerk. I don't know if the others could outvote him. Unless we establish our wishes legally."

"How do I keep missing all this?" she said, wrinkling her forehead. "None of it's penetrated my consciousness."

I traced her jaw with one finger. "I love you, Sarah. At our foundation, that's what matters. But the legal stuff will help with our future." I sighed. "You know, when I came home, I couldn't imagine a long-term relationship. Not after losing Azar. I thought I could go back to my old life. One-night stands. Fucking for fucking's sake. Working with Emily, I realized I wanted more."

I moved my hand to her neck, that wonderful little hollow at its base. "And then you were standing here, in my home. Ready to leave. Looking so alone. Sad. I knew I wanted you in my life. As my lover. Forever."

"Damn miracle, wasn't it?" Sarah asked, brushing away tears. "What would've happened if you hadn't kissed me that day?"

"Hell if I know. You were the straight woman. Widow. Everything in me said 'don't.' Right after that first kiss, when I looked at your panic, I thought I'd lost you as a friend. I hated every sexual impulse I had."

She captured my hand and moved it down to her breast. "I think I was attracted to you from the time David Paria came, and we crossed paths again. Before our first kiss, Win. I just didn't know what to do with it."

"So you didn't think about it."

"Of course not." She kissed me and filled me with desire. "I didn't know what being lesbian meant. I had no idea. Lesbian was just a word that painted images of an island in the Mediterranean, an exotic place with naked ladies lying around eyeing each other."

"Shit, Sarah. You heard the other words. Lezzie. Dyke. Queer. Rug-licker." I sighed. "But you didn't think about those either."

She shook her head. "Sometimes I think I've refused to become intimate with myself for self-protection."

"I have a feeling you're right. But that's something we can work on together, you know. As we go deeper, you can share with me things you're discovering. I can do the same." I moved my hand under her shirt, felt her soft skin. So warm. Such an invitation. I swallowed. "I think it's time to go to bed, Sarah."

"We don't have to be conventional, since we're not anyway."

Rather than explaining that statement, she took off my shirt and began kissing my neck, her hands already busy with my buckle.

CHAPTER TWENTY-FOUR

Sarah

"Every time we make love, how come it's like the first time?" I asked Win as she packed for her trip in a tiny duffel she could sling over her shoulder.

She looked up at me with a big smile. "We haven't gotten better at the details? Not become more attuned to one another's bodies?"

"You know what I mean," I said and tossed her underwear at her. "I mean, that first time, the passion and the feelings were so overwhelming, at least for me."

"Me too." She jammed her underwear in the bag. "Difference is, now I don't have to worry about reinjuring your shoulder. You're very nicely healed."

"I wonder if we're the only lesbian couple in the country who can compare bullet wounds?" It wasn't an empty question. I had one, Win two, plus a thigh torn up by shrapnel. "Do you have a lawyer in mind? I can contact her today, set up an appointment."

Win stopped fussing with her bag. "Seriously?"

"I do listen to you, Win. It just takes me awhile to decide you're right about almost everything."

"Almost?" She zipped her bag. "I'll send you her contact info while I'm waiting to board. I'll have to wait to catch a ride back, so I'll see you tomorrow or the day after. Let you know as soon as I know."

She opened her arms and I walked into them.

"I'm not going into battle." She kissed me. "You take care. Don't lose concentration on the moment. Don't get complacent. Please."

We kissed again, and I could've stripped her of her traveling clothes in less than a minute. "I know," I said, leaning back. "Our morning delight was too delightful and you're running late. Take your own advice, Win. Come home safe."

She let me go, slung her bag over her shoulder. "Take Des on a long walk today when you get home, would you? She's not getting enough exercise with both of us gone. Or busy doing other things."

"How about I take her into the office today? She'd be around more people, more activity."

"Good idea." She kissed me again, then was out the door and in her truck.

* * *

I delivered the probable cause affidavits to the judge, both for arrest and property search. He read them over slowly, nodded occasionally and then signed them. "Good work, girl. I hope to hell he's the one and spends the rest of his days behind bars. Go get him with my blessing."

I thanked him, though I wished he'd stop calling me "girl." I headed to the office to pick up John and to arrange backup close by to the arrest scene.

"You want to take Des?" John asked. "Give her some purpose like the old days?"

I looked down at her. She grinned and wagged her tail. "I suppose we could. But where can we get a canine vest? If she thinks we're on an op, she won't stay in the car."

"I heard Greenglen PD got a dog. Let me call."

He came back ten minutes later with a vest and Des danced like she'd been born to wear one and had been deprived of the privilege way too long. Then she stood still, eyed John and whined. He fit it on her, clipped the lead onto her collar. She woofed.

When we got in the car, John set the GPS, but I didn't need it. The small hamlet we were looking for lay southeast and off the state road on a poorly maintained county road. My last trip through, Crothers Chapel had been nothing more than a remnant of history, ten or twelve homes with their occupants waiting to die. Interesting that Will Harrison chose this place when he'd returned from Florida.

"I never got to tell you what Harrison's boss at the plant said," John said, flipping his notebook open. "He worked there from two thousand nine until midwinter last year. He was let go at that point because his supervisor thought he'd started drinking on the job. Said his speech was slurred, and he had trouble walking a straight line. Harrison wouldn't let them do a blood draw, so it was adios. He's living on Social Security and a small pension from GPD now."

"John, call Doc Webster and ask him if those might be symptoms of ALS." I turned onto the county road even though the mechanical voice was telling me I'd made an error. "Shut off that damn GPS."

I didn't listen to his conversation but instead watched the rolling fields of corn and soybeans. We were almost at midsummer, the crops growing at a record pace and yet every farmer I knew was holding his or her breath. Just as I was holding my breath over this arrest. Everything was going great, but I couldn't help fear the worst would occur. The belly laden clouds hanging so low didn't help my state of mind either.

John closed his phone with a snap. "Doc said it could be ALS symptoms, but without seeing Harrison as a patient, he couldn't say for sure."

"If he saw Harrison as a patient, he couldn't tell us anyway." I slowed as a rusted sign announced Crothers Chapel. "Two thirty-seven South Maple." I'd passed Maple before I'd seen it so took a left at the next street. A boarded-up store sat on the corner, the sign too faded to tell what they'd sold. I took the next left, and then the next. Stopped at the country road again.

"God, what a depressing place," John said.

"I feel it too. Hard to think this was a bustling small town. I remember coming here for the Fourth of July parade when I was a kid. A guy on stilts, dressed like Uncle Sam, was the highlight for me."

"They have fireworks?"

I shrugged. "I always hated fireworks because they were too damn loud."

I crossed the road, barely tapped the gas until I saw 237. I pulled over and parked. Des, who'd been riding like a true professional, stuck her head between the headrests and whined so deeply in her chest I barely heard it. Her ears pitched forward, flicked to both sides of the street.

When we got out, I adjusted my new vest that Win had given me for my birthday and secured the neck fastener. I took Des's lead, gave her the alert command and walked toward his house. To call it a bungalow would've been generous, and I doubted if it contained more than two small rooms, or three tiny ones. The last time it had been painted must've been during the Nixon administration because there was nothing left to peel.

Des started growling, ending in a yip and seating herself down on the pavement in front of 237.

I looked at John. "She senses danger. Let's use protocol. Call in backup."

I took the left side of the porch, John the right, both of us avoiding the sidewalk. We stepped up quietly, took position on either side of the door, weapons drawn. I kept Des on a short lead behind me.

I tapped on the door with my Glock. "Mr. Harrison? This is Sheriff Pitt and I'd like to ask you a few questions."

Silence. Then a roar as the front door exploded outward.

CHAPTER TWENTY-FIVE

Win

Bill handed me a packet before he saw me off. "None of our players are moving or talking to one another."

"You think they know we're watching?"

"No. But if we're going to get them to relax and resume the game, we need more activity from the sheriff's office. Don't ask me what. I don't have the foggiest."

"I'll call Caleb when we land. We've held off on pulling Noor in for questioning, hoping to get a line on her direct involvement. But maybe we can build a smokescreen."

"Flight's ready. Be careful, Win."

I slept all the way out to Tucson. I let my dreams range from making love with Sarah to walking a narrow path in the mountains of the Kush. Noor appeared now and then, never with Kemat. Never with another woman. The dreams ended when my seatmate shook my shoulder.

"We're about ready to land," he said. "God, I wish I could learn to grab a nap like that."

"Did I give away any government secrets?"

He laughed. "No, but you smiled a lot."

As I walked down the stairs, I scanned the tarmac for my contact. Only one woman in a marine uniform was visible. Must be Major Laura Wilkins. I walked toward her, wondering how she managed to keep so crisp in the heat that attacked from above and below.

"I wasn't expecting someone in civvies," she said as she shook my hand.

"Win Kirkland, MCIA, retired. I need to make a few calls. You have a cool office?"

She walked me to a Jeep with a driver. We sped off to a small, squat building at the edge of the base. As we entered, she turned to me. "You need to fill me in. I've complied with the general's requests, but I don't like operating blind."

"Understood, Major. Let me make the calls, then we'll talk." I shifted my bag to the other shoulder. "You might want to lose the uniform if you're going to accompany me."

She opened the door to a spacious office with its own bathroom. "Are we in disguise or normal residents?"

"Just what you'd wear when your off duty," I replied as I took out my phone. Even though it was his day off, I dialed Caleb's office and waited for him to pick up. "Hey Caleb. Don't you ever take a day off?"

"You called me to see if I was working? Hell's bells. We've got an op going on and Sarah just called out our SWAT team."

My stomach dropped. "Oh, shit. Is she okay?"

"Doing fine, situation's under control. What can I do for you?"

I told him about Bill's thoughts on creating a smokescreen. "Could you send out a couple of detectives to start questioning the faculty and maybe grad students at CELI?"

"Let me check the duty roster before I give you an affirmative, but that sounds reasonable. You want to start today?"

"That would be lovely. But just concentrate their questions on trying to find if Kemat had enemies at IU. I could work out a list of questions if you want." I heard papers rustling.

"No, not necessary. We've got it handled. I've got two detectives I can send today, and if things resolve here quickly, I'll join them. Enough smoke?"

"Perfect. Caleb, please let me know what happens with Sarah. Text."

"Don't worry. She's got plenty of backup, and she's always careful, Win. But I'll let you know."

I hung up with a knot of fear tearing up my stomach.

The major, dressed in cowboy boots, jeans and a casual short-sleeved shirt, watched me with a raised eyebrow. "Who's Sarah? Or is that need-to-know?"

"My wife." I held up my left hand.

Her eyebrow still didn't go down. "Does that mean all those stories about you aren't true? The week-long parties? Cutting a swath through the women of a certain persuasion everywhere you went?"

"Why? Were you hoping for a little partying here?"

She colored slightly, shrugged. "Can't fault a woman for hoping."

"Most of the stories you heard were probably exaggerated. Though I will admit to exploring possibilities of a deeper understanding of local culture. But I made a vow to Sarah that I won't break." I glanced at my watch. "Let me call my contact, then I'll fill you in."

I called Bassir. He picked up after four rings. "I'm in Tucson. Where would you like to meet?"

"Gold Rush Restaurant on Drachman Street. It's down the street from the Borderland. Half an hour?"

"Fine. I'm going to send you two photos. First one of me, second of a woman who'll be shadowing us. She's MCIA and will be there to protect both of us. Is that all right?"

"Yes."

He hung up. I used my phone to take a selfie, then one of Laura. Sent them. "Let's go."

On the drive, I tried to give her as complete a picture of what led me here. "I don't know why Kemat was assassinated. Nor why they hit her in McCrumb County. We have a couple of leads on who—the name Mohan Shamsi ring any bells for you?"

"Aw, shit. Whac-A-Mole-Shamsi. He's been popping up in our files for a number of years, but a lot more in the last two. I'll pull his file when we get back."

"You know what Bassir looks like?"

"I do. We've been looking for him, afraid somebody had gotten to him."

"Why?"

"We got intel that he'd picked up a story in Syria that would blow the whole thing to bits."

"What 'thing'? Assad? The Free Syrian Army? Our involvement? Other country's?"

"I'm not avoiding, I just don't know, Win. Maybe all of the above." She glanced at me. "Bill knows. Ask him."

She pulled the car into an open parking space on the street. "The Gold Rush is down there. How do you want to do this?"

"I want you to go in first, find a seat where you can keep an eye on our table, but more importantly, on the door and other diners. Anyone who seems to have an interest in us? Get their photo. Follow them. Text me what's going on and your location. Let's do a clean op."

* * *

My first problem was how to approach Bassir. Lover? Sure way to get off on the wrong foot. Old friend? Probably not. Business acquaintance? Best choice. My clothes would work for casual Friday, but this was Monday. I turned around to scan the backseat. A scarf and a briefcase. Better than nothing. I grabbed both, wrapped the scarf loosely around my neck. Checked my watch. Time to go.

When I pushed my way into the Gold Rush, I immediately spotted Bassir in a back corner booth. He rose when I approached. I shook his hand.

"Let us order, then we can do business," he said, signaling the waitress. When she left, he examined my face. "My mother has great respect for you and for the work you do for women. She also trusts you."

I couldn't put this off any longer. I told him of her death. Tears gathered in his eyes. He sobbed once. Then took a deep breath with his jaw clenched.

"Please let me extend my condolences, most deeply felt. She was a force of nature, grand, sweeping, soft, gentle and fierce. I have profound respect for her, Bassir."

"As do I. She taught me her values, and I try to honor her in everything I do."

"Do you know why anyone would want her dead?"

Tears welled in his eyes again. He quickly wiped them away. "Because I sent her a copy of my files for safekeeping. I caused my mother's death."

I waited. Let him gulp in air, trying to gain control over his emotions. "Here comes our lunch."

We ate with only a few general remarks about nothing we were thinking. After the waitress cleared and gave him the bill, I said, "This article you're doing, does it have anything to do with Shamsi?"

His face transformed. Every feature fractured into pure hatred. "That seventh son of the seventh devil."

I wasn't sure of the reference, but his meaning was clear. "The story you're writing?"

He smoothed his features. "A series of articles for the *Washington Post* and *Reuters*. I sent your friend all my notes. If I live long enough, I hope to make it into a book. And yes, Shamsi is one of the players. How did you come across his name?"

"My own research. I'll share it with you, but not here and not now." I forced myself to lean back. "You're not safe here. Nathan wiped your number from your sister's call, but I wouldn't be honest if I left without saying it."

He buried his face in his hands, rubbed slowly. "I know. It is only a matter of time. All I need is another few days to finish. Then I will disappear."

"Bassir, that's not only dangerous, but foolish."

He frowned. "There is no reason for me to stay here, but every time I move, I risk exposure." He brushed his beard with long, thin fingers. "Why are you concerned?"

"I failed to protect your mother. I owe it to her to try and protect you."

"You didn't know she was at risk. I did."

"So we're sharing a load of guilt."

I caught movement out of the corner of my eye. Laura coming in our direction. Rapidly.

"We've got to get out of here quickly," she said, leaning toward us. "Mr. Zulficar, if you'll come with us. Threat level is very high." She looked at me. "Win—now."

"Come with us, Bassir," I said. I had to trust Laura was on the up-and-up. That we weren't going to walk into a trap. I got up, took his arm and followed Laura down a corridor and out the back door.

She handed me a Glock and broke into a trot until we reached the end of the alley. "Stay back, I'll get the car." She was off.

"What is going on?" Bassir asked, eyes darting from one side of the street to the other.

"I have no idea. Honest." My hand was on the Glock Laura had given me, my eyes scanning the area behind us.

Her car pulled up. I looked at Bassir. "This is an act of faith for both of us."

He nodded, opened the back door and I got in the front. Laura took off, watching her rearview mirror as much as the traffic in front of us. We'd gone no more than a half block when a percussive boom echoed off buildings.

I ducked, covered my head, waited for the next explosion. And eternity.

When it didn't come, I sat up and looked out the back window. A pillar of black smoke hung over the area where the Gold Rush had been.

CHAPTER TWENTY-SIX

Sarah

I heard the pump of another shotgun shell being loaded. I mouthed "Call SWAT out" to John and watched him duck around the side of the building. Damn. I dug my recorder from a pants pocket and held it up as close to the door as I could without getting it blown up by buckshot.

"Mr. Harrison, I don't want to see anyone hurt here. I want you to put your weapon down and step outside."

"Cold day in hell!"

His words were slurred. Drunk? Or was it the ALS? Damn. "Will you answer my questions?"

"Got nothing to lose. Ask away."

"I have to warn you, Mr. Harrison—"

"I know my rights. Was a cop. Waive 'em."

"You waive to your rights to have an attorney present?"

"Yes!" he bellowed. "I killed those goddamn gypsies. Dumped 'em at Alert."

"You killed thirteen women here and buried them at the Alert State Wildlife Area?"

"Yes."

"How many women in Florida?"

"Eight."

"Can you give me the names of these women?"

"Took their IDs. In here."

I heard a "psst" from behind me and turned to see John motioning me over. I back-stepped quietly, tugging Des with me. "What?"

"Our backup's here and did recon." He motioned to the backyard. "Harrison's blacked out all the windows, so there's no sight line in, except through the door he blew apart."

"Back door?"

"A bird's nest on it. Looks like it hasn't been used in years. SWAT's on the way, ETA five minutes."

"He sounds awful, speech slurred and I don't hear him moving around at all."

"The ALS?"

"Could be. But we can't take chances. I'll try and record as much of a confession as I can, but I really want to take the sonofabutt alive. See if the neighbors can give you any information on the layout of the house and the back door."

"You want me to put Des in the car?"

"Too hot. When you come back, you can hold onto her." He took off, and I returned to my place at the door.

"At ease, soldier," I said to her. She flicked her ears and sat, but I felt how tightly wound she was. Me too.

"Why don't you start at the beginning, Mr. Harrison."

"Beginning. Those damn gypsy sisters killed my father. Stole my parents blind. They lived outside city limits, so I reported the abuse to that fat deputy sittin' at the desk. Who did nothing."

"So you took the law into your own hands?"

"I *was* the law."

"No. The law gave you the right to arrest a suspect—not try, convict, and execute, Mr. Harrison."

"Every time I came home, Dad had more bruises. My mother was missing more of her treasures. No one would do anything. What would you do if someone killed your father in the next county?"

I took a deep breath. "I wouldn't kill a whole group of innocent women. You are under arrest, Mr. Harrison, for multiple counts of murder one. Please step outside with your hands up."

I could hear him wheeze. A laugh?

"Sheriff?" The whisper came from behind me.

I turned off the recorder. "We will wait until hell freezes over for you to come out." I eased back and stepped off the porch.

Willy Nesbit, my SWAT leader, nodded at me.

"I heard some of that," he said. "Man's not coming out."

"He doesn't want to because he wants us to go in."

Willy frowned. "Suicide by cop?"

"He may have ALS, which means he's facing a tortuous death. He saw his father become debilitated, and I think he doesn't want to go the same way. We can't just wait him out. He's got a shotgun and, if he's got the strength, he can turn it on himself."

"Jesus, Sarah. We have a layout of the interior?"

John popped up behind him. He showed us a drawing of three small rooms. "Neighbors say he nailed the back door shut and the refrigerator's in front of it. He's got stuff in front of the two side windows too."

"Shit," Willy said. "We can lob a couple of flash-bangs in through the door, go in as quick as we can."

We heard a shout from the house. "Hell ain't freezing over, Sheriff. But it's going to real soon."

"Get set," I said to Willy. "I'll try to keep him busy in the meantime."

I eased back to my position by the door. "Mr. Harrison, I'm not sending my people into a situation where you can slaughter them. Do you understand?"

"All I got is a shotgun. You've got automatic weapons and armor."

"If you believe that, why not just come out?"

"Stop the chatter, Sheriff. It's now or never."

Des flew by me and through the opening in the door.

I heard the shotgun discharge, Harrison screamed and Des growled. I didn't even think. I kicked open what was left of the door, weapon at the ready, finger on the trigger. I pulled it off, lowered my Glock. Des had Harrison pinned to the floor, a low growl rumbling in her throat. The shotgun lay on the floor amid a pile of debris from the ceiling.

CHAPTER TWENTY-SEVEN

Win

I was shaking. Couldn't control it. My teeth chattered. Breathe, Win, breathe. Suck it in, hold, let it out slowly. In, hold, out.

"Are you okay?" Laura asked.

"Too many IEDs in my past." My voice shook too. "What the hell's going on?"

Ignoring my question, she addressed Bassir. "Mr. Zulficar, do you need anything from your motel room?"

"I have everything with me that I need."

"Good. With your permission, I'll take you back to Davis-Monthan. In case Win didn't tell you, I'm with MCIA and my office will be a safe place for you." She watched him in the rearview mirror. Evidently he nodded. "Good."

I kept concentrating on my deep breathing. Finally, I uncoiled my body, leaned my head against the headrest.

"PTSD?" she asked.

"Yeah. Thought I had most of it licked. Now, how'd you get the heads-up?"

"Spotters. They recognized a couple of locals we've had eyes on. They had backpacks."

"Locals? Affiliated?"

"Not that we could see."

"You need to dump all those files to Bill ASAP." My head was beginning to ache and the sharp desert sun wasn't helping. I closed my eyes, concentrated on my breathing. I wasn't in operations mode. Even though I was in the middle of an op that had turned.

When we pulled into Laura's parking space, I was still shaky. Bassir was quickly out of the backseat, opened my door, helped me out. "Sometimes I forget it is not only our people who carry the scars of war. Let me help you in."

I took his arm gratefully, collapsed on a couch in a small conference room. Laura brought in a couple of painkillers and a blanket. "Does this happen often?"

"Never happened like this. Shakes, yes. Headache like this, never. I open my eyes and it feels like a dagger through them. Shit." I closed them, threw my arm over them for maximum dark. "Tell me what's going on with the op."

I could hear her pull a chair close. "There was a second explosion at Bassir's motel room."

"God, I'm glad we weren't close enough to hear it. Same bad boys?"

"Looks like it."

"Tell me about them."

"They're young, late teens and early twenties, second or third generation kids of immigrants from all over the Middle East."

"Radicalized at a mosque? Or Internet?"

"Internet. We didn't think they'd done any bomb-building or we'd have turned them over to local law enforcement." She got up. "Try and get some sleep, Win. Bill wants us at Atterbury. I can stall for a while, but you're in no shape to fly right now. If you need anything, let me know."

She turned off the light as she left. I lay there, humiliated. One boom, and I couldn't function. Shit. I dreaded the nightmares starting again. Needed Emily to tell me everything would be all right. Wished Sarah was here to run her fingers over my forehead. Heal the pain. Kiss me and make the world go away. Think about Sarah. Feel her touch. Rest in her.

"Win. Win, wake up."

I cracked open my eyes. The room was still dark, but streams of sunlight slipped through the blinds. I sat up. Eyes open, no pain. Sitting up, no dizziness. "What time is it?"

"Almost four thirty. Do you feel well enough to fly?" Laura asked. "Any headache?"

"Pretty much gone, but I need to walk around. Could I get something light to eat?" I folded up the blanket and stood up. "So far, so good. How's Bassir?"

"Silently brooding," she said as she opened the door. She held up a pair of wraparound sunglasses. "For you."

I took them, stuck them in a pocket. "Please tell me we're not flying a C-130."

"Same plane you flew in on." She opened the door to her office. "I'll get you something to eat."

I walked into her office, aware that the blinds were open. The light didn't hurt.

"You are feeling better?" Bassir asked from a chair in the corner.

"Yeah. Sorry about the performance. I'm usually a little more levelheaded and balanced." I dropped into a chair across from him. "Do you know anything about the men who placed the bombs?"

He shook his head. "There are angry Muslim men all over the world, and the radicals do everything they can to fan the flames. But why would they target me? There is no answer to that question."

I nodded. Noted that I could do that without losing my equilibrium. "You're coming back with me?"

"With us," Laura said as she handed me a sandwich and cup of coffee. "The local agencies are scrambling to explain the explosions, and Bill thinks I should be far away from questions. He's bunking Bassir with a man named Micah Barrow. You know him?"

"My father-in-law. Former sheriff. Very shrewd man. Bill's putting other security in place?"

"Of course. He wants me to stay with you."

"Why?"

"Bassir, Mr. Barrow and a Mr. Cloud will work on gathering intel. I'm assigned to you to work on Shamsi. I hope that's okay."

I wondered what the hell Bill had up his sleeve. Right now, it felt like nothing good. Okay or not, Sarah and I would have a guest.

CHAPTER TWENTY-EIGHT

Sarah

"Win's going to kill me when she sees this," I said. I closed my laptop and rubbed my temples. Front page of the online *Sentinel*: Des smiling like a fool, still in her vest. The article related the story of the arrest of Harrison, dubbed the "Burial Ground Killer," and Des's part in it.

"You solve one of the grisliest serial cases in Indiana history, and you're worried Win's gonna yell at you 'cause Des saved your life?" Caleb said, grinning. "Man, talk about bein' whipped."

John snickered.

"Don't—either one of you." A part of me really meant it, another was glad they'd tease me like any other married person in the department.

Dad tapped on the doorframe. He was toting a pizza box. "Reckoned you might want some celebratory dining." He set the pizza on the desk. "Have at it, folks."

Dad stooped to hug Des, who looked more interested in the food than more praise. He took off her vest and ruffled her fur back into shape. "Thank you for savin' my daughter's life." He took a chew out of his jacket pocket and offered it to her. She was still more interested in the box but accepted the chew with great dignity.

Caleb walked back in with paper plates and napkins and we dove in. Another one of those times when I didn't realize how hungry I was until food appeared in front of me.

"Bill called," Dad said. "Asked if I'd be willin' to put up a guest for a few days."

"Who?"

"I dunno. Guess we'll find out when they show up. An' Win called. Said to tell you to expect a guest too."

"She what? When?"

"Said she'd tried you, left a message, but when she had to board, she was worried you wouldn't turn your phone on until she was already here. Probably true."

I picked up my phone, which I'd turned off before we'd started up Harrison's walk. Three messages from Win. "When will she be in?"

"Said she'd be home 'bout ten tonight."

"All right. We can finish the rest of the paperwork in the morning. It's going to be a hell of a trial—a media circus—and I sure am glad I'm not the prosecutor."

"You find the stunbolt gun?" Dad asked.

"Yeah," John said. "And the IDs of every one of his victims. The two unidentified victims from here were Katya and Miliaka Korzhu, but we haven't run down any relatives yet. Names ring a bell for you?"

Dad shook his head and leaned against the wall. "Can't help thinkin' if Adult Protective Services took the case serious-like, them murders never woulda started."

"Maybe," I said, wiping my hands on a napkin. "But I can't help wonder if that hadn't been the trigger, something else might've been. He wasn't married, living at home with two disabled parents. High stress job."

"Don't do any good to go back, play guessin' games. Just be glad you nabbed him." He glanced at his watch. "You better head out if you wanna beat your better half home."

* * *

About ten minutes after I got home with Des, I heard Win's truck pound up the drive. Two doors slammed, and I heard two women's voices. I opened the door, Des started to charge out, but put on the skids when she saw the other woman. She sat, looked at Win.

Win made the formal introduction, instructing Laura Wilkins on proper behavior. Laura wasn't as tall as Win, but was another striking woman. Short, brown hair streaked with blond, muscles toned and a spectacular smile with very white teeth. Did Win only know beautiful women?

I sought her gaze across the space, but she watched Des get familiar with Laura. Shadows beneath her eyes, a wary way of moving meant something had happened. In trying to wrap up our case, I hadn't watched the news, national or local.

"This is Major Laura Wilkins, MCIA," Win told me. "This is Sarah, my wife."

I nodded to Laura and held the door open for both women. Des swarmed in after them, looked at me as much to say, "When are you going to tell her?"

"Have you eaten?" Hell, I sounded just like June Cleaver. Damn good thing I still had my uniform on.

Win nodded and crossed to the couch. I showed Laura to the guest room and hurried back to Win, whose hands were sunk deep into Des's fur, head buried on her shoulder.

"What happened?" I asked as I sat down next to Win.

Win let go of Des, gave her a kiss on the muzzle and leaned back. "There was a bombing, and I fell apart."

"A bombing? Where? In Tucson? I thought this wasn't supposed to be an op, that you wouldn't be in danger." I put my arms around her. "Are you okay?"

"I fell apart, Sarah. We heard the blast from about a half block away. I couldn't function." She was shaking.

"I'll call Em."

"Already did. I see her in the morning. Just hold me."

I did, rocking her in my arms, murmuring the nonwords every woman is born knowing. I could feel her trembling. I heard footsteps in the hall, the bathroom door close and the shower run. I hated the pain she had to suffer again and again. At the moment, I hated Bill and Laura, and maybe even Kemat, for dragging Win back into a war she'd have to fight the rest of her life, the rest of our lives. And the only damn thing I could do was hold her. She'd done enough for her country, for this county and for me.

She quieted, stopped shaking. She sat back, wiping tears away with her hands. "Let's go to bed. Give me a good fuck and I'll be fine in the morning."

"Win!"

She gave me the evil eye and stood up. She held out her hand to me. "This isn't something I can talk through right now. It'll recall the incident and relive it. I'm exhausted. Don't want to think. If you don't want to fuck me hard, could we please just make love? I need your comfort."

I stood up, kissed her while my hands cupped her butt to pull her close. She was so open to my touch, so ready to surrender to our desire. With my arm around her, I walked her down the hall and into our bedroom. I almost forgot to close the door, corrected course and turned on the bedside lamp. Win stood, waiting for me, her eyes pleading with me to take the lead tonight.

CHAPTER TWENTY-NINE

Win

When I woke, I stretched like a satisfied cat. I reached out for Sarah, but all I found was the imprint of her body next to me. The digital clock on the nightstand read 8:24 a.m. Well, hell. I didn't feel like getting up, so I stretched again as I remembered last night. Sarah had taken me slowly, building my response one exquisite sensation after another.

The bedroom door was open, and I heard voices from the kitchen. Then the reason for my neediness last night came back to me. I sat up. So far, so good. Swung my legs off the bed and let my body follow. I showered, grabbed my terrycloth robe and headed for the kitchen.

Sarah looked up. "Good morning, sleepyhead."

I gave her a kiss. "Thanks."

"You're feeling better?" she asked, her forehead creased.

"I am." I poured myself a mug of coffee. Turned to Laura. "Thanks for driving last night. I was really wiped out."

"Don't blame you," she said. "That damn explosion came out of nowhere and scared the shit out of me."

"Win," Sarah said. "I called Em, and she made an appointment at eleven so you can catch your breath."

"Thanks." I took a couple of deep sips. Noticed Sarah was in uniform. "Isn't today Tuesday?"

"I wondered when that would register," Sarah said with a smile. "We arrested the serial killer yesterday, and I'm going in to finish up paperwork. I'll be home in time to take you to Em's, if you want me to."

I grinned. "Don't mind being coddled at all."

Sarah blushed.

I turned to Laura. She was staring at the floor. I still wasn't clear why she was here. "You going up to Camp Atterbury today?"

"I didn't think you caught my explanation," she said. "We're supposed to work on Shamsi. From here. Bill said you had a safe satellite service. He, Nathan and Micah will work with Bassir. Debrief him and help him fill in any blanks he's got left. Bill wants the articles printed and then stand back and watch the shit fly."

"Do you know what's in the articles?"

She shook her head. "Couldn't tell you if I did."

"Fuck you." I grinned so she'd know I was just giving her a hard time.

Sarah's cell beeped, and she stepped into the living room to talk. Came back with a smile on her face. "Caleb said the paperwork's finished and delivered to the prosecutor. I don't have to go in. Oh, and he said he'd come out here tomorrow to go over the detectives' interviews at CELI with you. Okay?"

"Our quiet home, cop central." I sighed. "Yeah, okay."

I wanted to take Sarah back to bed, return the delight she'd given me last night. But our guest was at loose ends. A long walk with Des? "Laura, I think you should sign in with Bill, meet Nathan and Micah. Know the lay of the land here."

"I was thinking the same thing myself. Can I call a cab? I mean, do they come all the way out here?"

Sarah giggled. "Sorry, but a cab is the last thing I'd think of. Neighbors, yes. Cabs, no."

I found my keys hanging on their proper peg. "You can take my truck, and I'll program the GPS for you."

We walked outside and I wished I'd put on shoes. She watched as I put in coordinates. "This isn't tricky, Laura. One county road to the next."

"You're lucky, Win."

I glanced at her, but she was looking at the house. "Because I live in the country?"

"No. Because you've got a woman like Sarah. She's grand. Smart and funny and so attuned to you. I watched her calm you last night when we got here. You really lucked out."

I examined her eyes that were still focused on the house. I saw envy there. Desire. Interesting. "All set." I got out. "Laura, Sarah gets one day off a week. Tuesdays. We get to spend the day together, and I treasure the time. I'm sorry if we…if I made you uncomfortable."

"I caught the vibes, and it's fine. I just didn't know where to go. I won't be back until dinnertime. Promise."

I walked back into the house wondering if Sarah had any idea of the effect she had on Major Wilkins. I sincerely hoped not.

"She fled our home," Sarah said when I returned to the kitchen. "I thought I'd made her feel welcome."

"You did. But she knew we had certain, uh, business to conduct." I hooked a finger in her belt and tugged her to me. Kissed her.

She leaned back. "Are you really okay today?"

"I know I need to talk about what happened, but you soothed me in a way talking couldn't have done. I needed some distance from bombs."

"Laura said you had a bad headache right after—has that ever happened before?"

"No."

"How many explosions were you close to?"

"You think I've got brain damage?"

"Just tell Em. Please."

"Promise. Now, let's get you out of your uniform and into something more comfortable. Like naked."

* * *

After I talked through the trauma with Emily, she sent me to the hospital for an MRI. She hovered with a doctor as they looked at the scans. Shit. This wasn't how I'd planned to spend my day with Sarah. Brain damage? Shit, shit, shit. I wanted to take Sarah's hand, hold on to her in this antiseptic world. But her ring was back on its chain, tucked away from hostile eyes.

"Waiting in a hospital gives me a headache," I said. "Think I should tell them that?"

Sarah smiled. "Relax Win. Can you?"

"No."

Emily walked up and took the chair next to me. "It looks clear for you, Win, though one of them thought there might've been a very small bleed."

"Which means what?" Sarah asked.

"Which means it was probably an extreme form of tension headache caused by the stress of being close to another bomb explosion."

"Probably?" Sarah asked.

"Win, did the driver brake suddenly?"

"Don't remember, but we can ask her." At Emily's raised eyebrows, I thought I'd explain. "Laura's staying with us. We're supposed to be gathering data on one of the players."

"Interesting." Emily squinted.

"Quit. Can we just go home? Please?"

"Yes. But take it easy, Win. No heavy physical activity for a week or so. If you feel another headache coming on, get yourself here right away. Understood?"

"Yeah. But could you define 'heavy physical activity' for me?"

"Well, running, splitting wood or tae kwon do. Oh, uh, just don't go banging your head around when engaged in sex."

Sarah blushed and I grinned.

The ride home was quiet. Sarah focused on the roads. I focused on Sarah. She was thinking about something. "What?" I finally asked.

"I realized today why seeing a lawyer is so important. If Em hadn't been there, I don't know if the doctors would've talked to me at all."

Score one for our side. "When's the appointment?"

"Thursday after my shift. You think you'll be able to make it?"

"I'll make the time, Sarah. We can go to dinner at Ruby's after. Maybe take Laura in, introduce her around."

"Laura's gay?"

"Woman, you're going to have to learn to develop your gaydar." I adjusted my seatbelt. "I think she's attracted to you."

"What? Stop kidding around like that. I'll end up feeling funny around her."

"Is that such an impossible thought for you? That I'm the only fool in the world who thinks you're hot?" I asked.

"Do you? Really?"

I didn't answer, just ran my hand along her thigh. Listened with satisfaction at her sharp intake of breath. She *was* hot. I saw the glances that followed her when we walked into Ruby's. Lingered on her figure. I saw the way Laura looked at her. I had no problem admitting I got the same kind of looks. Enjoyed them. Genetics had given me my looks, hard work my body. Why not enjoy the perks?

Des greeted us enthusiastically when we got home.

"She's got a definite spring in her walk," I said. "What've you been feeding her?"

Sarah groaned. Opened my laptop and found a page. Turned it around so I could see.

A photo of Des grinning hugely. In a Kevlar vest. The headline read, "Serial Killer Arrested by Retired Canine Officer."

"Oh, fuck. Please tell me you did not do this."

"I didn't mean to, honest. It just kind of happened, Win. I thought John had her lead and he thought I had it. But she saved our lives—the first shotgun blast could've killed us."

"You took her into an op you were running? In a vest? What the hell were you thinking?" I slammed the laptop shut. Walked into the bedroom and slammed the door behind me. I was shaking. This time with anger, not fear. When Des had a vest on, she was at work. I'd told Sarah that. How could she have been so damn cavalier?

I lay down on the bed, pummeled the pillow. This was not how I'd envisioned the bedroom this afternoon.

CHAPTER THIRTY

Sarah

"Where's Win?" Laura asked when she got back late in the afternoon. "I've got intel I should tell her soon."

"Um, I think I'd wait on that. She's pretty angry with me right now, and she needs time to cool off."

"What'd you do? Make her get a brain scan?"

"No, Em did that. I took Des into a dangerous situation without thinking about her training. Win's royally pissed, and I don't blame her. Story's on the *Sentinel* website."

She walked to the laptop and opened it. There was Des, looking proud. She read the article, whistled. "Wow. Des is a hero, and so are you. Congrats on the bust, Sarah. You do this kind of thing often?"

"Des rushed the guy who was holding a shotgun. Do you realize what an up-close blast could've done to a leaping dog?"

"Well, uh—"

"Have you ever been in combat?"

"A little, right after basic training. But then they transferred me to Intelligence to do analysis."

"Harrison's first blast took out the front door, which was solid pine."

"But it turned out okay. Neither of you was injured."

"That's not the point, Laura. I screwed up. Now Des has stationed herself outside the bedroom, won't let me close because her bond with Win is so strong. My thoughtlessness could've gotten Des killed." I hoped liked hell they both would forgive me. I didn't blame her for her anger. I hadn't been thinking about Des's safety. I'd been concentrating on a clean bust of a predator. "Are you ready for dinner? Salad and sandwich?"

"Yeah, sure. Let me help."

I got her started, then went to check on Win. Des didn't growl, so I tapped on the door and wondered if I should plan on sleeping on the couch tonight. Or bunking with Laura. I snorted at that last thought.

The door opened, Win grabbed my hand and pulled me into a bear hug. She kept murmuring, "Sorry, so sorry," into my ear. I hugged her back, as hard as I could.

"Win, I never should've brought her along. Never. You were right, I was wrong."

She pulled back, and I saw her tears. She drew a deep breath. "I was so scared, Sarah. Not just for Des, but for you. Either one of you, or both of you, could be dead. It overwhelmed me."

I wiped her tears with my thumbs. "You got angry to banish the fear. I get it. I'd taken Des to the office, everything in the case came together and all I could think about was getting that sonofabutt behind bars where he'd never kill another woman. Thing is, he's in his own prison—his body. I should've let him rot in his own house. I wasn't thinking beyond the bust."

We hugged again, then Des woofed and swarmed us. We bent down to reassure her. Kissed.

"I'll read the article," Win said.

"Des saved my life. We thought it was a standard arrest of an old man. If it hadn't been for Des, I would've knocked on his front door."

"Good girl, Des, good work." Win ruffled her fur. "But I think I'm going to have to explain to her what 'retired' means. Again."

"You're the last person to explain retirement. I watched the news coverage on the Tucson bombing. It was bigger than Boston. Were you close to that restaurant?"

"We'd been *in* the restaurant. Laura got a tip and hustled us out the back."

"It was that close? Hell, Win." I leaned against her. "Maybe we both should retire for good and move to Vermont."

"You mean that?"

"It's a thought. Right now, I want to get things straight between us."

"Straight?" She kissed me. "Level, maybe. Never straight."

* * *

I went into work early and tried to diminish the stack of paper I needed to sign off on. I found my thoughts drifting to home. To Win, always. But to Caleb and the progress he'd made on Kemat's murder. Copies of the detectives' reports were at the bottom of the pile, a carrot to keep me on track.

John tapped on the doorframe and leaned into the office. "Harrison said he'd plead guilty if he's guaranteed the death penalty."

"Hell. Suicide by cop doesn't work, so he goes for suicide by the state. What did Tod say?"

"Our esteemed DA is disinclined. But he does want to do a press conference today with you. One o'clock. Courthouse steps."

"You'll be there, too, I presume."

"Shoulda worn my good uniform," he said as he backed out of the door.

I went back to work, doubling down because time would be eaten up by the press conference. The phone rang, I threw my pen down and answered in a voice that demanded brevity.

"Hey, Sarah, this is Lloyd. After the news conference, could you stop by the *Sentinel* for a minute?"

"You want an exclusive?"

"No, nothing like that. It's about an anonymous note I received. Won't take more 'n a minute or two. Promise."

More time gone. "Okay, I'll see you then."

I hung up, closed my door and returned to the paperwork with renewed vigor. I was halfway through the detectives' reports when John opened the door. "Time to go."

We walked across the square, entered the back door of the courthouse and met up with Tod Morrow in his office. He gathered his notes and put on his suit jacket. "We're not going for the death penalty. I want to get ahead of his request, so I plan to take some time dealing with that."

"Good," John said. "That bastard should die a long and painful death. Thirteen women here, eight in Florida. Jesus H. Christ."

We walked into the glare of television lights, Tod made his statement and then turned it over to me. I made a brief statement, officially thanking Dr. Elspeth Mackintosh and the work our deputies and detectives had done. We answered questions for an additional fifteen or twenty minutes. I hadn't seen Lloyd there, though his one reporter asked several questions.

"Hey Lloyd," I said as I entered the *Sentinel*'s office. "Didn't see you at the press conference."

"Zoe was there. She enjoys them." He beckoned me past the low gate. When I sat across from him, he handed me three plastic bags. "These came in the morning mail."

I looked at the document in the large one: my marriage license from Vermont. I felt like I'd been bushwhacked. The second held the envelope, and the third a short note printed in block letters: *The whore lied. Print this.*

I took a deep breath. "I don't know how this person got hold of the document, but it's real, Lloyd. Win and I married in January. Maybe it's time I started wearing this." I pulled out the chain with my wedding ring. "I'm so tired of hiding Win and how much I love her. Go ahead and print it."

"I'm not going to do that, Sarah, not to spare you, but because I never publish anything anonymously. But I thought you should know someone out there is rabid enough to get this document." He pointed to the plastic bags. "I bagged them as soon as I realized what they were, in case you want to track down this idiot."

I took them. "He hasn't broken any laws, so I can't use the department's facilities or personnel to find out who he is. But thanks for the heads-up."

He leaned back in his chair, an old oak one that creaked an unheeded warning. "I don't really know Win, but I've known you more years than I'd like to admit. You're still the driven law enforcement officer, but you seem happy, content maybe, in a way

I've never seen in you before." He creaked forward. "I'm an old dog, but this has got me thinking in new ways about marriage equality. So I'm not ready to toast your union, but I sure as hell won't condemn it."

"I couldn't ask for anything more." I stood. "You know, Lloyd, Win took me by surprise. I never thought I could fall in love with a woman."

He took off his glasses, wiped them with a big, white handkerchief. "Zoe's been wanting to write a series on marriage equality. Think I'll give her the go-ahead. If you know people she could interview, shoot me a list. I won't mention where it came from."

I nodded, swallowed hard. "Thanks, but if she needs contacts, send her to talk to me."

I walked back to the office scared shitless and simultaneously feeling my shackles had been broken, at least a little. I wanted to ask Win if coming out to friends ever got easier, but I had a feeling I already knew the answer.

CHAPTER THIRTY-ONE

Win

My home had become a cop-shop. I wasn't comfortable with it, but I figured it was only for the moment. Sanctuaries shouldn't be violated.

"Okay then," Caleb said. "We'll pick up Noor Bhatti in the morning, bring her back to Greenglen for questioning. What about the other one?"

"Rafi Jilani," I replied. "We don't necessarily want to tip him off. But unless Nathan finds something, I don't think you have legal grounds to pick him up."

"Glad to know legalities are important to you, Win." He held up his hands. "Just kidding, but you know, after all the stories we heard about torture and renditions and black ops, well, it makes you wonder."

"MCIA doesn't do that stuff. Never has." I swiveled my chair to face him. "Sorry, but what you said makes it harder for all of the other intelligence agencies to do their job. I will never justify what the CIA did. Just realize, Caleb, they are one agency among a whole bunch. Besides, living with a sheriff has made me a tad more aware of how you need to build a case."

"Peace," he said. "So what do we do about Rafi Jilani?"

"Put a tail on him." I swiveled a little more. "You up to tailing a suspect, Laura?"

Her eyebrows shot up. "I haven't been out in the field for years. I don't know, Win."

"We can partner," Caleb said.

At that, my eyebrows rose.

"Why not, Win? We can shift back and forth, double-team him. As far as I can see, we've gone just about as far as we can with this stuff. I guess I could watch you grill Ms. Bhatti, but getting a better handle on Mr. Jilani might provide a better use of my time."

"I'll call Nathan, have him start a deep background on Jilani. Anything else? Laura?"

She'd been quiet most of the time we'd been working. She should've been throwing out ideas, suggestions and new directions. Instead, it seemed to me her mind was elsewhere. Maybe she was uncomfortable working with local law enforcement.

"I feel like I'm missing something that should jump out at me," she said with an impatient slap of the desk. "Anyway, can you pick me up in the morning, Chief Deputy?"

"Please call me Caleb. Pick you up about eight." He scooped up the papers he'd brought, shuffled them together. He stood and stretched. "This is the kind of work that drives me batty. See you ladies in the morning."

I listened as the sound of his truck faded down the driveway. "What's going on with you?"

Laura jumped a bit. "Guess I've been a little out of it, haven't I? Sorry, promise my head will be in the game tomorrow."

"I'd bet you've been in the field plenty. What's with the 'I-don't-know-how-to-tail' business?"

She rose. "How about I take Des for a walk? She's been quiet all afternoon."

I gave her a long look before responding. "Fine."

While Laura was outside, Sarah came home. "Where's everybody?" she asked.

"We finished up. Caleb and Laura are going to tail Rafi Jilani tomorrow. Detectives will pick up Noor and bring her to your office tomorrow morning early." I took her hand. "You wouldn't have a basement room of some sort we could use for interrogation?"

"Basement? Where no one can hear her screams?"

"No. Where Noor will assume no one can hear her screams. I want to get her as off-balance as I can, that's all. You don't really think I'd torture anyone, do you?"

She shook her head. "I guess *I'm* just off-balance." She handed me some evidence bags.

I scanned the document in one. "Our marriage license?"

"It was sent to Lloyd at the *Sentinel*."

"Shit." I read the note. "Fuck it. What's the *Sentinel* going to do?"

"Lloyd won't print anything submitted anonymously, but I know this isn't the end of it."

I held up the bags. "Shouldn't these be with your CSIs for fingerprinting?"

"No laws broken, so I can't use the department to find the sender. I brought my fingerprint kit in. Why I don't know. I can't run the prints."

"Print it. Laura can run what you find through the MCIA databases." I hugged her, rubbed her back. "You nail a serial killer who's been operating for twenty-plus years, and this is the thanks you get. It really sucks, Sarah."

She leaned against me. "Yeah, it sucks. I hate sneaky people. But I told Lloyd it was true, that we're married."

I held her at arm's length. "Are you sure that's wise?"

"I made a vow with you, and I'm not lying about it." She pulled me close, began kissing me with small tentative brushes of her lips. Her hands slipped to the back of my neck. Her lips bore down and I felt the flood of desire.

The front door opened, Des dashed in and swarmed Sarah. She laughed, went on love attack with the dog until Des snorted and walked over to me. She licked my hand, went to her water bowl in the kitchen.

Laura still stood in the doorway. Gaze fastened on Sarah. That woman might be getting dangerous notions.

"Let's get the prints, Sarah." I cleared off the desk, turned on the light. I stepped back as Sarah pulled on gloves and motioned Laura over. "Would you run these prints?"

"Part of our case?"

"Personal favor—you have a problem with that?"

She pursed her lips, shook her head.

I fixed dinner. Sarah joined me when she'd pulled the prints. Laura scanned the images in and began the program that would do the comparison. It was still running when I went to bed.

I heard Sarah and Laura talking, but couldn't decipher the conversation. I hoped it was about fingerprints. I didn't like the way Laura seemed fixated on Sarah. I'd seen the way her hand brushed Sarah's breast when we were cleaning up after dinner. Sarah, I thought, dismissed the touch as accidental.

Des nudged the door out of her way. Went through the circling ritual until she collapsed on her bed with a satisfied sigh.

Sarah followed, closing the door behind her. "You still awake?"

"Wide awake, waiting for my wife." I watched her strip off her uniform, lay it over the back of a chair. I let my gaze run over the contours of her body as she moved.

When she was in bra and panties, she turned. "Would you like to finish this? We don't have any stripping music."

"Just go with the music in your head." I raised my eyebrow. Though Sarah had shed most inhibitions with me, she was still shy about getting naked while I watched. So what followed wasn't a tease. It was expedited clothing removal. I held the sheet back and she slid in next to me.

"I love you," she said as she drew me down onto her. "Profoundly. Forever."

"When we're really all-the-way-out, will you dance naked with me on the courthouse steps?"

"No, it's against the law." She reached up, caressed my cheek. "But I will encourage you to screw my brains out tonight."

* * *

We left early the next morning, drinking coffee on the way in. Sarah had agreed to my plan, though I knew she wasn't completely comfortable with it. When I'd put on black cargo pants, a black turtleneck, and my black boots, she'd frowned.

"What the hell is that outfit for? You look like a marine ninja or something."

"This is what I wore in the field when I didn't dress like the local population. I sure as hell didn't wear a standard uniform, Sarah."

"You sure as hell aren't active duty either."

I didn't put on my silver bird, figuring Sarah would give me double hell. But I put it in my pocket. For later.

When we got to the department, we emptied what had been the forensics lab in the basement of the few odds and ends left. Moved in a table and two straight-backed chairs. Rigged a camera and mic. Waited for the deputies to pick up Noor. Sarah had notified the sheriff's office, Bloomington's PD and the campus cops.

"I know you're not going to torture Noor," Sarah said as we sat in her office. "But I still don't see why you can't use our interrogation rooms. Bill could watch from the monitoring room. So could I."

"I don't think we're going to get much from Noor." I locked my hands behind my head. "It's more of an exercise in turning on the lights, see where the roaches run to."

"You need to use a dungeon to 'turn on lights'?"

"Sarah, relax. The only dungeon I've ever been in was made for pleasure, if you get off on pain."

Sarah blushed. "When we're both eighty, I'm going to ask you about that kind of dungeon. But I worry—"

"I'm not going to do anything illegal. But you can bet if Brandon Westin had gotten control of this case, things would've been different. Noor Bhatti is suspected of being a foreign agent? Poof! No more Noor."

Sarah shifted in her chair. "What happened to Westin? He went 'poof' too."

"Back at the CIA as far as I know. I keep telling you, Sarah—MCIA is authorized to work abroad and in this country. We have to follow the law. We do."

"We?"

"Slip of the tongue. They. Okay?"

"Just remember that." Sarah looked out at Courthouse Square. "It's the law I'm sworn to uphold. I'll stop you if you cross a line."

I hated to see an interrogation come between us. But I knew how to crack Noor's facade of junior academic. I knew how to panic her. These were my skills. I would skate as close to the legal border as I could. But I would never cross it. Never. If we were ever to bring Kemat's killer to justice, I had to shake up the players.

Sarah's line rang, and she put it on speaker.

"Deputy just called in," Dory said. "ETA ten minutes for Ms. Bhatti. Any special instructions?"

Sarah looked at me.

"Have them report to you and when they do, tell them to take her downstairs," I replied. "Have them look uncomfortable at that point."

"As well they might, seein' we got no interrogation room in the basement," Dory said.

"Thanks Dory." Sarah ended the call and looked at me. "Ready?"

"Are you?"

"No. She's in my custody, Win. What the hell do I tell her? I have no charges to file against her."

"That you simply wanted to ask her a few questions about Kemat since Kemat sponsored her visit. But a federal warrant just came in to hold her. Be apologetic."

"Does a warrant exist?"

"Yep, a FISA warrant. Bill's bringing the hard copy for your files." I pulled up the document on my phone and showed it to Sarah. "I set up a viewing room across the hall. In that small room?"

"In the closet? You're putting me back in the closet?"

I grinned. Shrugged. Back to business. "I'm not going to speak to Noor in English, so you won't understand what I'm saying. I sincerely don't want to bully her. She's had enough of that in her life. I recognize that, so if you see something that crosses the line, come in and end it."

We rose and walked downstairs. I stood behind Sarah, in the shadows that described the basement. Put the silver bird on the fold of my turtleneck. When Noor saw the symbol of my rank, she'd know I wasn't messing around. I heard clattering on the stairs and two deputies appeared with a very wary woman between them. Their discomfort was palpable.

Sarah opened the door and motioned Noor inside. "Thank you, Deputies, I'll take it from here."

When I walked inside behind Sarah, Noor stood by the table, her eyes huge, her breathing already ragged.

"You cannot hold me here, Win." She raised her chin. "This is America. There are laws."

"Yes, laws. You fall under the PATRIOT Act, my dear. A law, duly passed by Congress." I smiled. "Sit."

She hesitated. "You have no power. You are retired from the marines."

"Is that what your boss told you?" I threw my notebook on the table.

She said nothing, sat at the table with her hands on her lap.

Sarah handed her a bottle of water, explained the situation and apologized for the room. "We finally got paint donated, and our normal interview rooms are still in process. The paint fumes are awful. So sorry, Ms. Bhatti." She glanced at me and left.

I sat down at the table, waited a few beats. "Hands on the table," I said in Urdu. She complied.

I ran through a list of questions I'd worked up. Simple questions about her background. Which she should have down pat. The trick was, I changed language and dialect with each question, each follow-up. She stumbled on some, indicated she didn't understand with others. She tried to answer each question in Kashmiri, but I thought she lacked the vocabulary.

I threw down my pen, folded my arms. "You are so full of shit, Noor. You're not from Kashmir. Not even close. You were born in the tribal area, maybe Gupis or Yasin. But I imagine you spent the majority of your life in Islamabad."

She said nothing, but a vein was pulsing on her neck. She refused to meet my gaze.

I slammed my palms on the table. She jumped. "You think Shamsi gives a shit about you? Once you walk out of this station, you're a dead woman. Listen to me, Noor. We know."

Her hands clenched. The vein pulsed faster.

I put as much of a growl in my voice as I could. "We know. We have all the phone records. Complete conversations. We know."

She wouldn't look up, but she was using her clasped hands to stop their shaking.

I leaned back. Let my gaze rake her body. "It's such a shame, Noor." I let my voice fill with desire. "You are such a beautiful woman."

She looked up.

"Your skin is as soft as a rose petal, your lips as red, your breasts roses in full bloom. Your magic cave lined with pink rose petals. Ah, your body is truly a palace of all delights."

She caught the reference and white-knuckled her silence.

I stood. "But, no matter how beautiful the rose garden, like any rose that's plucked, you will turn to dust."

I walked out the door.

* * *

I nodded to the deputies. "Make sure she doesn't take off."

They assumed a guard's stance and I slipped into the closet.

I pulled Sarah to me, kissed her with all the passion my words had stirred in me. "You are my only rose, Sarah."

She raised an eyebrow. "What the hell was all that?"

"Snippets of Persian poetry. I needed to soften her up. The rose is a symbol of beauty—as in 'you are my only rose.' I used those images of her body so the last one, the Palace of All Delights, would shake her."

"The expensive brothel. Is that where she grew up?"

"Probably. It explains a lot. Particularly her connection to Shamsi. I imagine he began training her early on."

"He bought her?"

"Maybe. From her parents. Or he became her patron. Backed her. Made sure she had the best education, probably developed a relationship with her."

"He screwed her, literally and figuratively. Hell and damnation, it just makes me sick, Win."

I pulled her close. "I know. That's what Kemat was fighting with her network."

"Do you think she sold Noor to Shamsi?"

"No. My guess is that he made the purchase when she was a child, sent her down to Islamabad for training. I think Kemat tried to get Noor out. Shamsi found out and took advantage of the situation." I rubbed Sarah's back. "Do you ever lie to a suspect?"

She stepped back. "Like what?"

"Tell a suspect you've got a piece of evidence you don't really have? Or exaggerate the truth a bit?"

"What do you want me to do?"

"Go in and tell Noor she'll have to stay put until the feds take her into custody. Nothing you can do."

"Anything else? Do you want me to play good or bad cop? Oh, wait—you've already played both. Reckon I'm supposed to be the country bumpkin from Mayberry."

I tried not to laugh, but she caught my grin.

"Wipe that smile off. Win, we can't hold her without charges."

"Don't you have seventy-two hours or something?"

"Not for Noor."

"Can we keep her until dinnertime? The point of this exercise is to shake her up. To build distrust with her cohorts. Now go. She'll have to stay put for a while."

She scowled at me, but went on mission.

CHAPTER THIRTY-TWO

Sarah

I delivered Win's message, which shook Noor thoroughly. She asked for a lawyer, and I said I didn't have charges against her pending, so there wasn't anything I could do. "This is just a courtesy to the feds," I said. "Need anything else?"

She shook her head, sagged against her chair.

I left her alone, probably wondering how she'd found her way to a basement room in the sheriff's department in the middle of nowhere. So did I.

I poked my head in the closet. "Remember, we have an appointment with a lawyer this afternoon."

"I need to do another round with her, then Bill's taking over. I'll be able to leave whenever you're ready."

"She looks so pathetic," I said. "So lost."

"That's part of her game, Sarah. I know I sound cold, but she *is* the kind of woman who would slip a knife through your rib cage without emotion if she was told to."

I shivered. "I'll be in my office. Call me when you go in again."

I went up to my paperwork, all the daily chores I needed to get through. But my thoughts kept drifting to the small woman in the basement. Was she involved in Kemat's murder? Was Noor culpable? Knowing her background, I didn't have an answer.

At lunchtime, Caleb called. "Tell Win we think Jilani's on the move."

"Let me transfer your call. Is Nathan monitoring his phone?"

"Yeah."

I transferred his call, looked out the window. I trusted Win not to break the law, but I knew she was operating close to the edge. As close as she could. Was she dragging Caleb along with her? And the whole department? I'd be glad when Bill got here, when I could wash my hands of this whole thing. Or could I?

There was a tap on my door and I turned to see Win watching me.

"I'm ready to do the second round," she said. "I'll do it all in English, so you can follow."

"Is this plan working? Or am I putting my department at risk for a fishing expedition that's coming up with minnows?"

"Minnows when there are sharks out there? I can't guarantee anything. I understand what a delicate position your department's in. I do. I'm staying within your rules." She leaned against the doorjamb. "My gut reaction is that we've shaken things loose. Will all those leads end up in a conviction? Don't know. I'm working for the same end you are, Sarah. The arrest and conviction of the person or persons who executed Kemat. And those behind it."

"Okay. I just worry, Win. You know that."

"Yeah, I do. This is going to be a short session. Then I'm going home. Try to look presentable for the lawyer. Oh, Laura called. She's going to join us at Ruby's. Okay with you?"

"Sure—but isn't she going to keep tabs on Jilani?"

"Bill's sending down two teams to do that. They'll be in Bloomington about the time we get out of the lawyer's."

"So, if I get home a little early, we'd have time to mess around a little?" I asked.

Win raised an eyebrow. Smiled. "Oh, woman. Don't distract me now or we'll never make it home."

* * *

We walked out of our lawyer's office hand in hand. I knew Win was relieved and after going through the process, I was glad we'd done it. We still didn't have the rights straight couples had, but we'd covered all the bases we could. The lawyer would draw up the documents and we'd go back on Tuesday to sign. She would also investigate if Win could put me on her benefits. But it would take time to sort out procedure.

I prayed nothing would happen over the weekend, no shoot-outs, no chases, no bombs—just quiet times for paperwork.

"I'm glad you pushed me to do this," I said as we got into my truck.

"I'm glad you agreed to it. Nobody ever wants to think about the rough stuff. You especially. So I'm glad you manned up."

"Manned?"

"Drive, Sarah. Womanned up doesn't sound right. How about faced up to it?"

I found a place close to Ruby's and when we entered, Laura was sitting at the bar, waiting for us. We walked her out to the patio and found a table in the far corner.

"Nice place," she said. "Is the food decent?"

"Above decent," Win said. "Good. Just avoid eye contact with the woman who's bringing the menus."

I glanced up and saw Julie bearing down on us. She still flirted outrageously with Win, but I thought most of it was bravado. Still, she made me uncomfortable. She handed out the menus, put her hand on Win's shoulder and then moved it up to the back of her neck. Win shook it free, so Julie started in on Laura. I found myself fascinated, watching Julie advance, Laura slip around her flank, so to speak. Julie got tired of the game, took our orders and flounced over to another table.

"What a frigging harpy," Laura said. "I hate dykes like that."

"Like what?" Win asked.

"Grabby. Pushy. Don't notice when you're not interested. You know?"

"Um," Win said.

I glanced at Win, who was frowning. The only woman I'd seen paw her was Julie and Win handled it easily, even though they'd had a brief affair. There was something in her eyes. A warning?

I pushed the thought away as our food was served and we tucked into it with gusto. I'd missed lunch again and so had Win.

We decided to wait for the DJ, stay for the first set and then head home. I went into the backroom to get a table while Win took Laura around and introduced her to some single women, though she did stop at Paige's table. She and Laura sat down, and I thought Win might be looking for academic gossip about Kemat or Noor. I began thumbing through the thin file I had for Kemat's murder in my head and lost track of them.

Win found me, sat down and slipped an arm around me. "I offered Laura my studio for the night, just in case. She didn't bite."

"She's not going to be in the area that long. Maybe she's looking for more than a quick hookup."

"She's got a crush on you, Sarah." She turned the ring on my finger. "I know, you think I'm crazy, but I see the way she watches you. You don't."

"I don't encourage her." I hesitated, still not sure of myself. "Do I?"

"No, but unless you were a dragon lady, I don't think she'd notice." Win rubbed her thumb over my shoulder. "She'll be gone in a few days, so don't worry about it. I want our house back. I feel like we're hiding in the bedroom."

"We are, at least as far as making love. Maybe this is the time to try a three-way." I watched Win's face as she processed the thought.

"Are you serious? Sarah, please tell me you're not serious."

I laughed so hard I almost slipped off my chair. "Damn, sometimes you are so gullible."

Laura walked to the table with another woman I'd seen here on a couple of occasions. Maybe she'd get lucky and we would have the house to ourselves tonight.

"This is Gerry Oldfield," Laura began the introductions. Turned out Gerry was a state cop, but not in Greenglen's district. A table full of cops and spooks.

Lights dimmed, the music started and Win and I stepped onto the dance floor. Her arms around me, her lips on my neck, I felt this was a close as we could get to making love without taking our clothes off. I lost count of how many songs we danced to, but when the tempo turned fast, we returned to our seats.

I snuggled into Win, turned her chin to me, and kissed her—a promise for later. We settled back and watched the dancers. Gerry was a natural, Laura much more controlled. When they came back to the table, Laura took off to get drinks for the table.

"So you're the sheriff who nailed Harrison," Gerry said. "Jesus, what a great job. You should get a promotion."

"Thanks, but a promotion's impossible, Gerry. Sheriff is as high as we go."

"McCrumb County's pretty conservative, isn't particularly welcoming to gays. Are you out? I mean, to the general public."

"No, but that may happen." I gave her the brief outline of the note Lloyd hah received.

"You ever think of joining the state police?"

"I'm happy where I am, for now. Future? Who knows."

Laura brought a tray of beers and we chatted, as much as we could over the music. I was waiting for some more slow dancing. When it came, Gerry invited Win onto the dance floor and I was left with Laura. Which made me nervous.

"You feel like you made progress on the case today?" I asked her.

"Let's not talk business, Sarah." She stood, reached for my hand. "Let's dance."

Hell, why did Win have to accept Gerry's invitation? I got up, but didn't take her hand. When we stepped on the dance floor, she wrapped her arms around me. I didn't know what I'd expected, maybe something out of ballroom dancing classes from my youth, but I hadn't thought close body contact was part of the deal.

When her hands dropped to my butt and her lips to my cheek, I said, "Whoa, Laura. Totally inappropriate. Let's sit down, please."

"Sorry," she said. "I didn't think you were..."

So uptight? Such a prude? We sat down, but when the song was finished, Win grabbed my hand and swept me into a slow, sensuous dance.

"Told you, didn't I?" Win said into my ear. "Let's make this the last dance and go home."

"Did you pay Gerry to take Laura home?"

"Should've. Didn't think of it. Gerry's okay, didn't come on to me, just danced. She seems nice. Centered. Loves her job, broke up with a longtime lover about six months ago."

"How'd you find all that out?"

"We talked, not groped, Sarah. Now hush your mouth, and let's enjoy the music and being close and loving one another."

I closed my eyes, felt her body against mine and the rhythm we shared.

As we got ready to leave, Laura and Gerry were still on the dance floor. Laura was pretty much draped over Gerry. Gerry saw us, motioned for us to go on home. She winked.

"I don't get it, Win," I said as we drove home. "How could she just jump into bed like that? With somebody she doesn't know?"

"You never have gone to bed for some recreational sex?"

"Okay, I get the point. But still, it seems like her attention shifted awfully quickly."

Win sighed. "She's using Gerry as a substitute for you for the physical part. I doubt fucking somebody else is going to end her crush. Watch out, wife."

CHAPTER THIRTY-THREE

Win

Nathan had been sending me a feed, but I'd turned off my phone after dinner. Now, on the ride home, I turned the phone on. He'd sent a whole bunch of texts. I thumbed down and gave a whoop. "Noor contacted Rafi Jilani. And Shamsi. Hot shit!"

"You didn't expect that?" Sarah asked.

"Not so soon. I wasn't expecting Shamsi. He usually keeps a distance from his operatives." I kept going through the messages. "Bill's got both Noor and Jilani under surveillance."

"Proving what?" Sarah asked as she slowed for an intersection. "Is any of this going to lead to an arrest? One that I can make? Or will these people go 'poof' too?"

"Don't know. I've never seen Bill cooperate with local law enforcement like he does with you. He's got ears on them. He could turn those recordings over to you for prosecution. That is, if you have grounds for prosecution."

"Could?"

"He doesn't have to." I reached the end of the messages. Put the phone in my pocket. "Maybe he feels he owes you one for never giving you the credit for Scotty's capture."

"That's a military court-martial," she said, turning onto another county road. "I didn't expect him to."

"Still." I shrugged, though I doubted Sarah could see me in the glow from the dashboard. "You have a sense of fair play I admire."

"One that you don't subscribe to?"

"When you're up against an enemy who doesn't play by the rules at all, fair play could get you killed. But I've never broken the law stateside."

"Abroad?"

"In most areas I was in, there were no laws. No courts. I know it's hard for you to understand. The most I can say is that I always acted honorably."

She reached out for my hand. "You have a code of conduct, and so do I. I can't tell you what I'd do if I faced the situations you did."

"I'm glad you never had to." I took her hand in both of mine. "Now, can we talk about what we're going to do with what's left of the night?"

"Maybe Laura will turn up anyway, so don't make a bunch of elaborate plans beginning at the front door."

"I didn't have anything elaborate planned. But I was thinking about starting at the front door." I brought her hand up, kissed it. "I love dancing with you. All foreplay. I vote we get right down to the rest when we get home."

"How's Laura going to join the task force in the morning?" Sarah asked. "We have a meeting at nine thirty. Does she know?"

"I was talking about making love. Where the hell did that come from?"

"Stray thought," Sarah said with a small smile. "I'm trying to maintain control until we're parked in front of our home. I welcomed stray thoughts."

"Well, here's one for you. Gerry's off duty this whole weekend. So Laura's not our responsibility. Either she shows up or she's getting some really good sex."

Sarah turned into our drive, pulled up in front of the house. As soon as she cut the engine, she turned to me. Moved her hand to my thigh. "I vote we begin before the front door."

* * *

"We're trying to collect enough evidence for you to prosecute, Sarah," Bill said the next morning at the task force meeting. "Our wiretaps are solid, all have warrants."

"FISA warrants?"

"Yeah, and all obtained before we put the first tap on."

Sarah squirmed in her chair. "I'm a bit hazy on the law. I know you can collect evidence against anyone in the US, but don't they have to be involved in espionage or terrorism?"

"Hazy, my foot." Bill leaned against the whiteboard. "We know Shamsi's trafficking arms in Afghanistan, arms obtained illegally in this country. We also suspect he has other plans up his sleeve."

"Other things you can't talk about? But pertain to this case?"

"Yes and yes." He pushed away. "All assignments clear? Anything to add?"

He was met with silence. Then people filed out of the conference room. "Sarah, I'm really trying to work this one so you can put these folks up on charges. I don't mean to tell you and your people less than they need to know, but I can't spill all the intel."

Sarah pushed her chair back, stood. "The last time you said that, we ended up with a WMD in our backyard. Please, Bill, don't spring something like that on us again."

She walked out. I rose to follow.

"Win, a moment please," Bill said. "What's with Laura? She's usually so damn focused, but today she was in a fog."

"You'll have to ask her."

He frowned. "I'm asking you. I know Laura's gay. Has she suddenly gotten involved?"

How much could I divulge? "Maybe. She met a good woman last night." I stared at the whiteboard.

"What aren't you telling me, Win?"

I sighed. "She's got a crush on Sarah. Don't worry. Sarah's made it clear she's not interested."

"Aw, shit. I'm tempted to send her back to Tucson, but we're stretched thin here." He rolled his neck. "I hate this kind of crap. You're sure this 'good woman' is okay?"

"I didn't run a background check, but my assessment is positive. Maybe she'll settle Laura down." I crossed my arms. "Now I have a question for you. How close are we to an arrest? What the hell is the subtext of this investigation."

He sat on the table. "That's two questions."

"Shamsi's involved in something big, or you wouldn't want him so bad. What kind of arms?"

He shook his head. "Re-up and I'll tell you."

"Fuck you."

"I deserve that." He ducked his head. "We have a feeling Noor's going to contact you soon—"

"Feeling?"

"Intel. Anyway, if you decide to meet her, I was going to use Laura as your backup. Is that a problem?"

"Why not Sarah? I'd trust her with my life any day of the year. You've seen her on ops. Cool under pressure, focused as a hawk on a rabbit."

"For this operation, she's a civilian."

"And I'm not. Shit, Bill. Get it straight. Either I am or I ain't."

"Don't you trust Laura? Please, be honest."

I exhaled slowly. "It's complicated, Bill. I think she's infatuated with Sarah. Given the chance to 'save' me as opposed to 'collecting the widow' might slow her reaction time. She wouldn't even be aware of it. I would. I'd be checking my six all the time."

"Shit. Suss her out as well as you can. That call may come in the next day or two."

"A setup?" I asked.

"Possible. That's why I want you to be sure of Laura. Really sure, Win."

CHAPTER THIRTY-FOUR

Sarah

We got home late after a long day of combing through phone logs and tracking Noor, Jilani and Shamsi. My eyeballs ached and my shoulder muscles were so taut, I thought they might break. Win had been chewing on something since the task force meeting this morning. I hoped she'd spit it out soon. Des huffed off to her bed, probably fed up with both of us and our inattention during the day.

I was still heading for the couch as she walked down the hall to Laura's room. She came back to the living room with a note in her hand. "Thanks for the hospitality," she read. "Found other accommodations. Will be in touch. Laura."

"She's gone?" I asked.

"Probably at Gerry's." She wadded up the paper and threw it in the fireplace. "She can't go running off on a lark. We're in the middle of an op. I've got serious problems with her conduct since she got here."

"Do you think it's a lark, or she's just embarrassed? Our lovemaking has been a bit noisy lately."

"She couldn't stand the thought I was fucking you—and you were enjoying it."

"I'll stick with noisy, Win." I sat down on the couch and patted the cushion beside me. "Let's talk about this rationally."

"How can we talk about it rationally when her actions are totally irrational?" Win got her phone out and speed-dialed a number. "Do you know where Laura is? Has she let you know she's changed her billet?" Win walked over as she listened to the answer. "Probably with Gerry. But that's only a guess. I've forgotten Gerry's last name and don't know where she lives."

Win listened a bit more, then ended the conversation. "Shit. That woman just sank her career."

"She didn't tell Bill?"

"No."

I put my arm around her, felt the muscles on either side of her neck. They were as tight as mine. "Why don't you call Paige? She knows everyone and can probably give you Gerry's last name, maybe a phone number. I mean, wouldn't it be better to check?"

"You think something else is going on?"

"Maybe, but I'm only a bumbling bumpkin rural sheriff—what do I know?"

Win shook her head. "Shit, Sarah." She switched phones, called Paige to get Gerry's number, and immediately dialed it. Her face clouded over as she listened to what Gerry was saying. "So you brought her back here this morning, waited, dropped her off at the sheriff's office. Haven't heard from her since?" Win listened. "Shit, Gerry, I don't know. She was at a task force meeting this morning, but I don't remember seeing her this afternoon. I assumed she was working a lead." Win nodded a couple of times. "If you hear from her, call me right away. Please."

She closed the phone. "Gerry hasn't heard from her. Doesn't have a phone number for her either. Oh, and said last night wasn't so hot."

"They looked like they were getting along pretty well when we left."

"A lot can happen between the dance floor and later," she said. "Not all of it good. Can you call your people and see if they remember seeing her this afternoon?"

"Dory, our all-seeing dispatcher." I got up, found my phone and called Dory at home. Her answer was quick and precise. "Dory said she left at twelve thirty and didn't come back."

"Shit." She switched phones again, told Bill what she'd found. "I can't think of any reason for behavior like that, Bill. Something's wrong. Can you track her phone? She didn't? Double shit. Can I have Sarah put out a BOLO? Will do."

I called night dispatch, asked for a BOLO on Laura. I was able to give her physical description, but had no idea what she was using for transportation. I asked that John get onto rental firms as soon as he came in tomorrow morning. "Done. What's next?"

"Hell if I know."

I stood behind Win, kneaded her shoulders. "We'll find her, Win."

She groaned as I hit a knotted area. "I'm glad you're sure."

"We'll get deputies started on a canvass as soon as the stores on the square open. People would notice her because she's not a local. Probably the one advantage of living in a small town."

She took my hands, turned around. "The only reasons agents disappear are if they're kidnapped, dead or they've turned."

"Not good choices. Which one do you think?"

"Not a guess, Sarah. I need to review my conversations with her. Go on to bed. I'll be in soon."

"Not a chance in hell. I won't talk, but I'm working on your back until you relax."

* * *

Bill joined us early the next morning, pacing my office in a way that made me dizzy.

"Sit down," Win said. "You're making Sarah crazy, and I'm not far behind. Can you get deeper background on Laura?"

"Why?" he asked. "You think she's turned?"

"I tried to recall our interactions before we came back here. I remembered feeling uneasy with her at the restaurant where we met Bassir. Later, wondered why she deployed spotters. Who were they looking for? Her intel said the bombers were angry young men with no affiliation to terrorist organizations. Why would spotters give an alert on them?"

"Good questions." He turned to me. "You have a quiet place where I can make some calls?"

"Quiet or safe?" I asked. "We've got a lovely room in the basement that's safe."

Win snorted. I asked her to show him the way, then turned to reports that were beginning to dribble in from deputies.

John walked in. "Major Wilkins didn't rent a car anywhere in the county or in the Bloomington area. You want me to extend the search?"

"No, she left here on foot." I drummed my pen on the desk. "Would you shift over to the canvass? Try people walking on the square, and if you don't get any hits, try again at noon."

He nodded and left. I sat and thought. How could a woman disappear without a trace? My gut told me we were dealing with something other than an agent gone wild or bad. On a prayer, I called the bank manager at home, asked if they still had their ATM camera recordings from yesterday. They did, and he'd get them to me later.

Win walked in and plopped down on the couch. "Bill's working all his sources. Told me to vamoose. Shit, I feel useless."

"Come with me to the Rise 'N' Shine. I think we should talk to Aunt Tillie. Martin Kline said he'd open the bank for us after church."

"After church? You're kidding. Shit, Sarah, is that the only camera in town?"

"The ATM outside the pharmacy has one, but the focus is too narrow to do us any good. This isn't New York City or even Indianapolis. County government doesn't have the money to put in a camera system, Greenglen less so. Be grateful we have two."

"Sorry. I'm feeling particularly frustrated this morning. I don't know if it's Bill playing it so close to the vest or you worrying. But I think the clock's ticking for Laura."

"I thought you suspected her of going over to the other side."

"It's a possibility that has to be explored. If it's true, she has a limited shelf life. She's an asset only if she's an active service member." Win raked her hands through her hair. "If she's been abducted… "

"Then let's go. It doesn't do any good to sit around worrying. A really wonderful woman has told me that several times." I held my hand out to her, and when she stood, I gave her a quick kiss.

We crossed the square no longer holding hands and entered the diner to a noisy Sunday morning crowd. I spotted Tillie at the helm and one empty table at the back by the counter. We sat down and Tillie brought menus. Win opened hers right away.

I looked up at Tillie. "You have time to talk to us for a couple of minutes?"

"What does it look like? Use your eyes, Sarah Anne. Should slow down a tad by the time your order's up. That is, if you're gonna order."

"Two eggs over easy, bacon, toast and coffee," Win said.

"Oatmeal and coffee for me."

Tillie went back to the counter.

"We get in the bank—after church. We get to grill Tillie—after her diners are taken care of. Shit."

"Win—"

"I know. I told you I was frustrated. I'll try to rein in my desire to ride to the damsel in distress and concentrate on food."

The waitress brought our food and said Tillie would be with us in a minute. I watched Win dig in, wishing I'd ordered the same. We were just finishing when Tillie sat down.

"Well?" she asked.

"Did you see any strangers in here yesterday?" I asked.

"You mean like two swarthy men who babbled in a foreign language? Twern't Spanish. I'd say Arab talk, but you'd accuse me of profilin'."

"What time were they in here?"

"Round about noon, sat up front, didn't order nothin' but a coupla Cokes. Nursed 'em. Sat there an' took up valuable real estate durin' lunch rush. Which is why I recall 'em."

"You didn't happen to notice if they met with an attractive woman?"

"Nope. Just that they left an' I got to seat regular customers." She stood up. "Anythin' else?"

"Which way did they go?" Win asked.

"That a-way," Tillie said, pointing toward the west.

Win got out her wallet, started to lay a twenty on the table.

"On the house, Win," Tillie said, putting the money back in Win's pocket. "You both got free meals here for a year. Only weddin' present I thought you two could use."

"Thank you, Tillie," Win said with a big smile. "Perfect present."

As we walked west toward the bank, I remembered Dad had said Tillie'd been a hard case to crack. She wasn't actively antigay but harbored reservations about two women getting married. "Don't see no need to go trottin' to the altar" was what Dad had reported. Maybe she spoke from her own experience.

Martin Kline was waiting on the steps of the bank, let us in and led us back to the security room. "Any particular time of day?"

"Start a little before noon, if you would," I responded.

We watched as he fast-forwarded the digital counter until 11:45 a.m., then slowed to regular speed. People walked by, and I wrote down the names of those I knew. A couple of people used the ATM. Then at twelve thirty-five, two men appeared with Laura walking between them.

"Shit. Stop it there," Win said. "Those are the two guys I saw at the Sherry Hour. Talking to Noor. I assumed they were faculty. Can you send me the image?"

"Um, our tech probably could," Martin said. "I can call her."

"Would you trust me to take a try?" Win asked.

Martin looked relieved. "Be my guest."

Win sat down, started clicking keys. In a couple of minutes, my cell phone buzzed. I checked it, and there was the video. "Good job."

"Who should I send it to in the department?"

"John and Caleb."

She did, then toggled in for separate shots of the two men. Again, my phone buzzed. "Laura doesn't look happy."

"She wouldn't, not with a gun in her side. See?" She zoomed in on the man on Laura's right. Then she turned to Martin. "Can I burn a DVD of this?"

"Of course. Use anything you need."

Win started the burn.

"Run it a little longer," I said. "We need to know who else was on the street."

Win nodded. While the DVD was being burned, Win turned to me. "We have an abduction. The clock is ticking, Sarah."

CHAPTER THIRTY-FIVE

Win

We hotfooted it back to the station and found Caleb and John already in Sarah's office, sending out a BOLO for the two men.

"We figured it'd be okay to go ahead and alert the troops," Caleb said.

"Fine. It's an abduction, all right," Sarah said. "We may not have much time left to find her. John, here's a list of people I recognized on the street around the time. Caleb, will you go through this with John, see if both of you can recognize anybody else." Sarah handed him the DVD. "Then start calling them and see if they saw where the men went. I'll shoot this over to the *Sentinel*, see if they'll post it."

"Sarah, can you check the CELI faculty? Pictures are on their website."

"Sure. And you're going to…"

"Talk to Bill. He's left us in the dark too long."

I thundered downstairs, threw open the door of Bill's new office. "Who the hell are these guys?" I threw down the photos I'd printed out.

He scanned the photos. "Rafi Jilani and Imad Reza."

"Shit." I started pacing. "You never gave us photos of them. Why the hell not?"

"I was trying to keep this situation under control."

"By not letting Sarah—or me—in on what the fuck's going down? What the fuck were you thinking? You *know* me. You *know* Sarah." I slammed my hands on the table, leaned forward. "If you'd shown me photos, I could've identified them as two men who were talking with Noor. Right before she hit on me. At CELI. What the hell were they doing there?"

"You're not going to listen to an apology now, are you?"

I glared at him, crossed my arms. "Laura could be dead."

"You didn't trust her."

"I said I had questions. Elimination of possibilities. Your rule. Now, what the fuck is this about?"

"Drones." He motioned me to the chair. "Not the toy ones. Military variety."

"With the ability to target and fire missiles?"

"Yes."

"Does Shamsi already have them?"

"Unfortunately, yeah. A baker's dozen."

"Holy shit. He could sell to anybody, Bill. Homegrown terrorists, right-wing nuts, not to mention buyers overseas. Well, fuck."

"Not to mention the damn things can be controlled from anywhere in the world. Plus," he paused, took a deep breath. "There's a shadowy group of Americans who are putting money into Shamsi's operations."

Group of Americans? Shadowy? Shit. "What does Kemat have to do with this?"

"She was a lifelong enemy of Shamsi, without tipping her hand," Bill said. "From time to time, she'd tip us off on some of his operations. She wasn't working for us, Win. Nor the CIA."

The first truth Bill had told me since this started.

Arms. Sex trade. Drugs. Shamsi was making a fortune on his regular business. Why would he go out on a limb to steal drones? I had another question. "What does Bassir have to do with this?"

Bill frowned. "His story is about the activities of the CIA in Syria, but he also picked up a trace of the American backers. One they don't want publicized."

"Shit. I don't believe in coincidences. That's got to be important, but hell if I know why."

"There is one connection—Shamsi's one of the major players in Syria. He's selling to both sides, and Kemat passed the word to us."

"The CIA is a player?"

"CIA is cooperating with Shamsi."

I sat still. I couldn't believe it. It was a fucking contradiction of what this country stood for. Preached about. Using scum like Shamsi was unjustifiable. An abomination.

"Sorry Win. It's a shit situation."

"You're hoping to clean house at the CIA with the story?"

"Yeah. From the intel we've got, it's a couple of high-level rogue agents. They're probably getting a payoff from Shamsi."

I felt a knot in my stomach getting tighter. No wonder people didn't believe the government anymore. "Back to Laura. Why would they kidnap her?"

"To find out how much we know about Shamsi's project." He stood, started his patented frenetic pacing again. "We've had a leak somewhere, which is why Shamsi's always a step ahead of us."

"You thought *I* was the leak? Fuck it all to hell, Bill."

"No, I never thought that. Not once. But I needed to keep you and Sarah out of the drone investigation so I could find the leak."

"Did you?"

He nodded. "Now, anything I can do to find Laura, help Sarah find Laura, I will. I've asked Nathan to come in."

"Is Bassir safe? And Micah?"

"When I found out Shamsi had drones, I sent the appropriate countermeasures down."

I knew that's all he'd say. Patriot missiles on the farm? Fuck it all. "You want to come upstairs and join our task force now?" I stood. "Without a lot of resources, they're doing one hell of a job. Be nice if you could add to it."

"One more thing. Bassir sent his mother all the evidence he'd found on the American backers. Somebody's got to be looking for where she hid it."

* * *

We'd left the task force busy in the conference room and ducked out to the square for some private conference time. I wanted to fill Sarah in on the whole story, let her decide how close to her vest to play it. She was as shocked as I had been. Sarah went quiet, sat on the bench. Patted the seat beside her. We were quiet for a few minutes, Sarah obviously thinking through how the new information fit with the old.

"I still don't understand why Laura left our house," she said. "Especially since Gerry didn't invite her for the weekend."

"Maybe she'd had enough of our 'noisiness.' But it does seem out of character somehow. Let's get Nathan onto her cell phone usage that day."

"How'd she get in our house to get her stuff?"

"I didn't set the alarm. Figured that black spangly top she had on was not exactly office wear."

"The woman's got cleavage."

"You noticed." I quirked an eyebrow. "My, my."

"It was difficult not to notice, Win. Anyway, we found out Jilani rented a car in Bloomington—of course, not under his own name. Do you think Kemat knew he was one of Shamsi's men?"

"I don't think so. There's still some missing links for me. Like Noor. Kemat must've been onto her. Why'd she bring her to CELI?"

"Keep enemies closer than friends?" Sarah frowned. "My question is the other two men. They're not on the faculty list. Did they drop in on Noor to give her some new directive? If so, why in such a public place?"

"It's not that I don't believe what Bill said, but he's holding back. All of the questions you brought up need to be answered. Maybe we should get back and ask."

"Storm's coming," Sarah said, looking at the horizon beginning to cloud up. "God I hope we find her in time."

When we walked in, Caleb was sticking a red pin in the map of Greenglen. "Last sighting," he said.

I followed the trail of pins from the square to what used to be a factory and warehouse area by the river. "Which buildings are empty?"

"Bunch of 'em, Win."

"Nathan, can you find out if any cell phones you're tracking are in any of these buildings?" Sarah pointed at two particular ones. "These are either abandoned or empty at the moment."

He threw a map up on a large monitor and began his search. I looked from one map to the other. Paper and electronic. Push pins and electronic pings. Somehow they worked together.

Little green dots began popping up on Nathan's map. Sarah leaned toward the screen. "Five in the old sausage factory?"

"Burn phones, I think," Nathan said. "Wait, there's one more. A little off from the other ones." He clicked more keys. "Registered to Laura Wilkins."

"Shit," Bill said. "I'm going to call out the troops."

"How long 'til they can get here?" Sarah asked.

"Hour or so."

"That's too long. We can deploy our SWAT team in under a half hour."

"Okay, your team leads. I've got some stuff stashed in the trunk of my car that'll help. Do you have floor plans for the place?"

"We don't, but..." She turned to John. "Call the county recorder. Request she come in and help us. Why the hell isn't this stuff digitized?"

"Unbelievable," Bill muttered.

"Screw you, Bill Keller," Sarah almost shouted, hands on her hips. She leaned forward into his space. "You've got all the fucking equipment in the world and yet this is the second time we're cleaning up after you. This is my patch, and you didn't even have the moral sense to tell me what the hell was going on." She turned on her heel and stomped out.

Bill was red in the face. From anger or embarrassment, I couldn't tell. Not one deputy would look at him. I wondered if they blamed me for complicity. I glanced at Caleb. He grinned and gave me a thumbs-up. I breathed a little easier.

"You better get your stuff," I told Bill. "Now would be a really good time."

He left the room. John and Caleb shared a knuckle bump.

"Do you have a wire?" I asked.

Caleb's eyes opened wide. "Yeah."

"I probably have a more sophisticated setup, one with camera too. I'll get it." Nathan turned to leave.

Caleb shook his head. "I don't think I even want to know what you're planning."

"Good. You better get on the horn to SWAT. I'm going to find Sarah."

CHAPTER THIRTY-SIX

Sarah and Win

Sarah

Win caught up with me as I crossed the square, heading for the back door of the courthouse. "Congratulations," she said. "Bill got a double-barrel blast from both of us. Hope to hell he gets it."

"You reamed him out too?"

"Sure did. He knows both of us. Known me for years. There's no reason he couldn't tell us. Maybe an earlier heads-up would've stopped Laura's abduction before she was taken."

Kay Castle, our recorder, stood holding the door as we headed up the walk. "Know exactly where the plans are," she said as she started down the hall to her office. "We had another inquiry a couple of months ago."

"By whom?" Sarah asked.

"Any of these people?" I flicked through the images on my phone.

"Yes." She pointed to Jilani's photo.

"Has he bought it?" Sarah asked.

"No deed transfer." Kay opened the her door, flicked on the lights. She disappeared behind the counter, returned in two minutes with a roll of fading blueprint pages. "Please bring them back, Sarah. Otherwise, commissioners will skin me alive."

I thanked her and headed outside. I made a quick call to Caleb, asked that we rendezvous a block away from the old factory. Caleb said SWAT was on the way and would meet us there. Win leaned over and asked that they not forget the wire.

"A wire? What the hell for, Win? Please don't tell me you're planning to go in by yourself. Please."

"It worked the last time, didn't it?"

"This is different. We haven't had time to scope out the place. We don't know where they are in the building, or if they've made changes to it. Plus, we don't have the marines here."

"Let's go—we can talk about this on the way." Win touched my hand. "It's your op. I'll abide by your decision. But please hear me out."

"Okay, but you better talk fast."

We trotted across the square, watched as squad cars drove out of the lot and flagged down Caleb.

"Silent approach," I told him as I dove in the backseat.

We squealed away, met SWAT and other members of our team behind the tallest building around, an old granary.

Win had indeed talked fast, and we huddled with Willy Nesbit, ex-SEAL and team leader, over the blueprints.

"It might work," he said. "How much time do we have to get set up?"

I glanced at Win.

"Half hour max?"

He motioned his team over.

Bill walked up with Caleb and Nathan. "Personally, I think you're crazy. But here's what we've got from infrared." He ran playback on a Thermal-eye 250. "Our group of five is actually four, all on the first floor. There's another person on the second—looks like he might be here." He pointed to a place on the blueprints.

"Sniper?" Win asked.

"Probably. Thing is, there's another hot spot here. Could be Laura."

"That corresponds to the place where we spotted her phone," Nathan said. He began to take Win's ear studs out, and she slapped away his hand. He opened his hand, which held another pair. "Mic and camera."

She handed me the studs and put in the new ones.

"I've got an Apache on the way," Bill said. "Just in case. It won't get close enough to be heard inside."

"Best way in for me is here, on the river side," Win said. "An old door that used to open to a short wharf. Remember? We used to swing off a hoist beam into the river on hot summer days."

Nathan snorted. "*You* used to jump in the river. Sarah and I watched."

Bill shook his head. "I believe it." He turned back to the blueprints. "SWAT planning to enter from the roof?"

"Right."

"I've got an extra vest," Caleb said.

"I can't," Win said. "It's important they think I've come alone. A sheriff's department vest would blow that idea. If I had my old vest with me, I'd use it. At home, sorry."

Nathan began handing out equipment for the com sets. "We need to try these out."

Win didn't take one.

I pulled her aside. "You can't be without body armor and communication."

"You'll be able to hear and see everything that's happening." She took my hand. "I know how well you know me. Nobody else would sense small messages."

"Can I follow you in?"

"Can you lose the uniform shirt? Wear a plain ball cap?"

"I'll find something." I swallowed. "I couldn't bear to have something happen to you—"

"Gotta leave that behind, Sarah. You've got to be cool, professional. Always looking for the upper hand. Deal?"

"Shit, Win."

Win

We all huddled once more, then SWAT took off. Sarah and I went upstream, worked our way back down along the shore. We made it to the corner of the building without exposure. The windows on the first floor had been blacked out. I looked up at the door I remembered. It hung slightly ajar. I nudged Sarah, pointed.

She looked up. "Is that the way you remember it?"

"Yeah. Too much of a coincidence?"

She raised an eyebrow. "Wouldn't somebody like Jilani not leave an obvious weakness in his perimeter?"

"Let's test it."

"Wait, Win." She grabbed my arm. "SWAT's almost in place. We need their cover." She fingered her earwig. Finally nodded.

I threw a grappling hook on a long line up to the beam. It wrapped itself around the beam. Held. We both ducked behind some bushes. Nothing. Either they hadn't heard anything or they were baiting a trap.

"Watch how I do this—that is, if you're still going in. You don't have to, Sarah."

"I won't let you out of my sight."

"Unless I'm discovered. Please hang back and assess the situation." I hugged her hard.

"That's supposed to make me cool? Detached? Oh, Win. We shouldn't even be here, doing this."

"When we get home, we'll talk." I tested the rope again, worked my way far enough that I could swing over to the door. I hung beside it, glanced inside. Nothing but darkness except the slight ray of light from outside. A dusty floor. No footprints. The blueprints indicated this was a loading dock for the original building.

I used the toe of my boot to ease the door open. It squeaked. Good, no recent oil. I balanced the other foot on the sill. Examined the doorjamb. I couldn't see any trip wires, infrared or otherwise. I swung myself into the dock. Silence. I unfastened the rope, sent it back to Sarah. I shone my Maglite over the floor. Nobody had been in here in a very long time. Double doors ahead. Locked?

I heard a slight scuffling behind me. Sarah swung herself into the opening. She tied the rope around the doorknob. Scanned the room swiftly. Nodded. We walked to the doors. I tried a knob. The door squeaked open. I left it ajar, slipped through. More darkness. Sarah followed, her Glock in her hand.

I whispered in her ear. "First priority, Laura."

She nodded, pointed to a corridor on the left.

"They may have a surprise for anyone trying to get to her," I said. "When we get close, please, stay well behind."

She fought to control her rebellion. Nodded. But her blue eyes darkened and she frowned. I squeezed her hand.

We eased down the corridor until we came to a large storage area. "Fuck it," I said.

"What?" Sarah whispered.

"Coffins," I whispered back. "What they pack the UAVs in. And over there, Hellfire missiles."

"My God." She leaned toward my ear. "SWAT—no flash-bangs! There's enough ordnance in here to blow half of Greenglen to bits." She waited, nodded.

When she looked at me, her eyes were even darker. I could feel the heat of her rage. I motioned Sarah to follow as I moved on down the corridor. It met with another one and I leaned to look around the corner. I saw an open door to a room that faced the front of the building. I tucked back around the corner. "That's the approximate location we have for Laura. Door's open. About twenty-five feet on the left. Corridor goes all the way to the other end of the building."

"Damn," she whispered. "If they hear us, we'd be trapped."

I crouched down, leaned forward and scanned the floor. I could see footprints going into the room from the opposite direction. I scooted back. "Cover me from here. I'll make entry." Or die trying.

I moved as quickly and quietly as I could. Stood by the doorway, slipped the Maglite onto my weapon. Took a deep breath and swung into the room.

It was empty but for Laura. She hung forward from a chair in the middle of the room. Her blouse was open, bra cut in two, her breasts horribly red and blistered. She was barefoot and the floor was damp beneath them. I saw a truck battery sitting beside her. I swallowed the bile that had risen in my throat. I moved to her side, found a light pulse. As much as I didn't want to, I stepped back to the door, waved Sarah to come.

She moved silently until she stepped into the room. She gasped. "Oh, my God."

"Get her buttoned up." I took out my knife, moved behind the chair. They'd used a plastic tie cuff, which was now covered in blood. I cut it, pried it loose from the flesh on her wrists. "Can you do a fireman's carry?"

"It's going to hurt her more."

"She won't feel it now. I'll cover you. Get back to the door we came in. We'll figure out how to get her down when we get there." I went back to the doorway, tucked my flashlight back in my pocket. I heard a grunt from Sarah. Peeked out the door, weapon ready. The hall was still empty. I motioned her to go.

I felt her pass behind me, moving quickly for the weight she carried. When I looked in her direction, she was just disappearing into the other corridor. I followed, weapon still trained on the hall. As I tucked around the corner, I heard a door open and heavy footsteps in the hall I'd just left.

I crouched down. I knew SWAT wanted us out of the building before they made their assault, but damn. The footsteps stopped just about where the open door was.

"She's gone!" said a male voice in Pashtun. He didn't move but a step or two. Which way?

"Now would be good time for SWAT," I whispered. Waited. The footsteps began to come toward me.

I dove into the hall, both hands on my weapon, finger on the trigger. Imad Reza held a bullpup with a large magazine. I pumped three shots into his chest. His finger jerked the trigger and a line of bullets pocked the floor in a line heading for me. I pulled back, felt something hit my cheek.

Sarah

I was struggling to get the door open while I held on to the rope and balanced Laura on my shoulders. It seemed the wind had changed and was pushing to keep the door closed. The storm? I leaned Laura carefully against the wall, kept her propped up with the same hand holding the rope and put my shoulder to the door. It suddenly whipped open and I teetered on the sill.

When I regained my balance, I realized the wind was a downdraft and I looked up. An Apache helicopter hovered above. The pilot gave me a thumbs-up, and a guy in a flight suit and helmet began to descend toward me.

Jesus, now all I had to do was keep Laura upright, keep hold of the rope and wait. I heard three rapid shots from a sidearm, then a series of shots from a heavier automatic weapon. I looked back. Come on, Win, tear through those doors. Come on, come on. I looked over my shoulder and saw the guy on the line was almost level with the sill. Then it seemed like all hell broke loose from the bowels of the building. SWAT or Win? Come on, Win. Please.

"Ma'am, could you reach for my hand?" the guy on the line yelled.

I did and pulled him into the opening.

"Is that our victim?" he asked, moving toward Laura.

I nodded and he slipped a harness on her, then attached it to him and to the line. "I'll need a tiny push—really tiny—when I give you the signal. Okay?"

I nodded again. He lifted her to the opening, got a good grip on her and extended one leg over the river. He signaled the copter, the line tightened and he gave me the signal to push. I did, hoping my "tiny" and his matched.

He swung out a tad, then up, and I got another thumbs-up. I turned to the double doors, Glock in hand and moved as quietly as I could. I heard something move out in the hall, so moved behind the open door. Win raced through, stopped when she saw an empty room.

"Don't shoot," I said. "It's me."

"Thank God."

"Shit, Win—you've been hit!" Blood ran from her cheek and forehead.

"Splinters, we'll worry about it later. Come on!" She holstered her weapon, held out her hand and began untwining the rope from a peg I'd found. "Let's swing together."

CHAPTER THIRTY-SEVEN

Sarah

By the time we made it back to the granary, the firefight was over and reports were beginning to filter in. The number of emergency vehicles, all with lights flashing, amazed me and I wondered how many were military. I handed Win off to the EMTs to get cleaned up and probably stitched up. I searched for Caleb and found him huddled with Bill and Willy Nesbit.

"Are your guys okay?" I asked Willy.

"Andy caught a shot in the leg. He's on his way to the hospital. Nonlife-threatening."

"Thank God, I was worried."

"We were worried about you. We heard Win, then the firing. Put fire in our butts."

I gave him a brief hug. "Just glad you're all right." I turned to Bill. "Did they take Laura to the local hospital? She was in bad shape."

"Don't take it on your shoulders, Sarah. Your people went above and beyond in getting her to safety. As well as getting these terrorists."

"Where are they?"

"Two are on their way to the hospital, three dead," Willy answered. "Win took one of them out."

My breath caught, but I forced myself to nod. "Bill, I need to explain what all of this is to the good citizens of Greenglen. We're not going to sweep this one under the rug."

"Couldn't if we wanted to. I'll prepare a press release, but go ahead and talk to the press if you want to. Just try not to mention the UAVs or Hellfires specifically. You can say 'major armaments' or something."

I looked back at the old sausage factory, its brick facade rosy in the afternoon sun. It appeared as idyllic as a painting, maybe a Norman Rockwell. Within it, ugliness of the gravest variety.

"Everybody on scene who should be?" I asked Caleb.

"Yep."

"Can I get a ride back to the station? I want to pick up my truck and head to the hospital. Maybe talk Win into getting more than butterfly bandages, but I really want to check on Laura."

Willy turned to Thea. "We'll need to debrief at the station, but I want to check on Andy first. Give you both a ride to the hospital, then back to the station?"

"Deal." I went to find Win.

* * *

"You're getting those stitched up by someone who knows what they're doing," I said as Win and I rode with Willy to the hospital.

"What? You think I'll become Scarface?"

I squeezed her hand. I couldn't say she was so beautiful, it would be criminal to not have a plastic surgeon do the best for her. I wasn't sure how Willy would take it.

"You listen to your old lady, Win," Willy said, leaning forward to look at her. "My old lady goes in if she gets a pimple, afraid it's gonna leave a scar."

Win laughed. "Ah, Woman, thy name is vanity."

We found a parking place near the emergency entrance and went to the desk. Andy was resting upstairs, Laura still being treated. A short woman in scrubs walked up, turned Win's face so she could see the damage.

"Dr. Elaine Condron," she said. "Let's get you into room five and I'll stitch you up so that in a couple of weeks, you won't have a reminder of how you got this. Move."

Win threw up her hands and followed Dr. Condron down the hall. I rode up in the elevator with Willy to visit briefly with Andy.

"You're lucky you married Win. She's a hell of a good woman. So are you." Willy watched our progress upward. "If you guys hadn't gotten Laura out—which was one hell of a move—we couldn't have had such a clean op. Took the extra hostage worry out of it. I sure hope she's okay."

"She's not good, Will. She was tortured."

"Shit. If I'd known that, I would've taken the other two out."

The door pinged and opened. I walked with him down a sterile corridor that smelled like disinfectant had been spilled and left to evaporate. We stopped outside Andy's room. "I'm glad you didn't know. We may get some additional information out of them, and that's important."

"I wouldn't have taken them out anyway, but I can think about what I'd do to them. No excuse for torture. Not us, not them."

We walked in. Andy was in good spirits and said he'd be out tomorrow. "Basically, it's a flesh wound."

Willy glared at him. "A through-and-through isn't a damn flesh wound. Could've hit an artery and you would've bled out before we could get help."

I glanced at Willy. He was shaken but still cool. We talked a bit, then I headed back downstairs to find Win and check up on Laura's condition. I peeked in the exam room Win had disappeared into. The doctor was still working on her. I backed out at the glare Win gave me. I went to the ER desk and asked the head nurse for an update on Laura.

"She's in three oh three. She hasn't regained consciousness yet, Sheriff. They've put her on pretty heavy pain meds. I don't know how the hell human beings can do that kind of shit to one another."

"I don't have an answer for you, Mel. Is it okay to go up?"

"You'll have to be quiet, wait for her to wake up. May not be 'til morning."

I thanked her. Win was walking toward me when I turned around.

She tried to smile, but it was lopsided. "Pain shot. Can't move this side of my face. Fuck it. Can we see Laura?"

"Yeah." We headed back to the elevator and I punched three. When the doors closed, I kissed her and she giggled.

"Half a kiss, Sarah. Hope the numbness wears off soon."

I kissed her again, harder and deeper. I felt her arms around me, drawing me closer. She was alive and I never wanted to let go. "Screw the numbness," I said when the door pinged.

We got out and walked to the nurses' station and signed in. "Mel told me she's not awake, not likely to be soon."

"When she wakes, she'll be disoriented," Win said. "Probably terrified. I'd like her to see a face she knows."

The nurse looked up at us. "I'll try and find a couple of more comfortable chairs for you since you'll probably be spending the night."

"What room?" Win asked.

"Three oh three," I told her. "But I'm going to have to get back to the station soon and start the after-incident reports."

Win searched for the room, found it and we walked down the hall.

"Win, what did they do to her? I was so focused on getting her out…"

"Put her feet in a puddle of water, used jumper cables to attach her nipples to a battery. I really don't want to talk about it. But it could've been worse."

"Worse? Her breasts were—"

"They hadn't gotten to her genitals yet." Win stopped at the door to Laura's room. "Enough, Sarah. I don't want to talk about torture. Seen too many of the results at the hands of our enemies."

I watched Win walk in, pull a chair close to the bed and take Laura's hand in hers. From what I could see, Laura's chest was swathed in bandages and her face was beginning to show deep bruising. Five men against one small woman. Send them to hell for all eternity was the only thought I could make coherent.

My phone buzzed and I stepped out of the room. Willy said he was ready to head back to the station and did I want a ride or should he send someone back for me later?

"Give me five minutes, and I'll meet you in the parking lot." I hung up and stepped back into the room. I walked to Win, kissed her again.

"You've got to go?"

"Yeah, I need to start the debriefing and get the paperwork flowing. I need to find out what the media's doing with this." I fingered her cheek. "All I want to do is lie by your side and thank the heavens we both got out of there alive."

"We'll do that," Win said with her cockeyed smile. "Probably not until tomorrow, though."

"I'll be back tonight. Promise."

CHAPTER THIRTY-EIGHT

Win

I didn't envy Sarah her job, paperwork up to her eyeballs. Reporters feeling like they had a right to know every last detail. If they could manage it, the vultures would probably take photos of Laura's breasts. Unfortunately, I had those images seared in my mind.

The night nurse had been in every hour to check Laura's vitals. Marked the charts. Left. So when she'd marked the chart the last time, I was surprised when she turned to me.

"She seems to be coming up."

"Coming up?"

"Out of a mild coma. In addition to the wounds on her chest, she had a slight concussion. You can see the bruise on her temple." She closed the chart. "I know you can't talk about this, but I've never seen anything like the damage to her breasts. She's probably lost all sensitivity. It's…Jesus, it's awful."

"Torture. She was tortured. But don't spread it around. If she thinks all of you know, it'll make things worse for her."

The nurse closed her eyes. "I'll pray for her, and I promise I won't mention this to anyone."

She left. I rubbed Laura's hand, shifted my position in the chair. The hospital had been true to their word. I now had a comfy chair. But still, my arm ached from keeping it extended. When I had awakened in a forward hospital after the IED explosion, a guy from our unit was there. Holding onto my hand. It had meant the world to feel his presence. To see his face. They told me later he hadn't left my side. A little achy muscle was the least I could do for another wounded warrior.

The door opened again ten minutes later. With the low light, I couldn't see her face. But I knew it was Sarah.

"I didn't think you'd still be awake," she said.

"Nurse comes in every hour. Hard to fall asleep."

She came over and sat on the arm of the chair. Put her arm around me. Kissed my forehead. "Want me to take over the hand-holding for a while?"

"Mine or hers?" I traced her chin with my free hand. "You look dead on your feet."

"Not dead, Win. Just really tired. Sick. Besides what they did to Laura, they killed Noor. Tortured her, raped her and slit her throat."

I felt like I'd been hit with a medicine ball in my stomach. "No, no, not Noor. Fuck 'em. Fuck 'em all to hell."

Sarah rubbed my shoulders. "She must've known too much."

"Or they weren't sure of her. I still can't grasp how Kemat figures into all of this. But I'm too fucking tired to think about it tonight."

"Today. It's four in the morning."

Laura groaned, tossed her head back and forth. Reliving the torture, I was sure.

"The nurse said she was coming out of a coma. But they don't know what she went through. They should increase the meds."

Sarah reached over, pushed the call button. The nurse came in a minute later. I explained the situation. She checked the vital signs again. She gave her a mild tranquilizer and waited until Laura lay quiet again.

"We can't do much of this," the nurse said. "She needs to regain consciousness."

"How close do you think she is?" I asked.

"Close. I'll wait with you."

Sarah hadn't moved. Didn't look like she was going to. The nurse—I'd finally managed to read her nameplate, which read Shirlee—sat in the other visitor's chair.

Time was so fluid. Waiting, it moved like a creek in summer's drought. Trickled. In action, it was a tsunami. The waiting after-action was torture.

As it got light out, Laura started moving again. Small actions, not the terror that had gripped her before. At almost eight, she groaned again. Her eyelids fluttered. Shirlee stood, moved to the other side of the bed.

"Sarah, move to the end of the bed where she can see you," I said.

Laura tightened her grip on my hand. Opened her eyes. Screamed.

"It's Sarah. You're safe, Laura. You're safe. It's over."

The screams ended, she whimpered. She looked between Sarah and me. The sobs began. I held onto her hand until she quieted.

"The nightmare's over," I told her, keeping my voice soft. "We'll stay here until you feel safe."

* * *

After Sarah had gone back to work, I'd grabbed a nap. I watched the television coverage of the bust while I ate in the cafeteria. Including a brief news conference with one tired Sheriff. Bill stood behind her, in full uniform. He answered the military questions. Everybody avoided specifics. While a hostage was mentioned, Laura wasn't named. I could see the newshounds slavering for more details. Fuck them. What I wanted to know was what had happened to Shamsi.

Laura alternated between an uneasy sleep and wakefulness. Every time she woke, I could see the momentary panic in her eyes. She was going to have a long road to recovery. I wondered where she'd start the long walk. Something to talk over with Sarah.

It was after six when Sarah picked me up. We were both too tired to talk, to do anything but tumble into bed when we got home. To sleep, spooning each other to oblivion.

"We haven't made love for a couple of days," Sarah said when we woke up Tuesday morning.

"We're becoming an old married couple." I yawned.

"Hell to that," she said and touched my cheek lightly. "What do you want to do first? Eat or make love?"

"Shower. I'll bet you took one at the station before the news conference." I pushed back the sheet, swung my legs onto the floor. "I'm one stinky broad."

"Be careful of the stitches, Win. The doctor said not to get them wet."

"I need to wash away the pain. Too bad it doesn't work on memories." I rose and started for the bathroom. I stopped at the doorway. "I'm sorry you had to see Laura like that, Sarah."

"That could've happened to you, couldn't it?"

"Only if I'd got caught alive."

Sarah was quiet as we ate a really late breakfast. I didn't know if she was replaying Laura's rescue or feeling guilty about still having beautiful breasts. Which I'd ravished once I got out of the shower. All the fear of yesterday, perhaps of two lifetimes, had been concentrated in our lovemaking. Fierce gentleness had marked every kiss. Every touch.

"With all that's been happening, do you remember we're supposed to sign our wills and all that stuff today?" Sarah asked.

"Completely forgot. You want to go to Ruby's for dinner?"

"No. I need to lie low for a while. Lloyd said he's gotten a couple of calls from Indy TV stations about my orientation."

"He what?"

"He said they'd gotten copies of our marriage license."

"Shit." I poured another mug of coffee. Spilled coffee all over the counter. "You have any idea who's doing it?"

"I have plenty of ideas, but no evidence. Besides, there's still no law broken, Win. I'm too tired to fight right now. Too overwhelmed by this case." She frowned. "Is that okay with you? I mean, it's not just my decision."

"Whatever you do, I'll stand beside you. Always. You know that."

She was still frowning. "It's so damn demeaning. A woman was almost tortured to death, there were enough missiles to explode the county and all they want to know is which way I swing."

"Without a lot of details which you can't release, there's bound to be speculation about the case. Sometimes about the wrong things. Just think what they'd do if they knew about the bomb. It's always a thin line between security and the right to know. They'll go away when the next big story hits."

She took the mug from my hand, enclosed me in her arms. "I want to come out, Win. I want to wear my wedding ring every day. I want to be proud of our love."

She kissed me hard. I could feel all of her frustration. Fear. Love.

"I'm afraid I've waited too long," she said as she moved her hands to my sides. "That people will think I lied to win reelection."

"You answered honestly, Sarah. You didn't know where we were going then. It was all so new."

"I knew I loved you."

I rubbed her shoulders. "You shouldn't be forced to let McCrumb County into our bedroom."

Sarah giggled. "Should we sell tickets?"

I hugged her. "When the time is right, we could do an interview with Zoe. She's been running that series on marriage equality. You could explain what coming out has meant to you. How you had to come to terms with it before you came out to the whole county. How hard it's been. How many questions you've had to face."

"With you at my side. You've been so patient with me. I can't tell you how grateful I am that you've given me the time to get clear."

"What other choice did I have? It's your life, your decision. I can never tell you how much choosing our love means to me." She wrapped me in an embrace. "So, dinner at Ruby's?"

"Oh, hell. Why not? Maybe an evening out will recharge my battery and make me feel human again."

CHAPTER THIRTY-NINE

Sarah

"Here's to Laura," Win said, holding up her bottle at Ruby's. "And a thorough recovery."

"To Laura." I clinked my bottle against hers.

We'd gone back to the hospital to check on her before striking out for Bloomington. Laura had been pretty foggy, doped up on pain meds, so I didn't even try to get a statement from her. Nor would I until she had regained a bit of equilibrium, a little bit of the old Laura, if ever she could.

"Do you think she'll ever come back to her old self?" I asked.

"No idea. She'll have visible scars to remind her the rest of her life."

"Like yours?"

"These are battle wounds, Sarah. Different. We still don't know what intel she gave up, if she did. So there might be a layer of guilt on top of the pain."

"Guilt? The pain must've been excruciating. You've seen torture like this before?"

"We're supposed to be recharging batteries." She took a long swallow of beer.

There were things in Win's past I'd probably never know. Things I should learn not to ask about. I took her hand in mine. "I trespassed. I'm sorry."

She entwined our fingers. "There's ugliness out there that I never want you to know about, Sarah. Protect you from. But when it's in our own backyard, that's kind of a useless notion, isn't it? Yes, I've seen the results of torture like this, but never on a woman before. They usually don't inflict pain on women, but Laura is an agent. Guess they figured it was justified."

"I understand the reasoning, but Jesus."

"Do you?" She gazed at me with troubled eyes. "It's about surrender. Who surrenders first, the torturer or the victim. The torturer has nothing to lose—except his victim might die before he gives out the intel. So he takes the prisoner as close to death as he can, again and again. I kept seeing the men who've been tortured. Couldn't keep them away. Now I can add Laura to those specters." She raised her bottle. "I used to want to get drunk. But that didn't work. I couldn't pass out quick enough."

I felt her grip tighten. I put my other hand over hers. "You're not alone anymore. You don't have to carry this burden by yourself. You don't have to protect me—but you already know that, don't you? Anytime you want to talk, I'll listen."

I saw tears form in her eyes, but she blinked them away. We sat for a while, connected by our hands twined together, as were our lives.

"What's the word on Shamsi?" Win asked.

"Not much. Whatever Bill knows, he's not sharing. If Shamsi was behind the murders, he seems to have escaped without consequences."

"He lost his merchandise, his cell of operatives. Probably a half a billion dollars. I'll bet he's pissed. Really pissed."

"Something to worry about?"

"Worry does no good," Win said. "Just stay alert. If something stinks, look for the skunk."

"You sound like Dad."

She smiled. "How's Bassir doing?"

"Dad said he's already mailed off the first three parts of the article and should be packing up for parts unknown by the end of the week."

Win examined the label of her beer. "I know we should be out of this now, but I'd like to talk to Bassir. I still can't fit Kemat into the scheme, especially her connection to Noor. Now we can't ask Noor any more questions. I feel like I handed her to them."

"I feel awful about that. I had nothing to hold her on, certainly not murder charges. I didn't think about putting her in witness protection, and I should have." I remembered the conversation I'd had with the Bloomington PD and took a deep breath. "But we're making connections between her murder and Shamsi's men."

Win twisted the bottle around and around in her hands. "If I were you, I might put extra deputies on the two guys in the hospital. Or ask Bill to." She stopped playing with the bottle, looked up at me. "Shamsi's angry at his losses. He's got two men wounded but not dead. Guys who might talk."

"You think he might try something? What?"

"Yeah, I think he'll try to eliminate them. How? Could be anything from an IED to turning a nurse. He's got a hell of a reach." She looked across the room. "You need to talk to Bill. I have a feeling he's thinking the same thing. I'm surprised he hasn't moved them to a more secure location."

"One's in critical condition, and I think the other isn't in much better shape. Transporting them now might kill them, and everything they know will disappear." I sipped my beer. "This is supposed to be our night out, Win. Can we use my old dodge and think it about it tomorrow?"

"Yeah, but tomorrow, definitely think about it. Tonight, no more talk about crime, criminals or law. Except maybe the law of mutual attraction."

We clinked bottles again. "What's on the bill tonight? A DJ?"

Win grinned. "A drag queen show."

"Oh." I took another sip. Something else I didn't understand. "Do they ever have the opposite?"

Win hooted. "What? A drag king show? Yeah, but not around here." She started giggling again and couldn't stop.

"I'm driving home."

That sent her off into peals of laughter. A good way to banish the specters.

* * *

I called Bill as soon as I got in the office the next morning. I was kicking myself for not having thought the way Win had. She'd always had to think two steps ahead, while I was content to wrap up an investigation and hand it over to the courts.

He assured me they had the situation well in hand. "We've moved both of them out of ICU into a room farther back in the building. All of their medical personnel are military. We've also got personnel sprinkled throughout the hospital, just keeping eyes open. And on Laura. Anything else?"

"Sounds like you've covered all the bases, Bill. Are they going to be tried in federal court?"

"No definitive word yet," he responded. "Are you worried your county won't get a swing at them?"

"Just wondering how many resources I should use to collect evidence. What I should tell our prosecutor. It takes a lot to go to trial. We've got limited resources, and I'd hate to waste them on something that'll never get to a county courtroom."

"No decision's been made yet. What if I send down a couple of investigators to help you? Temporary assignment to the sheriff's office? Under your control."

"CSIs? We only have two and they're up to their ears with the factory."

"I'll get two down there by noon. Okay?"

"Thanks Bill. Should I give our DA your number?"

"No, give me his."

I did and hung up feeling like I'd gotten stonewalled. Before I dug into the paperwork, I clicked on the *Sentinel*'s website and went back over the series of articles Zoe had done. She was giving equal coverage to both sides, but the antigay side seemed to have only one argument: it's wrong because the *Bible* says so, and because of that, it'll destroy the institution of marriage that God gave us.

I had two things on my mind when I called Dad.

"McCrumb County Rehabilitation Center," Dad answered.

"I must have the wrong number. I thought I was dialing an old reprobate who'd never get himself rehabilitated."

"You did, huh? Reckon you got the right number. Hell of a job you done with them terrorists or whatever the devil they are. Smooth operation, Sarah. You need to talk to Bassir?"

"Win would like to. Can you have Bassir call her, set up a meeting?"

"Sure. What else is on your mind?"

"Somebody got hold of our marriage license from Vermont and has been sending it to news outlets. Lloyd got one awhile back and asked me about it."

"Ain't seen nothin' in the paper, Sarah Anne—you ask him to quash it?"

"I told him to do what he wanted, but he wouldn't touch it because it was sent anonymously. He said he's gotten a couple of inquiries from Indy TV stations lately."

"You figurin' on beatin' 'em to the punch?"

"I'm tired of hiding, Dad. I told Win I wouldn't lie if someone asks." I shifted the phone to the other ear. "Have you been reading Zoe's series in the *Sentinel*?"

"You gonna contribute to the series?"

"I was thinking about it, but not without your blessing."

"Course you got my blessin', don't ever think otherwise. You do what you think is right when you think it's right."

"Win says the same thing."

"Now the light's penetratin' this old, befogged mind. You want somebody to tell you what to do. Ain't me. Ain't Win. All on your shoulders, Sarah Anne. You're the one wearin' the badge that's on the line."

"Thanks a lot, Dad. Great talking to you."

"Always been honest with you, with any luck, always will be. One thing occurs to me. With all the attention on your action at the factory, you may be gettin' questions sooner than later. If you wanna get ahead of 'em, best talk to Zoe soon. Now go back to work, Sarah Anne, an' stop fussin'."

"How does Bassir like your cooking?"

"Low blow, Sarah."

I laughed as I hung up. Took a deep breath. Then I called Zoe.

CHAPTER FORTY

Win

I strapped on my sidearm before I left the house. Why, I didn't know. I'd have to ask Emily if it was a bad sign. Probably was. But I hadn't had any nightmares. Maybe because Sarah was beside me as I slept. Good juju against ghosts and specters. Or maybe because I was finally working my way out of the terrors of the past. At least part of it.

My stitches had moved from throb to ache, and I didn't have to see the surgeon again for a couple of days. I took Des for a long walk before I left. She was pissed at being left behind too much. I tried to explain, but she just snorted and ran off after a squirrel. I thought I wasn't a very good example of retirement and Des knew it.

After I showed my ID to get on Laura's floor, I walked into her room expecting to see her asleep. She wasn't. Her bed was raised, and she was watching TV. She saw me and snapped it off.

"You're looking better. How do you feel?"

"Foggy," she said and tossed the remote onto her lap. "I hear you saved my butt."

"Sarah and I were the last of a tag team." I sat down in the chair. "A lot of people were looking for you. I'm sorry we didn't get there sooner."

"Yeah, well…" She clenched her hands. "You here to debrief me?"

"No. Sarah will take a statement from you. When you're ready. She won't push, Laura. She's had to deal with me, so she understands."

"The PTSD?"

"Yeah. I only came to sit with you."

"Were you here when I first came to? Holding my hand? And Sarah was here?"

"I know how important it is to wake up to a familiar face or two."

"You were wounded?"

"The hospital trip was from an IED. My thigh resembles a topographical map of Afghanistan."

"That doesn't bother you?"

I leaned forward. "Why should it? I'm still the same soul. It doesn't bother Sarah. In fact, I think it makes her more…tender. It hasn't bothered any lover I've had since I got out of the hospital."

"They won't even let me look at my boobs. They come in, change the dressings and say 'Wait a few days, hon.' If they look as bad as they feel, maybe I'll never look."

"Your breasts will heal. So will you. Do you have family you can stay with when you're released?"

She shook her head. I thought there was a story there, but right now it wasn't my business.

"Do you remember what intel they were after? What they asked you about?"

She shook her head again. "It's all a blur, and I really don't want to think about it. Sorry."

"Let me know when we can talk about it." I leaned back in the chair. Disappointed. I wanted to say "Step up, marine," but I knew that wasn't fair. The experience was too raw. And one she'd never expected.

"Sarah doesn't have any idea she's so hot, does she?" Laura asked.

I could follow the thread of her thoughts: from her breasts to Sarah's. Shit.

"I mean, her body's so toned and curvy. And those eyes. Incredibly blue."

"She got her eye color from her dad, Micah. The nose, too, although it's tempered by her mom's."

"Shit, Win, is that what marriage does? Makes you think about genetics instead of being swept away?"

I stood. "I have an appointment. But let me offer you some advice. Don't substitute some fantasy about Sarah for dealing with your own pain."

I left feeling like a real bitch. But I remembered the crush I'd developed for the surgeon who'd put my thigh back together. It didn't matter that she was married. To a man. With kids. I'd spent my energy constructing the scenes where her hand slipped from a medical exam into a wild sexual fantasy. I'd stuffed down the explosion, the smell of explosives and burning human flesh. The screams of wounded marines and bystanders, the sight of a five-year-old girl's eyes staring, seeing nothing. Stuffed it down until I couldn't anymore.

I turned back to Laura's room to apologize. Caught the sight of a man rounding the corner at the end of the corridor. I sucked in my breath.

* * *

"Are you absolutely sure it was Shamsi?" Bill asked.

"No. I saw him in my peripheral vision. By the time I had eyes on him, he was turning the corner. I have PTSD. I could've hallucinated him." I took several deep breaths. "I watched all the surveillance tape you had on Shamsi for hours when he first came into this. He's got a barely noticeable limp in his left leg. So did this guy. By the time I got to the end of the hall, he'd disappeared. I asked a nurse who he was. She'd never seen him before. But if it was Shamsi…"

"We're checking the security tapes, but I don't see how he could've gotten in here," Bill said as he leaned back in his chair. He'd commandeered a consulting room. "Everybody's been briefed."

"Did you have them look at the videos?"

"Just the stills."

"I can't be absolutely sure, but once you notice it, the limp's distinctive. Pushes off with his left foot in an odd way." I closed my eyes, saw the man again. "But if it was Shamsi, he might've been scoping out the layout on Laura's floor."

"Why?"

"I asked Laura what they questioned her about, but she wasn't ready to go there. Bill, that's the key. We need to unlock her memory. Besides being pissed, that's what Shamsi's after."

"I don't get it. What's the key?"

"Whatever intel they were trying to get from Laura. And no, I have no idea what it is."

"Doctors says she's pretty fragile."

"I agree. Putting on a big front right now. I know how that works. I thought I could give my shrink a call. She's into alternative stuff. Works with a lot of vets. She's been a big help to me, Bill."

"I don't know…"

I got up and walked to the small window. "We still don't know why Kemat was killed. We know the assassins were Shamsi's men. What had Kemat stumbled on? Was it connected with Bassir and what he sent her? Or was that Kemat's way of getting me involved in all of this?" I turned to face him. "For all the results we've gotten, there are too many unanswered questions. What they wanted from Laura is a big one."

"You've got good instincts. A long history of making the right guess at the right time."

"But?"

"It's just so damn thin. You're not even sure it was Shamsi. You questioned the sighting yourself. I don't want to push Laura where she's not ready to go."

"Fine. But don't blame me when this blows up in your face." I pushed off the wall and walked to the door.

"Wait, Win. Call your shrink and see if he can do something that won't hurt Laura's progress."

"She." I speed-dialed Emily. Outlined the problem, asked if she could help. "Okay. Can you come to the hospital?" I turned off the phone. "Can we move Laura?"

"Where?"

"Off that floor. Far away from her current room. Without anyone knowing?"

"Jesus, Win, when you jump in following your gut suspicions, you go all in. Let me see what I can arrange. When's your shrink coming?"

"Two o'clock. She's rearranging her schedule for this. She won't push Laura past safe boundaries. She's a healer. A certified hypnotist. If it doesn't pan out, at least we gave it a try. I can't shake the feeling this isn't over."

Bill examined my face. Nodded. "I got the same niggles, Win."

CHAPTER FORTY-ONE

Sarah

"Where are you?" I asked, after Win picked up my call.

"Hospital."

"Where in the hospital? I'm here and no one has the foggiest notion where you or Laura are. I brought Em."

"Where are you?"

"Lobby."

"Meet you in the chapel." She disconnected.

"I have no idea what's going on, but something is," I told Em. "We're off to the chapel."

The last time I was in the chapel, Win had wheeled me through on the way to a lovely courtyard with a fountain, all so that I could see the night sky. If she hadn't been by my side, I would've alienated all the hospital personnel I came in contact with, as well as the people who came to visit. The sound of the fountain, being outdoors, was a blessed balm on my soul.

"We need a place where we aren't going to be disturbed, Sarah," Emily said.

"This is about security for the moment, I think. I hope to hell nothing else has happened."

I opened the chapel door, didn't see Win, but there was a woman in the front pew. She was bent over, her hands clasped in front of her and wore a head scarf. Strange because the Muslim women living in the county didn't wear head scarves. I supposed she could be a visitor, but I was uneasy. I put my hand on my weapon.

The woman rose in a fluid movement, taking off the head scarf as she did.

"Glad to see you were suspicious," Win said, a grim smile on her face. "But your weapon should've been in a fire position."

"Why? What the hell's going on?" I asked.

"I'll fill you in, but first let's get Emily to Laura." Win motioned us forward, opened the door opposite the fountain courtyard, and led us across another courtyard to a door in another wing. She rapped on the door, and it was opened by a man dressed in janitor's overalls. He carried a machine pistol. We hurried up the stairway to the second floor, where we were met by another armed man in scrubs. I glanced at Win, but she was scanning the corridor.

She stopped at a door and turned to Em. "I know healing is your priority. I'd never ask you to do anything but help Laura. But we need to know what her captors interrogated her about. Do what you can, Emily."

Em didn't look happy as Win ushered her into the room.

"This is Emily Peterson, my shrink," Win said. "She's done so much to help me find equilibrium." Win ran a hand through her short hair. "Laura, you've got healing to do. Emily can help you begin the path. But you've got to help her."

Laura looked downright balky to me, her mouth somewhere between a pout and a frown. "I'm tired and—"

Emily walked to the side of the bed. "All I intend to do is show you a few techniques you can use to alleviate pain, Laura, before you get addicted to your pain meds." She glanced at the drip and its monitor. "You won't be able to function if you keep using at this rate."

Laura locked her gaze with Em's. "I'm fine."

Em squinted at her. "Can you escape the nightmares?"

"With enough of that stuff, yeah."

"I think you made Em's point," I said as I walked to the end of her bed. "I've worked with Em too. You'd be downright stupid not to let her help you—that is, if you want a future."

Laura shifted a confused gaze to me. "I remember you carrying me on your back from that fucking place. You saved my life."

"Which is why I'd like you to talk to Em. I hate wasted effort and risk."

Laura's eyes widened, then closed. A tear slipped down her cheek. "Okay."

Win reached for my hand. "Time we talk."

"Where will I find you two later?" Em asked. "We have a session scheduled."

"Give me a call," I said. "We'll find you."

* * *

Win hustled me into a conference room on another floor of another wing. "Thanks for giving Laura a kick in the butt."

"If I didn't think Em was so good, I wouldn't have, regardless of what intel you were after. Laura looks like a recalcitrant zombie. Now tell me what's going on."

Win motioned me to a chair at the small table and took another one. She told me about her sighting of Shamsi. "Bill went over the security tapes and confirmed it."

"He's here? Why the hell would he take the risk? From what you've said, he could send any number of people."

"Don't have an answer, Sarah." She closed her eyes and took a deep breath. "He's probably brought operatives, but this has to be really high-level to get him here. The payoff has to equal the risk." She reached out and took my hand in hers. "I never should've gotten involved in this."

"You had tremendous respect for Kemat. What else could you have done when she asked for your help? I'm sorry I didn't get to know her better. She was such a strong woman with such clear vision."

"A force of nature," Win said. She tightened her grip on my hand. "I've got a feeling Shamsi's here for some reason connected to Kemat. But I don't know what."

"Trying to get his drones back?"

"No way that's going to happen. They're under guard at Camp Atterbury, and there's no way in hell Bill's going to let them disappear again."

"Finish what his men began with Laura?"

"No need for him to be here to do that."

I drummed on the table with my free hand. "Revenge made sweeter if he does it himself?"

Win sighed. "Maybe, but he's done all sorts of revenge killing by remote control. It's got to be bigger than wanting his pound of flesh. Even if that's part of his motivation."

I took her hand in mine, kissed it. "I haven't had lunch. Can we eat?"

"Eat?"

"Dad taught me to put something on the back burner when I can't solve it right away. I thought if we could do something else, maybe some of the pattern would come together."

"You suggested eating lunch?" Win asked with a grin. "I can think of another activity that would keep everything simmering."

"Here?"

"Okay. A quick hug, then lunch."

CHAPTER FORTY-TWO

Win

The long hug and its closeness had just ended when Emily called.

"Go on and leave," I said to Em. "We'll meet you at your office. If that's okay."

I clicked off and turned to Sarah. "So—any thoughts?"

"Too many, Win."

The door handle rattled and I opened it to Bill.

"So? It work with the shrink?" he asked and glanced at both of us.

"Don't know yet."

"Let me know when you find out." He turned and walked down the corridor.

"We're meeting Em at her office?" Sarah asked.

"Yeah. You take the southern route and I'll take the back way in. Watch and see if you pick up a tail."

"I'm getting worn out by the cloak-and-dagger stuff, Win." She moved her holster slightly, finding that sweet spot where it was comfortable. "See you there, if you think I need to be there."

"Emily wants us both there."

"For a session?"

"Yeah."

She traced the bandage on my cheek. "You haven't been having nightmares that I've slept through, have you?"

I took her in my arms. "No. I don't think you could sleep through one anyway. But it won't hurt for both of us to review the feelings from the day of the raid."

"I, for one, could blot out that whole day without a problem," she said with a grimace.

"That's where the problems begin." I kissed her lightly. "See you there."

I took the most indirect route I could, checking the rearview mirror every few seconds. So far, so good. I saw Sarah's Escape tucked in a parking spot about a block from Emily's office building. I circled the block, finally pulled into the parking lot. Met Sarah in the lobby and walked upstairs with her. "Notice anyone behind you?"

"Nope. Guess you didn't either or you wouldn't be here."

As we opened the waiting room door, Emily opened her office door, and we walked in.

"So, did you get anything?" I asked.

"It would be good if you asked after Major Wilkins and her health," Emily said as she sat in her chair. She glared at me, then her face softened. "Sorry, I know you get fixated on the operation, Win. But Laura's in lousy condition. She's carrying the guilt for the Tucson fiasco, not to mention getting picked up so easily by her abductors."

"Can you help her?" Sarah asked. "I mean, will she see you again?"

"I think so. I need to talk to her CO, see if he'll allow her to recuperate here or if he wants to whisk her away to a VA hospital. She said she didn't have family."

"She told me the same," I said. "What she's been through is appalling. Worse than horrifying. Sarah and I both saw what they'd done to her."

"That's not going to get erased from my memory soon," Sarah said. "If ever."

"I'm not clear on the torture. Can you give me a better picture, Win?"

I told her how we'd found Laura. What they'd done to her. I didn't skim the details.

"It makes my stomach curdle." Emily took a deep breath. "What are you feeling, Win?"

The question took me by surprise. "Guilty that we didn't find her sooner and stop the torture. Glad we found her when we did. It would've gotten worse for her."

Sarah groaned. "I can't even go there."

"You won't have to," I said. "We got her out."

"You killed a man to do that?" Emily asked.

"With no regrets. He would've killed me. Came fucking close to it anyway. These stitches came from splinters that were kicked up by his shots. From a fully automatic weapon. I carry no guilt. I would've liked to capture him alive. That wasn't possible. I was covering Sarah's back as she evacuated Laura."

Emily's eyelids opened to their normal sight. "How about you, Sarah?"

"It's still a nightmare to me, not that I've been having any. But as I was getting her out, I heard gunfire, then this awful silence. I was trying to not drop Laura, the damn door wouldn't open, and I was trying to keep the rope in my hand."

"Rather a disjointed account," Emily said.

"I could give you a minute by minute account, but what I felt was fear we'd get caught, fear that Win was hurt and blinding frustration at the end because it was so hard to do the little things."

"But you succeeded in the small things, as well as the larger mission, Sarah."

"Does that really matter when we're talking about feelings? I was as close to despair as I've ever come when Win didn't show up right behind me and I couldn't get the damn door open. Along with the torture, that's what I'll carry with me."

Emily's gaze traveled between the two of us. "Okay. Normal responses from both of you. Do you think the situation helped your relationship?"

"Oh hell," I said. "What the hell do you think?"

"I'm not in your relationship. Question stands."

"I know I'd die for Win, and she would do the same for me," Sarah said quietly. "I'm not sure that's a new revelation. But I know that, not in theory, but in fact."

Emily smiled. "You both sound remarkably in balance for what you went through."

I glared at her.

"Laura was terribly resistant when I approached the torture, rightfully so because it's way too soon," Emily said. "She was a little clearer on what they were asking her."

I waited three beats. "*What*?"

"They wanted to know about MCIA's operations and where the list was hidden."

"What list? A list of our operatives? Targets? What?"

"She didn't know," Emily said.

* * *

"I think we should invite Laura to stay here to recuperate," Sarah said as she lifted her bare feet on the coffee table and snuggled into my shoulder.

"Oh, no. Not gonna happen."

She turned to face me. "Why not? Do you blame her for getting hijacked?"

"No, not her fault." I looked into those remarkable blue eyes. "She's had a crush on you since she got here. Then today spent ten minutes telling me how hot you are."

"Hot? You've got to be kidding."

"I'm not." I told her of the fantasy I'd constructed around a certain colonel who'd been my doctor in Germany. "It's dangerous, if she reacts like I did. I shoved away all the terror I'd felt when the IED exploded. Focused on a fantasy sex life. Those stuffed-down memories came back to bite me in the ass."

Sarah was quiet, resettled against me. "Did I ever do anything to encourage her?"

"You didn't need to. It's fantasy, Sarah. A dream you build up like a movie. Go back and change dialogue. Invent new scenes. You dwell there because reality sucks too bad."

She touched my cheek so lightly I could barely feel it through the bandage. "Never go there again—to the movies in your head."

"I'd be a fool to. I'd much rather make movies with you."

"You want to make sex tapes?"

"No." I paused. "Although…"

She smacked my shoulder. "Yeah, that's all I'd need. A sex tape published to the Internet. Which reminds me, I made an interview appointment with Zoe."

"Sex tapes for the paper?"

"Interview about coming out, Tuesday morning. Will you be here?"

"Of course. But she doesn't get photographs. This is our home. My sanctuary. I hope yours too."

"It is. The place I come to be safe. To love you, Win. Maybe we can go hiking or something if she really wants a photo."

"Or we could make a sex tape."

"Hell, Win. Stop with the sex tape." She rested her hand on my chest. "So have you figured out what Laura meant by the list?"

"I have one theory." I took her hand in mine. "Somehow Kemat got hold of a list of Shamsi's network and contacts. Maybe including his American backers."

"His employees?"

"Yeah, as well as people he used occasionally. Maybe couriers. The cells he's got scattered all over the world, ready to do his bidding. But I'll be damned if I can figure out how she got it. Bassir sent a short list of people he suspected with what evidence he collected along with his other notes. He doesn't think it's enough for further involvement by Shamsi."

"Noor," Sarah responded. "You thought Kemat might've turned Noor. Noor's death, the way she died, suggests they were looking for something from her."

"You said they tortured her, didn't you? I was so tired then, I don't think it registered." I remember sitting in Laura's room, waiting for her to regain consciousness. "If she was Shamsi's operative—and I think she was—she might've had access. More likely, she was closer to him."

"A mistress?"

"Part of his stable. I'm sure he has his women all over the world." I stroked her shoulder. "So if she gave the list to Kemat, where is it now?"

"You think it was paper or electronic?"

"Thumb drive, something like that. Paper's too hard to smuggle out, tote around. If Kemat got it from Noor, she could've hidden it anywhere. Did anyone search her home and office?"

"Not my people. Better ask Bill."

"I will." I absently thumbed the back of her hand.

"What?"

"That's why she hit on me. She must've heard I was MCIA and figured I could give her protection. I sure did a lousy job on that."

"Think that she was after the same thing with Pan?"

"Very few people know Pan's an agent. But she does have a reputation for very inventive sex."

"Hell."

I watched her struggle with trespassing on my past. Felt more than a pang of guilt for letting Pan get me into bed. Enjoying the sex so damn much. Distraction time. For both of us. "There's something else. The language intensive starts Wednesday and goes for two weeks. I'll be camped out at CELI for the whole time. Unless I cancel."

"Which you don't want to do because you owe it to Kemat."

"I'm just not going to be much help to you until it's over."

"Can I come visit?"

"Um, I'll be in a dorm room. We speak only Tajik for the whole time. Eat the appropriate foods, learn to cook them in the traditional ways. Listen to the music and poetry. Everything in Tajik."

"Dorm room? Hell."

"Well, we'd best make hay while the moon shines." I kissed her, moved her hand to my breast.

She moaned, but when I stopped kissing her, she giggled. "While the *sun* shines."

"You see any sunshine right now?"

CHAPTER FORTY-THREE

Sarah

Bill joined us in my office the next morning. He sagged onto my couch. He looked like he hadn't slept for a couple of months or shaved for a couple of days.

"News?" I asked.

"Not a lot. I don't know where the fuck Shamsi disappeared to, and that bothers the hell out of me." He rubbed his face. "We went back over Kemat's house and office and didn't find anything. Maybe she had it with her the day she was killed."

"I doubt it," Win said. "The whole gang's still here. If they'd found it, they'd be long gone. Including Shamsi."

"Could he still be in the hospital?" I asked. "Sleeping in one of the on-call rooms?"

"How about if he was admitted as a patient?" Win added.

Bill looked at us through dull eyes. "How the hell can you be so perky at six thirty in the damn morning?"

Win glanced at me and winked.

"Yeah, yeah. Well, I haven't seen my wife in two weeks, so stop being so cheeky, Win." He leaned his head back. "All we have are the disappeared—no Shamsi, no list."

"A suggestion," Win said. "Either Bassir or his sister Somera might know where their mother hid important things. I could call Somera. Talked to her before. She trusts me."

"And talk to Bassir before he leaves?" I asked. "He's due to leave today—you know where he's going?"

"Nobody does." Bill rolled his head back and forth. "Do it. But ladies, we're clutching at straws."

"It must be bad," Win said, glancing at me. "He called us ladies." She pushed off the wall where she'd been standing. She walked into the bull pen, sat at a desk and got on her phone.

"Can we go see Bassir?" I asked.

"Why not? Just be damn careful. I don't want Shamsi getting hold of Bassir."

"Even if the cat's already out of the bag?"

"He may not know it, Sarah." Bill rubbed his face with his hands. "That's the fucking problem. All we're doing is guessing. I'm used to playing odds, but all of this is so murky. We're not sure a list exists, what's on it or how Kemat got it, if she did. This is a toothpick house."

"Not completely," I said. "Shamsi was identified not only by Win, but by you from the hospital security tapes. He's here."

"Yeah. I'm just bone tired."

"Stretch out on the couch, take a nap. If anything world-shaking comes in, I'll wake you up."

He looked at me doubtfully.

"Cross my heart. What if I call Bassir instead of going out there? Would that make you feel better?"

"Yes."

I called home. Dad answered and gave me a hard time about missing Sunday dinner with him. "Tad bit busy, Dad. Can I speak with Bassir?"

"Don't even wanna talk with the old man," he said. "Things sure is sorry 'round here."

He called Bassir to the phone and I asked him the question. "Do you have any idea where Kemat might hide something important?" His first answer was he had no idea. I asked him to think back to his childhood. Anything? He was quiet for a long time. The answer he gave me surprised me. I'd always assumed Kemat was Muslim.

Win appeared at the door with a big smile on her face. "A Coptic diptych of the Virgin Mary."

"That's what Bassir said too."

She laid a picture on my desk. "This isn't it—just one off the Internet. But it should give an idea what to look for."

I turned to Bill. "Shall I send a deputy into Bloomington to recover it?"

"I'll have agents meet him there. We have a warrant. Home or office, Win?"

"Never saw it in her office. Must be home."

* * *

While we waited word from Bloomington, Win suggested we grab something to eat and leave Bill to nap in peace.

"Burger time," she said as we walked out of the station. "I need protein."

"How about chicken?"

"How about that new burger place by the high school?" Win walked to my car and raised her eyebrows. "Come on, woman, I'm hungry."

Neither one of us was particularly wacky about eating healthy, but I couldn't remember the last time I'd had red meat except lamb. I surrendered and hit the remote.

"It's more about getting away from this case for a bit than protein," Win said. "I'm like a small rodent on a wheel. Keep going over the same territory."

"I know what you mean." I pulled out of the lot. "If Shamsi's here, do you think he'd operate alone?"

"If? He's here. And no, he's got people here."

"Where do you think—"

"No more case talk, Sarah. Please." She reached over and touched my knee. "Rhapsodize about the countryside or the weather."

The Burger Barn was the kind of place that didn't have a drive-through. We entered, ordered and Win seemed content with chatter. My mind kept wandering to Shamsi. I'd met a few felons who were evil, but many more who'd done evil things out of pain or a sense of misplaced justice. Laura had identified Shamsi as one of her torturers. A man who could order torture was beyond my understanding. A man who enjoyed torture was beyond everything I knew.

I thought I better understood why Win didn't engage in S & M, or was never rough with me in our lovemaking. At times, I'd felt her teeth on different parts of my body, but she'd never applied strong pressure, never bitten down hard.

"I need to get these stitches out today," Win said.

"Weren't you supposed to go in the other day?"

"I did, Sarah. She told me to come back today to get them out. Could you drop me there on your way back?"

"I'll wait for you." I checked the time. "Leslie and Vincente aren't even at Kemat's yet. If they find anything, they'll call me on my cell. Maybe Bill will be less of a bear by the time we get back."

"Maybe he'll take a shower."

An hour later, Win walked out of the doctor's office looking a bit less like Frankenstein's monster. She tossed me a tube. "Remind to put the stuff on at night."

I read the use directions. "You're supposed to work it into the scar area three times a day."

"Yeah, yeah, yeah. You think these new scars make me one ugly broad?" she asked as we walked to the car.

"Nothing could make you ugly, Win."

She leaned over and kissed me on my cheek. "I rest my case. At night will do."

We were getting close to the office when my phone rang. I put it on speaker and let it sit on the console between us. "Hey, Em, what's up?"

"You haven't come in today to finish the after-incident evaluation like you said you would. Will you come in now so I can finish it? You shouldn't even be on the job today, Sarah, because I haven't cleared you for duty yet."

"Neither should you, be on the job, I mean. I thought this was a task force meeting day at the high school, Em."

I glanced over at Win. Em hadn't even mentioned an official after-incident eval yesterday. Win was frantically making a "cut" sign, and she flipped on my siren.

"Gotta go, Em. Call you as soon as I get clear." I disconnected. "What's going on, Win? She made no sense."

"She sounded stressed to me," Win said as she turned off the siren. "Plus, what she said was patently untrue. You don't even need to do an eval on this one, do you?"

"I could, but I don't have to."

"Call Nathan. See if he'll come in ASAP. With his equipment that goes with the earrings."

"Please don't tell me…"

She shook her head. "I can't. I think Shamsi's resurfaced. In Emily's office."

CHAPTER FORTY-FOUR

Win

"Are you sure?" Bill asked. "I thought neither of you have seen a tail."

"He's had operatives in the county for months," I answered. "Wouldn't be hard to follow Emily from the hospital visit or identify her from my visits."

"Em was sending me a message," Sarah replied. "It sure sounded like it was 'help' to me. Win agrees."

"Fuck it all to hell and back," Bill said and smacked the corner of Sarah's desk.

"Stop cussing and tell us who you think Shamsi's got with him," I said, knowing we didn't have much time. "How many?"

"We've lost eyes on three of his guys."

"You didn't think to tell us?" Sarah said. Right now, her eyes were dark and stormy. "Pull their pics, please."

"Let me get my team in place—"

"No," I said. "This is Sarah's op. The sheriff department's. Not yours. Not anymore. My shrink is in serious trouble. I know that office. So does Sarah. If we need help, we'll ask."

Bill's eyes widened. He opened his mouth, closed it.

"For what it's worth, I agree," Sarah said. "You've said all along, he's not expecting a rural sheriff to do any serious damage."

"After the sausage factory, he may have revised his estimation," Bill said.

"He'll mark it down to luck. Or you and MCIA. He's too arrogant to believe Sarah could've taken him down." I started pacing. "He's trying to get to you, Sarah. Doesn't want to try a frontal attack."

"No. He's trying to get to you, Win," she said. "Just using me for bait. How do you want to do this?"

"The riskiest thing is to make him believe you have no idea what's going on." I wanted to sweep her into my arms, take her home. "But it's also the best—with the earrings, we can have eyes and ears on what's going down in Emily's office."

Sarah nodded. "I agree, but we'll need covering officers close. I don't want Em and me dead."

I stepped behind her, put my hands on her shoulders. "I could always show up in your stead. It'd take Shamsi by surprise."

"It would also blow the fact that we were onto him." Sarah took my hand, held on tight. "Let's get down to planning. Get Willy in here and put his team on alert. Caleb too. And we need to talk to the building management company. Anything else?"

"Nathan."

"Here and accounted for," he said, ducking into the room.

I started taking Sarah's diamond studs out. She caught one hand. "Don't lose them, they were Mom's."

Within ten minutes, the rest of the team had arrived. The management company sent over a super's uniform and master key. Caleb was rehearsing his part. Willy was going over the floor plans of Emily's building. Things were moving. I couldn't rid myself of the growing ice pit in my stomach.

Sarah motioned me to follow her out of the office.

"It's time I made the call." She dialed Emily's office. Spun a tale about a drunk driver and having to stop at the hospital to get a blood draw. "I should have him booked in another fifteen minutes if he doesn't pass out again. Make it a half hour, and I'll be sitting in your office. That okay with you?"

We heard a small grunt. "Fine, Sarah Anne. Uh, just come on in, I'll leave both doors open."

Emily disconnected.

"She's trying her best to give you warning, Sarah. I hope to high heaven Shamsi doesn't realize she's succeeded." I took her hand in mine. She leaned into me. "I don't want you to do this. It's taken my whole life to find you. I couldn't bear to lose you now."

She gazed into my eyes. "As long as you've got my back, I'm not scared."

"Shit. That's a hell of a burden you're putting on me." The feeling in the pit of my stomach rolled up to my lungs, and I couldn't get my breath. "I love you."

* * *

Willy's team had picked up two of the three men Shamsi had deployed. The other one worried me. All we needed was one loose thug to fuck up the whole plan. Until Sarah provided us with eyes, we had no idea if Shamsi was alone while he held Emily.

Timing. Timing was absolutely critical to get everyone out alive. Caleb and I had com sets, so did Willy's team. Nathan, John and I were holed up in an office across from Emily's exit door. Sarah with Caleb down the hall and around the corner by Emily's front door.

Nathan was monitoring the camera and mic Sarah wore. Clear picture and I could hear her breathing. Even, regular inhalation, exhalation. If she was scared, she wasn't showing it.

"Unit Two, any sighting of our third man?"

"Negative."

"Fuck it." I glanced at my watch. Only five minutes until Sarah was due to go in. At two minutes to go, the com set came alive. "Third target down."

I breathed a profound breath of relief. "Roger that."

I watched the seconds tick by. Tried deep breathing, but found my breath was following the pace of the second hand. "Okay, go."

I watched the screen with the deepest set of mixed emotions I'd ever experienced. Every beat of my heart said, "Run, Sarah, run!" But I knew she wouldn't. There was nothing I could do. Except have her back.

"Em?" Sarah called out. She turned her head slowly. Good scan. The waiting room was empty. Emily's office door was ajar.

"Come on in." Emily's voice cracked.

Sarah walked to the door, opened it slowly. We saw Emily seated across from a clean-shaven, urbane-looking man. Mohan Shamsi.

"So sorry," Sarah said. "I didn't know you had a client. I'll wait." She started to back out of the room.

"I don't think so," Shamsi said. He had drawn a small pistol. Hard to tell from the screen, but it looked like a Ruger. Small but deadly. He stood. "Take your sidearm out very slowly, and drop it."

"I can't," Sarah said. "Drop it, that is. It's a Glock, and it could discharge."

"Then let me come to your rescue, Sheriff." He moved toward her, then in back of her. When he appeared again, he held her Glock. Casually. "Now, handcuff yourself with those lovely bracelets on your belt. Slowly. No sudden moves."

"What the hell is going on?" Sarah asked. "Em are you okay?"

Emily raised her hands. Bound with plastic tie cuffs. "I'm so sorry, Sarah. I thought I had a new client. Remind me to never take on someone new again. I called you because I didn't want to die."

While she'd been talking, Sarah had cuffed herself. In the front. Smart woman.

"Now, call your friend," Shamsi said.

"Which friend? I have a lot of—"

"Shut up. Call Kirkland. Tell her the doctor needs to see her too."

Pretty much what we had expected. Sarah was the bait.

"No, I won't call Win. Not so you can get her too. What the hell do you want with us?"

Ease back, Sarah. Don't push him, he's a sick bastard.

"I said call your little whore."

I saw the Glock rising, heard the contact with Sarah's head. Felt it. I saw the ceiling tiles, groaned. So did Nathan. Shamsi reached down and pulled her up by her shirt front. He looked at her chest. "What's this?"

I couldn't see what he had, but I could guess. Her wedding band. "You two will have to show me what you do in bed to believe this isn't some bad joke." He tore it off and flung it.

Sarah steadied, focused on Shamsi.

He walked over to Emily. Held the Glock to her head. "Call. Now. Put it on speaker."

She fumbled the phone out. Hit my number. Put it on speaker. She raised her gaze from the phone.

I let my phone ring three times before I took the call. "Hey Sarah. You want me to pick up something for dinner? Be quick, I'm halfway home."

"Uh, no. But Emily wants you here. In case you've forgotten, we have couples' counseling."

"Crap. Why didn't you remind me?"

"Because I forgot too. Sorry. But she wants to go over the sausage factory fallout with both of us at the same time."

"Traffic was heavy coming out of Greenglen. Going to be worse going in. Give me thirty minutes. Does that mean we only have to endure thirty minutes of questions from Emily?"

"Something like that."

I saw Shamsi reach over and disconnect. "Very well done. It sounded plausible. Now, sit down." He motioned to the chair next to Emily.

Sarah did. Shamsi remained standing. With his back to the exit door.

"Caleb, start banging on doors down the hall." I turned to John. "Key?"

"I used lock oil on it. It shouldn't make a sound."

Nathan picked up his unit and we all slipped into the hall. John slid the key into the lock, waited for my signal to turn it and open the door. On the monitor, I watched Shamsi, my weapon drawn and ready. I listened to Caleb working his way down the hall as he warned occupants the electricity would be switched off in fifteen minutes.

"Dr. Peterson?" I heard Caleb rap on the door, open it. "Hey, Doc, we're gonna be turnin' off the electric. Doc?"

"Answer him," Shamsi said.

"Okay, Auggie. I'm with a client. Should we evacuate the building?"

Shamsi shifted slightly to face the other door. Perfect. I motioned for John to open the door. I could hear Caleb outside the other door, babbling on. I stepped quietly into the room, took three silent steps behind him. Shoved the gun into the back of his head. "You make one false move and you're dead, Mohan. There's nothing I'd like to see better than your brain spatter on the ceiling."

He raised his hands, I took the Glock. Stuck it in my waistband. "Hands locked behind your head. Now. Widen your stance." I patted him down, taking the Ruger and Sarah's keys. Knowing what he'd done to Laura, what he would've done to Sarah, I felt a rage that overwhelmed me. I took a couple of steps backward before I disabled him.

CHAPTER FORTY-FIVE

Sarah

Win stepped back and kicked a field goal. Only Shamsi's balls were what Win's foot connected with. He screamed, clutched his privates, doubled over, then fell into a fetal position.

Win walked to me, held me. Her whole body was shaking, and I glimpsed the rage in her eyes. It scared the shit out of me. She let me go and handed me my key ring. "Clear," she said into the com set.

John came in the exit door, and I heard Caleb push open the other one. Both men trained their weapons on the writhing man on the floor.

"Anybody have handcuffs?" Win asked. "The one thing I forgot in the planning."

Caleb shook his head, so John cuffed Shamsi and pulled him to his feet. Shamsi screamed again. I wondered how much damage Win had done.

"Get him out of here," I said and motioned Caleb to help John.

After they'd left, I turned to Win. "Excessive force, Win."

"Fuck it, Sarah. Be glad I didn't shoot his balls off." She reached out, touched my forehead. Her hand came away bloody. Her shakes had calmed down to an occasional tremble. She unlocked the cuffs on my wrists and hugged me hard. "We need to get you to the hospital. You're still bleeding."

"Uh, I hate to spoil this reunion, but could you get these off me?" Emily asked. She held up her own cuffed hands.

Win took her knife out, freed Emily and helped her to her feet. "How are you?"

Emily rubbed her wrists. "That's my line, Win. But this experience has given me a lot of new insights. God, I'm glad both of you are alive. I wasn't sure any of us would make it out. Who *is* that man?"

"An international arms and drugs dealer—the man who tortured Laura."

"Oh my God!" Em's eyes widened.

"Let's get to the station," I said. "We can debrief there."

"Hospital first." Win walked toward Em's desk, bent over and picked something up. She carried the wedding band to me and placed it on my finger. "Chain's broken. I'll get you a new one."

I pulled her into a long, deep kiss. "This is where the ring belongs, Win. I'm not taking it off anymore."

Emily cleared her throat behind us. "Maybe we should talk about that."

"Not right now, Emily. Lock up your office, and let's get out of here."

* * *

Bill was waiting for us when we got back to my office. He'd napped, showered and found clean clothes. He actually smiled when we walked in, in a cat-and-canary kind of way. "Your people came through," he said, pointing to a Coptic diptych on my desk. "Kemat's list has already been sent to my people. We've begun picking up the major players in his network. But I'm not sure we can do anything about the American money, at least not yet. But it's a damn wake-up call for us."

"Glad to hear it since that's what Kemat died for."

"And Noor," Win added.

"You want Shamsi?" I asked.

Bill shook his head. "Go ahead, press charges and bring the damn fuckhead to trial. By that time, we'll know what additional charges we have grounds for. Man'll never breathe free air again." He saluted. "Nice job, Sarah. Win."

After he left, I looked at Win. "All I want to do is go home."

"But you can't. I know. We should do something for Emily, take her out to dinner or something."

"Find her a counselor." I collapsed into my desk chair. "You need to write out a statement. Start with Emily's call—no, with the beginning of the op."

"You should go to the hospital, have your head checked out."

"It's stopped bleeding, Win. Besides, we've got to get them booked and preliminary charges filed. Then we can go home."

I started the paperwork and Win settled on the couch with her laptop.

After twenty minutes, she stopped typing and cleared her throat. "I suppose I have to mention the kick. Could I say 'kneed' him?"

"No. Full disclosure, Win. But please explain the circumstances and that the only pair of handcuffs in the room were already on me."

Emily knocked on the door. "Finished my statement. Can I go now?"

"Could we take you out for dinner or something?" Win asked.

"I'll take a rain check, but thanks for the thought. I want to get home to Marty. We've got the whole weekend together, and it'll help me get back to an even keel. We'll set up a meeting next week, talk through all of it."

"I'll have a deputy drive you back to your car, or home, if you'd prefer it."

"No. I need to walk."

"Em, thanks for keeping a cool head and for the warning. I'm so sorry you were dragged into this."

"I'm just glad you picked up on the warning. Very glad. Win, you have my complete respect. I don't know how you existed in those kinds of situations for so many years. You're one hell of a warrior. But you might want to think about anger control."

"I did control it. I wanted to kill him."

She made a sad smile, close to a grimace and left.

We didn't get home until after dark, and Des was glad to see us, but truly pissed. Win took her out for a walk, which I suspected was going to turn into a run. She was wound up tight and needed physical exercise to let go a bit. I showered, trying to avoid water getting into the bandage Dory had applied after cleaning the wound thoroughly. It's hard to maintain one's dignity as sheriff when the dispatcher insists on doctoring wounds during her break.

My thoughts kept going back to Win, the look in her eyes when she'd come into Emily's office. Murderous was the word that kept circling around my brain. Could she have killed Shamsi in the moment she stepped inside? Yes. *But she didn't* was the thought that followed. Was I hanging onto that too much?

I combed my hair back and put on shorts and a T-shirt. We needed to talk. Tonight.

Win and Des came in as I was pulling two beers from the fridge. I held them up and headed to the couch.

"What?" Win asked. She went into the kitchen to feed Des her very late dinner.

"We need to talk."

"About this afternoon? Can't it wait until tomorrow morning? I'm bushed."

"You were an avenging angel—scared the shit out of me, Win."

She plopped down on the couch, took a long drink and then leaned her head back. "I haven't felt rage like that since they bombed the village and killed Azar. If I'd had a target then, I would've killed them. This time, I didn't kill. Even though I wanted to."

"Why? The situation was under control." I reached for her hand.

"What if it hadn't been? He would've done to you what he did to Laura. Only he wouldn't have stopped with your breasts. He would've put the cables on your clit, in your vagina. Then he would've let his men rape you again and again." Her eyes were closed, but the tears streamed down her face. "He would've enjoyed every bit of it. Gotten off on it. The man's evil. Evil." She turned her face to me. "I love you so much, and I was so scared that something would go wrong. That he'd be able to do that to you."

She grabbed onto me and began to sob. I rocked her in my arms, crying too.

CHAPTER FORTY-SIX

Win

Exhaustion seemed to mark the next couple of days. Sarah's as she finalized the case against Shamsi and tried to prove a case against his goons. Mine from coming to terms with planning an op that jeopardized Sarah. I was on the rodent wheel again. *How could you? Do you know what could've happened?*

We met with Emily Monday afternoon. It took every ounce of control I had to sit in Emily's waiting room. My thought wheel turned faster and faster. So did my breathing. Sarah reached over, held onto my hand with both of hers. I wanted her on my lap so I could hold her. Stay that way forever.

Emily opened her door and motioned us in.

I was surprised to see a fourth chair that closed the circle, Emily's desk chair. In it was a wizened woman with permed white hair. She looked like she could've been a hundred and five.

"This is Dr. Clara Wentworth, my shrink," Emily said. "I figured I needed some help working through this. You feel comfortable enough in here to proceed? You're not overwhelmed with the memory?"

"I'm okay," Sarah said as she sat down in her usual place.

I took a deep breath. "It's hard for me. Brings back the rage I felt. I wanted to kill him, plain and simple."

"That is a good insight," Dr. Wentworth said. "Sit, please. Your name is?"

"Win," I answered as I sat. This was the chair Sarah had been sitting in when I'd stormed the room. "Winifred Kirkland, ma'am."

"So, you must be Sarah," Dr. Wentworth said as she turned her head toward Sarah. "You are sheriff?"

"Yes."

Dr. Wentworth glanced up at Emily. "Emily, sit down. I am running this session, remember." She addressed us. "Emily has told me what she witnessed, no more. From that, we will proceed."

I examined the shrink's shrink. She had to be in her nineties. German accent. A student of Freud? Would we have to tell Mommy tales?

"Winifred, you experienced rage, yet did not kill him, just damaged him. Why?"

"It was Sarah's op. She'd have to face the accusation of using deadly force without cause."

"Yet you were enraged?"

"Yes. I never used to believe in pure evil. But through my experiences in the marines, I've changed my mind. Mohan Shamsi is pure evil. He killed a woman with a strong purpose, a purpose that was opposed to his interests. She was doing important work for women around the globe. He enjoys torture. The world would be better off without him."

"How do you know he enjoys torture?"

"Reputation. Besides, Laura told us." I gave her the story's background. "He would've enjoyed doing the same thing to Sarah. While he made me watch."

She cocked her head. "That was the heart of your rage?"

I shifted my position in the chair. "That and all the pain I've seen inflicted by men greedy for power and money. It all wrapped up in one flaming moment with my finger on the trigger. I could've blown his brains out without guilt."

"Yet you feel guilt, yes?"

This woman must be a witch. Or mind reader. "Yes. For sending Sarah into the lion's den. It was *my* plan. So many things could've gone wrong. Things I hadn't thought of. Planned for."

Dr. Wentworth transferred her gaze to Sarah. "How do you feel about Winifred's guilt?"

"It's bullshit. I knew what I was getting into because we planned the whole thing together. Win had my back. How could I not trust her to do her best? I had my deputies who've backed me so many times I can't number them."

"Did you feel safe? Or were you scared?"

"I was terrified, so scared I'd lose Win, that we wouldn't be able to grow old together. Face-to-face with Shamsi, I got mad." She reached out, touched my arm. "Win, I remembered Laura's wounds too. I hated him, but I had to let the scene play out."

"And you, Emily?"

"To use Sarah's word, terrified. I tried to warn her when I made the initial call. When she walked in, I thought I'd failed. I despaired until I saw Win come in."

"Did you think you were going to die?"

"Yes," Emily said. She wiped away tears. "I was of no use in the situation. I felt paralyzed."

"You stayed out of the way," I said. "Your reactions were perfect, Emily. Shamsi saw your fear and bought the scenario we played out. Shamsi's used to dealing with liars, cheaters and thugs. He's used to making quick assessments. Your paralysis saved not only your life, but Sarah's. Probably mine too." I took Sarah's hand. "And I'm not saying that to give you an easy time. Not after all the grief you've given me."

Emily caught my grin. Tried to return it.

Dr. Wentworth watched the exchange. "Emily, I will work with you on your guilt issues, but please register what Winifred just said." She rose in a remarkably fluid movement. "As for you two, I think you have built an extraordinary relationship, especially with the deep scars you both have. Keep your communication channels open with one another. I suspect, Winifred, you did not tell Sarah about the guilt you felt. But you already have formed the most important part of loving one another—trust. Do not let it erode in silence."

* * *

We hadn't made love since the op had gone down. I marked it down to our exhaustion and worry. My hamster brain had short-circuited desire. How could I possess the body of a woman I'd sent into danger? Into the possibility of losing her forever?

By the time we got home from our session with Dr. Wentworth, all I wanted to do was cover every square inch of her body with kisses. Transport her to orgasmic nirvana. We walked in, I shooed Des out and embraced her. Pulled her to me. Kissed her so she couldn't misinterpret my intentions.

"I love you, Sarah," I said as we came up for breath.

She held me at arm's length. "I'm so glad you said what'd been bothering you the past couple of days. I meant what I said—we planned it together. I knew what I was getting into and the risks. Besides, I knew if something went wrong, you were there to bail me out."

"Oh, Sarah. Blind faith can be dangerous."

"My faith in you isn't blind, Win. It's based on observation and experience. But please, let's try to avoid situations that test both our abilities."

"Amen to that." I kissed her again, found her willing. So willing, she had my shirt unbuttoned by the time Des came back in.

We never made it into the bedroom until after midnight. Even then, neither of us was sated. Finally, I rolled off Sarah. Curved into her body.

"We haven't had a night like this since…"

"Ever," I said. "Not with the intensity. Or, er, longevity."

"Is this what happens when we don't make love every day?"

I snorted. "No, this is what happens when I'm afraid to touch you because I sent you in there. Knowing you could die."

"Quit with the guilt—and I mean it. I was a willing partner in the plan."

"You've been a very willing partner tonight." I caressed her belly. "But it was eating at me. I didn't say anything because I thought you'd dismiss it. Besides, I knew how tired you've been."

She reached up and traced the healing scar on my cheek. "If I ever pooh-pooh what you're feeling, call me on it. I never want to diminish what you're feeling any more than I want you to do that to me."

I kissed her breast, rested my head on her chest. "Shit, Sarah. We've come a long way. I remember when I couldn't say how much I wanted you in my life. As my lover. As my partner."

"Or how much what I was feeling scared me. I kept thinking about you and you kept your distance."

I changed position so I could look into her eyes. "Did you fantasize?"

She blushed.

"Ah."

"Nothing like this, Win. Not in my wildest imagination. Maybe a longer kiss. Feeling your body against mine as we embraced without my parka on."

"That's all?"

"Maybe a bit more, but I didn't know how to…end it. I didn't know the mechanics."

"Mechanics. Shit, Sarah." I ran my hand down to her thigh. "This isn't mechanics. It's passion and magic and learning your body."

"And love. Don't forget the love, Win. That's what makes me open to you. Emotionally as well as physically."

I kissed her breast, teasing her nipple with my tongue. "It's a good thing we don't have to get up a dawn."

"Not too far past. My interview with Zoe is tomorrow."

In response to my groan, Sarah rolled me on my back, began kissing me. With intent.

CHAPTER FORTY-SEVEN

Sarah

Win and I sat on the garden swing, her arm casually draped over the back, Des at our feet. Zoe perched on a rather ratty lawn chair Win had bought when she'd first moved in. A digital recorder rested on the redwood table between us. I'd given permission with a shrug. Dad would've said, "In for a pence, in for a pound."

"If you don't want to answer a question, just say so and we'll move on," Zoe said. "I know this can't be easy for you."

"Not easy, no. If Win were a man, we wouldn't be doing this at all. We'd have dated, gotten engaged and married. Period. No questions asked. We even could've lived together without getting married, and it wouldn't have been an issue."

"Well, let's jump into the deep end," Zoe said. "Do you identify as lesbian?"

Sarah expelled a long breath. "When I was asked that during the campaign, I answered truthfully—I said I didn't know. I was trying to sort through feelings I didn't understand, come to terms with a world shifting under my feet. It's been a process for me, one that I think has been more difficult because I hold a public office.

"As much as I hate restrictive labels, I do identify as lesbian. At this point in my life, my emotional bond is with this woman."

"When did you identify as straight?" Win asked, her gaze directed at Zoe.

"I never gave it a thought," Zoe said. Then smiled. "Point taken."

"That's why it's so confusing. Most people never have to think about it," Win said. "I faced the problem when I was a kid. When you're in the middle of your life and face it for the first time? It's a huge shift in who you think you are."

Zoe turned to Sarah. "Sarah, you're a widow, you were married to a man. Did that add to the confusion?"

"I loved Hugh. I want to make that clear. He was a remarkable man. A long time after he was murdered, I finally tried dating again but found it…arid. So yes, never questioning my sexual identity before confused me more, if that was possible."

"But you've resolved the issue for yourself?"

"Yes. Or I wouldn't be talking to you today."

"Why are you? I assume you're out to family and friends, but this is a much larger step."

I took a deep breath. "We were legally married in Vermont because it was impossible in Indiana. I was wearing my wedding ring on a chain around my neck at work and around town. During the operation to arrest a felon, he ripped it off. If it had been on my finger—"

"He would've cut your finger off," Win said. "Sorry. Go on, Sarah."

I examined her face, felt the residue of anger. I squeezed her hand. "What I was thinking at the time was that if the ring was where it belonged, it wouldn't have happened. And how much I was still hiding my commitment to Win. So in the aftermath, when we found the ring, I put it on and swore I wouldn't take it off again. I can't hide anymore."

"The best description of what I've been feeling for years is in an old novel," Win said. "One of Karin Kallmaker's, *Car Pool*. I don't remember it word for word. Something like 'so that's what it feels like, to be treated like everyone else. To not have to make excuses and feel limited and restricted just because of who you love.' That's the heart of it. It's not just the energy it takes to hide, but the very desire every human being has to be treated like everybody else."

Zoe looked at her notes and brushed her hand over her eyes. She flipped through her notebook. "How about a lighter question—when did you two first meet?"

Win and I grinned at one another and said together, "First grade."

"We grew up together, were best friends and along with Nathan Cloud, were called the Three Musketeers. Win came out to me in high school. But when she joined the marines, we pretty much lost contact except when she came home on leave. Since her mother died, that wasn't often. The David Paria case brought us back into contact."

"Was it love at first sight this time?"

"No. We were at loggerheads for most of the time," I said. "Can we keep this part off the record? I mean, not publish the really private parts?"

"After I write it, you can read it. That's the best I can do."

"Months after the case was closed, when my house was finished and I was settled in, I invited her over to see it," Win added. "I was hoping we could renew our friendship—like it had been growing up. Nothing more."

"And?" Zoe asked.

I could feel the heat making its way into my face. "We shared a kiss—nothing passionate, but it surprised me. Took me off-balance. She got all professional and distanced. I couldn't stop thinking about Win. I thought…well, let's just say I was a mess. It was really hard to sort through the feelings. Win was no help since she wouldn't get near me unless it was in a public place."

"I felt awful," Win said. "I'd wanted to renew our friendship. I felt isolated and I knew that wasn't good for me. Then, after it happened, I thought I'd crossed the line. Destroyed Sarah's trust.

"Besides, I didn't want to get involved in a relationship with a straight woman."

"You've been out since high school?" Zoe asked.

"Not openly while I was in the marines, at least until the policy changed. I lived the shadow life. But yes, I've identified as lesbian since high school."

"So how did you two get together?"

"Sarah wouldn't let me avoid her questions. Eventually, we talked."

And more. "I never thought I'd fall in love again," I said. "It was a struggle, Zoe. I knew what I felt for Win, but I couldn't let anyone know. It was like I was living two lives, trying to tamp down feelings, failing, but I didn't have anyone to talk to but Win—and she'd been out so long she couldn't help me much.

"Finally, before anything physical happened between us, I talked to an old friend who's lesbian."

"Was she able to give you any insights? Help you sort through the issues?"

I fidgeted and wished this was a bad dream. "She brought up all the external threats to the relationship. Could I live a shadow relationship? If we were found out—"

"Fuck it, Sarah." Win leaned over and shut off the recorder. "You're playing nice for a pack of righteous bigots."

"It's nobody's business what I do in my private life as long as it doesn't affect my performance on the job."

"Yeah, right. This is about sex. Straight people think it's all we do. They screw up their pious faces and say 'ew.' Even if sex is a duty, not a pleasure for them. They try to shame us."

"Not all straight people."

"No, not all. Fewer every day. But here in the county, enough to make you afraid you'll lose your job. And that's a pile of shit." She kicked at the table and set the swing into motion. "Think about LGBT youth. This whole sex thing is so overwhelming to teens, then add words like pervert and worse hurled at them. Think about Natalie Elder. She had to hang herself to get away from her persecutors."

"Low blow, Win." I'd done everything I could to bring her justice, but I'd failed to give her solace or hope for her future.

"I didn't mean to raise ghosts. I agreed to this interview to give those kids a different image. Two successful women who love one another without shame."

I felt tears well up and brushed them away. Had I banished shame?

"Sorry, Zoe," Win said. "Didn't mean to rant. I almost died protecting this country, Sarah this county. You'd think that'd be enough."

"Enough?" Zoe asked.

"Enough to end the derision, general ugliness. Let us live the freedom we both fight for."

Zoe examined Win's face for a long moment. "Anything else? Or can I begin to record again?"

"Sorry. I'll shut up." She touched the back of my neck. "I've interrupted enough."

"You want to pick up where we left off?" Zoe asked.

"Where was that?"

"Why don't you talk about your job and peoples' expectations for the office?" At my nod, she restarted the recorder.

"I think I do a good job for the people of McCrumb County, and I don't want to leave the sheriff's office. That's been the fear I've had—that people would hate me for falling in love and vote me out at the earliest opportunity."

"You're both wearing matching wedding bands. Have people noticed?"

I took Win's hand, turned the ring on her finger. "Some. We were out to my family and the deputies in my department.

"You know, we partially married for legal reasons—all the ones you've mentioned in your articles. But mainly because I wanted to say 'forever' to Win. To make a commitment to her like my parents made to one another. They had a wonderful marriage and were an incredible example for me. That's what I want to share with Win. An incredible love that deepens over the years."

Zoe smiled. "Anything else you want to put out there?"

"Haven't I said enough?" I closed my eyes, took a deep breath. "To me, this is about equality before the law—a principle I'm sworn to uphold. Not to discriminate against the people I arrest, not to profile minority groups. I'm not asking anyone to change their religious beliefs, just to realize equality before the law is something we should all uphold. In this country, we have separation between church and state. I don't know how marriage equality's going to work out for the country, but it shouldn't be a legal issue and shouldn't have been from the beginning. We are all guaranteed to stand equally before the law."

"Okay." She shut off the recorder, stuck it in a pocket and pulled a digital camera. "A few shots?"

"There's a nice trail I've cleared where Des and I run every day. It's pretty anonymous. This is our sanctuary. I'd like to keep it that way," Win said. "Could we choose the one you use?"

"I'd normally say no, but for you, deal."

* * *

"Are you feeling particularly naked now?" Win asked as we lay in bed that night.

"I am naked."

"You know what I mean. About the article."

"It doesn't come out until Thursday, so I guess I've got tomorrow to feel…invisible."

"Are you sorry you did it?" Win stroked my shoulder. "It's not too late to call and cancel. Zoe said so."

"I'm not going back, Win. Besides, I really like the picture you chose."

"It was a glorious shot—Des jumping between us. I saw real joy between the three of us. That's good PR."

"I'm going to ask Zoe for a copy." I rolled over so that our legs were entwined. "We don't have any pictures of us together except from the wedding."

"I have images of you in my head that I'll carry forever."

"I think I'm glad you didn't choose one of those." I kissed her lightly. Our lovemaking tonight had been so different than last night's marathon. Slow, gentle, dreamlike, yet as intense. "I'm glad CELI canceled the intensive. I need you here when the story breaks."

She stroked my face. "Postponed the intensive. They moved it to the end of August, right before classes begin again. They'll have an interim director installed by then."

"You're going to miss Kemat. Will teaching at CELI be too much of a reminder?"

"Could be. Or could be a spur to continue her work. Would you mind? No travel, no one tracking me down, just reorganizing her network with mine."

"As long you stay safe and can help those women, I'll help as much as I can. But I don't have a network, Win."

"Yeah, you do. Here. In McCrumb County. Some of those 'women' are girls who have no future in their own countries. They're already marked. Plus, with our troops pulling out of Afghanistan, there are going to be a lot of war orphans who need safe homes and won't find them in Afghanistan."

"You're talking about international adoption, aren't you?"

"I want kids."

I sucked in a deep breath. "Oh, Win…"

"I know, Sarah. Not part of our deal." She brushed the hair off my forehead, brought my head down for a sweet kiss. "But I've been dreaming about them. All the kids I met over there. Bright eyes and smiles, even when conditions were shit."

"We're so new on this path—"

"I know. It wouldn't happen overnight. Takes about a year. But I'm afraid after the troops come home, the process could become a nightmare. I'd like to start soon."

"They'd let a gay couple adopt?"

"They'd let someone they know as trustworthy adopt. Especially someone who knows the languages, the customs, the culture."

I sat up. "Are you going to do this whether I want to or not?"

Win locked her gaze with mine. "No. Kids need to see loving parents. Two people who bicker, disagree, find a way to reconcile issues. Shit. I sound like Emily." She propped a pillow behind her back. "You watched Micah and your mom love one another. That's how you learned to love so completely."

"You love completely too. I can feel it, Win, every time you look at me, each time you touch me."

"Azar taught me." Her smile was filled with such pain and loss it broke my heart. "But I think it was the kids there who first breached my defenses. They're so full of life. Hope. Trust."

"You went halfway around the world to discover kids are neat? What about your nieces and nephews? I know you've got a passel. Didn't they ever 'breach' your heart?"

Win looked away. "I wasn't allowed around them."

"What?"

"My eldest brother told me in no uncertain terms." She leaned her head back on the pillow. "But those Afghan kids are so different from American. Pleased at such small pleasures. I'll show you pictures in the morning. I asked you once before to think about it. It's time to take that request seriously."

I gazed at her. The scars on her body reflected the scars on her soul. From battle, from loss and from family turning their backs. I moved next to her, took her hand in mine. "I'll think about it, Win, but no promises. Kids are a huge responsibility and, as you pointed out today, we're midway through our lives."

She smiled, this time without the sadness. "Can I set up a Skype account? So you can meet some of these kids?"

"You're incorrigible, Win." I stroked her hand, rubbed my thumb over her palm. "Please don't push too hard. It's a huge decision. Just think, with kids in the house, we'd never have had last night."

She pulled me onto to her. "I'm sure Micah would love to babysit his grandkids now and then."

CHAPTER FORTY-EIGHT

Win

The *Greenglen Sentinel*'s website crashed a little after noon Thursday afternoon. Their Facebook page, shortly after. I'd been monitoring it so I could give Sarah some idea of public reaction to Zoe's article. Comments had been coming in so fast, it'd been hard to keep a tally.

The phone rang, caller ID said *Sentinel*, so I picked up.

"We sure started one hell of a conversation," Zoe said. "You have any comment for a follow-up?"

"No. Not until I can sift through the comments that come in. When will you get your sites up and running?"

Zoe snickered. "Nathan's working on it. Jesus, Win, I never expected a reaction like this. I mean, we've gotten a good response to the rest of the series, but nothing like this. I think it's because Sarah and her family are so well-known. Lloyd wants to do a follow-up for the next issue, so think about what you want to say."

"I know what I want to say, and I don't think you could print it. Email me when it's back up, would you?"

"Sure, just don't expect a summary of comments from me right away."

I hung up and called Des for a walk. There'd been something rattling around in my brain since I visited Laura yesterday. Physically, she was healing well. Or that's what they told her. She refused to look at her breasts. From experience, the longer I refused to examine my damage, the longer it took me to come to terms with it.

Emily was looking for somewhere Laura could stay when she got out of the hospital. She agreed with me that Laura's fixation on Sarah wasn't healthy for any of us. Then asked the question that stumped me.

"Are you afraid Sarah will stray after the honeymoon period's over?"

I'd hesitated before I answered. "She's only known one woman's body. Mine. Only made love with one woman. Me. But she's awakened to the allure. I can see it when we go to Ruby's. She's noticing breasts and butts and legs."

"You don't?" Emily asked.

"I'm fully appreciative. But I can admire without the desire to possess. I'm not sure Sarah knows the difference yet."

Des charged off into the underbrush. I didn't hear any cries from small animals, so maybe this was a dry run. I couldn't imagine Des not getting her prey.

Emily's advice had been to keep communication channels open. Be willing to stay vulnerable. Know that Sarah might very well become intrigued with another woman. It was up to me what happened within our relationship. Could I withstand a storm and stay open?

I suddenly envisioned hordes of beautiful women assaulting our home. Me, standing at the front door with an M-16. Sarah within, guarded by Des. That would be so much easier.

Des charged into me. Knocked me down. Grinned and woofed. I picked myself up and followed her down the trail.

Sarah got home early. Collapsed into my waiting arms.

"Rough day?" I asked.

"Crazy day. I got a standing ovation from my people when I walked in this morning. Then the calls started. Dory stopped taking messages about nine."

"The *Sentinel*'s website crashed around noon. We seem to have caused something of a brouhaha." I hugged her. "Lloyd wants us to do a follow-up next week."

"Hell and damnation. You can do it and talk about how much stress this is causing your wife."

"It'll die down, Sarah. Who knows? Maybe all the gay people in the county will stand up to be counted. All the radical right will be scared they're outnumbered. Move to Idaho."

"Right. Like that's going to happen." She attempted a smile. "I can't take it back, so it's 'forward ho' into the unknown." She registered the aromas coming from the oven. "What are you cooking? It smells like Mom's lasagna rustica."

"It is. I called Micah for the recipe. Even though it's hot outside, I thought some comfort food might help."

"Dad getting many calls?"

"He said a ton. Didn't mention the percentage of supporters versus yellers." I held her. Gently. Trying to undo the bruises of the day. "Go take your shower. Wash off all the worry. By the time you're finished, we can sit down and eat with Micah—I invited him. With your Mom's spirit hovering over our dinner, you'll be surrounded with love."

Sarah put her hands on my shoulders, looked me in the eye. "I know I am. That's what's sustaining me. Tillie even sent over lunch so I wouldn't have to endure 'the gawking of them illiterates.' I love you, Win. When you hold me in your arms, I feel so fucking brave because it feels so right. But you know what? That feeling, feeling so right, seems to walk with me and protect me even when you're not close at hand."

As I watched her walk down the hall, I thought I was the luckiest dyke in the world. No matter the storms ahead, we'd both found a safe harbor with one another. With this house that was becoming home.

I looked down at Des. "Don't let me screw this up, soldier."

She snorted as if to say, "I cannot stop human stupidity."

I heard Micah's old beater climbing the hill outside. Dented, rusted and missing a bumper, it still ran strong. Just like Micah.

And my love for Sarah. I hoped that love would be enough to keep us secure through the storms to come. I knew they would. I could feel it in my bones.

About the Author

S. M. Harding has been a teacher at grade school, high school and college levels, a cab driver in Chicago, a secretary, an art director and a chef. She started writing fiction in the mountains of northern New Mexico during a long winter when the roads were closed by snow, and has been writing ever since and has published more than thirty short stories in various anthologies. She lives in Indiana and revels in a retirement that centers on writing, editing and teaching writing.

You can find S. M. Harding at:
www.smharding.webs.com, www.storytellersfire.wordpress.com and on Facebook at S. M. Harding.

Bella Books, Inc.

Women. Books. Even Better Together.

P.O. Box 10543
Tallahassee, FL 32302

Phone: 800-729-4992
www.bellabooks.com